WATCH ME UNRAVEL

A BLUE IS THE COLOR NOVEL

JULIA WOLF

Cover by: Amy Queau
Editing by: Monica Black
Formatting by: The Side Hustle

To everyone living with anxiety...you're not alone.

ONE

DAVID

IT TOOK me a minute to establish the reason for my return to consciousness. It wasn't the tit in my hand or the legs tangled with mine, but the constant buzzing coming from my bedside table. I reached out to smack it or kill it—anything to stop the sound.

There was no one who could possibly need to get in touch with me in the middle of the night. My boys were tucked snug in their own hotel rooms down the hall, so even in my altered state, I knew it wasn't one of them calling me to bail them out of jail or some shit—not that I'd be anyone's first phone call from jail.

I closed my eyes, trying to ignore it, and thank Christ, it stopped.

The tit in my hand started moving. I cracked an eye to get a look at its owner. She was staring at me, eyes heavy-lidded, looking hungry. Her friend on my other side was still fast asleep, but this one was cute enough. If memory served, she spoke not a lick of English, but she *did* lick cock like she loved it.

"*Cekc?*" she asked drowsily.

Ah, the universal language of love. Sex was one of the words

I knew in multiple languages. I'd found I didn't really need to know too many more to communicate my needs.

"*Da.*" I lifted her pretty little tit to my mouth, intent on sucking her cherry nipple, when my phone started buzzing again. Why the fuck hadn't that thing died yet?

Groaning, I rolled over to grab it. With bleary eyes, I checked the screen. When the name flashing finally hit my brain, I bolted upright, and my feet hit the floor. Cherry Tits giggled behind me, but I gave zero shits. I locked myself in the bathroom and hit "accept."

"Hello?" I answered, definitely louder than necessary.

"David?"

"What's going on? Is Emma okay?" I demanded.

I heard her shaky intake of breath, and my heart stopped. "She's going to be okay, but she's hurt."

I sank down on the tile floor. "*No.* No, no, no, no, no. What happened, Sylvia? Where is she?"

"She's in the hospital—"

"The fucking hospital?" I gripped the phone so hard, I was surprised it didn't crack.

"Stop interrupting me!"

"What happened? Just fucking tell me!" I shouted.

"Don't yell at me, David."

I took a deep breath. "You're right. I'm freaking out. Please, just tell me what's going on."

"She was in a car accident. Her femur is broken. She just went into surgery to have it repaired. Our little girl is really hurt." The same abject terror roiling in my gut was in her voice. But she was there, with our daughter, and I was on the other side of the world, in Russia.

"Fuck. I'm coming. I'm in Europe, so it'll be a while, but I'm coming."

"You don't have to—"

"Yes I do! That's my kid. Don't try to keep me away."

"I wouldn't," she said weakly.

I covered my eyes, exhaling slowly. "I know, Syl. I've gotta figure out flights and shit, so I'll let you know the exact time I'll be there. Just...let her know Daddy's on the way, okay?"

She choked out a sob. "Okay. I'll see you when you get here."

"Call me when she's out of surgery," I said urgently.

"I will."

I hung up and stared down at my phone in a daze, trying to breathe. My chest constricted with panic, and my limbs were limp. I probably would have sat there for hours had there not been a tap on the door.

"*Daveed...cekc?*"

The sound of the woman's voice pulled me out of my stupor. A pair of jeans lay crumpled on the floor, so I pulled them on before opening the door. Ms. Russia was naked, cherry tits pointed right at me, but I barely saw them. I went searching for my wallet and a shirt.

Once I found what I needed, I tucked my phone and charger in my pocket and raced for the door.

"*Daveed...*" Ms. Russia whined from the bedroom.

Without looking back, I tossed, "*Da svidania,*" over my shoulder and let the door close behind me.

Nick's room was two doors down, and I figured he was still awake, so I knocked rapidly. When he opened it, he had his cell phone to his ear and a scowl on his face. Normally, I'd have ripped the phone out of his hand to talk to his girl, Dalia, but tonight wasn't the night.

Before he could ask me why the hell I was at his door at 1:00 a.m., I said, "I need help. Emma's been in an accident. I gotta get home."

With his eyes on mine, he said into the phone, "Dal, I need

to call you back." He stood back, opening the door wide to let me in. I paced back and forth until he finally asked what was going on.

"Sylvia called, said she's okay, but in surgery...and I need to be there. I—" I yanked at my hair. "Fuck, can you help me get there?"

He took charge from that moment, waking our manager, Tali. Between the two of them, within an hour, they'd arranged a chartered flight leaving at six. I couldn't even begin to imagine what that had cost, but I'd pay pretty much anything to get to my kid.

Tali rode with me to the private airport near Moscow and pulled me into a hug once we got inside the terminal. I almost broke, but I held it together. "I'm okay. I'm just going kinda nuts here," I said.

"Has Sylvia texted back yet?" she asked.

I pulled out my phone for the hundredth time. "Not since the last one. She said it'd be a while."

Tali rubbed big circles on my back. I wasn't normally into the touchy feely shit, but damn if I didn't need it right now. "Emma's young and healthy. She'll heal up from this, good as new. You know that, right?"

I threw up my hands. "No, I fucking don't know that. You don't know that either. Don't try to blow smoke up my ass."

"I'm sorry. I'll just say I *think* she'll be fine. I *hope* she's not in a lot of pain. And I *pray* you get there quickly."

I hung my head, half pissed at myself for spouting off, the other half not giving one single fuck. "I left a couple women in my room."

"I'll take care of it."

"I'm not coming back for the rest of the tour."

She rubbed my back again. "It's fine. We'll work it out. We

only had five more shows to go, so don't let the band be a worry. Focus on your girl."

Once I was on the plane, I called Sylvia again. "Hey," I said softly when she answered.

"Hi. I was about to call. The doctor came out and said everything went well with the surgery. They had to place a ro—" her voice broke, and she took a deep, shuddering breath. "They placed a rod inside her bone to reconnect it and a plate and some screws to keep it in place. I'll get to see her in about an hour, but she won't be awake."

"Oh Jesus. She's got metal in her leg?" I sunk down in my seat, not even close to being able to stay upright.

She sniffled. "Yes. Just...just get here."

I pinched the bridge of my nose, trying to stymy the pain raging through my brain. "Ten hours, Syl. Even if she's not awake, tell her I'm comin'."

Leaning my head back on the seat, I closed my eyes, gripping the armrests with all my fuckin' might. If there were shit to smash, I'd have smashed it. At least I had enough sense to know I didn't want to do something that'd send the plane spiraling to its doom. Not when I was trying my damnedest to get to my girl.

I hadn't felt this helpless since...since Sylvia broke the news she was pregnant fifteen years ago. I'd been eighteen, about to graduate high school, no real plans other than playing music. A kid was the last thing on my mind. Then, this little slip of a girl, one I fucked once before she disappeared on me, showed up at my doorstep with a print out of a sonogram and a round belly.

Let me be perfectly fucking clear: if she'd told me about the pregnancy earlier on, I'd have been all over her to end it. I didn't know her. No way I wanted to be tied to a stranger for life. And no way I wanted to be tied *down* by a kid.

But, our story hadn't gone that way. Sylvia had been in denial until she could no longer hide her growing belly from herself or her parents. She was six months along by the time she had her first appointment with an OB. It took her another month to work up the guts to tell me.

We'd never been a couple. Nothing close. We were co-parents in a completely non-traditional way. I was gone seventy percent of the year, but I was there for Em as much as I could be. We had scheduled weekly phone calls or Skypes—but one of us usually called the other at least one or two other times a week just to say hey—and when I was in town, we did the shit teenage girls liked to do.

I was a screw up in a lot of ways. I had the maturity of a gnat. But if anyone was surprised I was a decent, committed dad, they'd never met my mama.

I'd be dead and buried if I'd even thought about being a deadbeat like my own dad. And my mama would've tap danced on my grave.

She didn't have to resort to murder, though. One look at my baby girl—a sniff of her sweet, brand-new smell—and I was hers.

My mouth hitched, thinking about how ugly Emma had been as a baby. She had been a scrawny thing, covered in baby acne with cradle cap under her sparse hair. Truly, the face only a mother—or lovesick father—could love.

She'd gotten a lot cuter pretty quick, and now, at fifteen, she was terrifyingly beautiful.

If I could've seen the future the day Sylvia showed up at my doorstep, I'd have been even more scared. That one day I'd be the father to a beautiful teenage girl...well, it served me right for all the hell I put my mom through over the years.

Emma was a good kid—so unlike me. She probably got it from her mom, but I couldn't be sure. 'Cause fifteen years down the line, Sylvia was still as much of a mystery to me as she'd been back then.

TWO

SYLVIA

I'VE HATED David Wiesel for a long, long time. Maybe just as long as I've loved him. The really hilarious—though, not at all funny—part was, I was fairly certain I barely existed to him. I was the person he texted to see his daughter. The name on the monthly child support check—although that was probably sent from an accountant or money manager...

I slumped in the hard, plastic hospital chair, staring up at the ceiling. I shouldn't have been thinking about him, but thinking about him was a lot easier than getting buried in the what-ifs—what could have happened today, how I could have lost her.

Emma still had another hour of recovery before I could see her. Knowing she was out of surgery, though...I was finally able to take a breath.

She'd never really been sick, never broken a bone or had stitches, and now this. One twist of fate, and here we were. My girl would be scarred for life, which wasn't a huge deal in the grand scheme of things, but I already knew she'd be devastated. Her self-image was decent, but no teenage girl wanted a scar on her leg.

Plus, we were looking at weeks of rehab. And who knew how long she'd be in the hospital.

I still couldn't quite wrap my head around what was happening. I was a little desperate to believe I was in a terrible nightmare. I hadn't even called anyone besides David—not that I had many people I could call. But David's mom, Gwen, would've been here in a heartbeat if I'd asked her. She'd be sitting here, holding my hand, petting my hair, telling me it'd be okay.

I wasn't sure I wanted that.

Mostly, I wanted a time machine. To turn back time to when Emma was four or five and thought I hung the moon and her daddy hung the stars, when the truth was, she hung the entire universe. To when she'd hold my hand when we crossed the street and squeezed my cheeks in her chubby little hands when she told me she loved me. Now, I was lucky if I got an "I love you too."

Having a teenager was a mind bender. I was so close to seeing if the decisions I'd made along the way had been the right ones, but I still had enough years to mess everything up. I *thought* I was a decent mother, but who the hell knew?

This was all a crapshoot.

Another hour of staring at the ceiling passed, then *finally*, a nurse came out to get me.

"She woke up for a minute, but we gave her something for the pain that knocked her right back out," she explained kindly. "All her stats look great. The doctor will be in in a bit to explain the details of the surgery, but I'd say she's going to be just fine."

I walked into her room slowly, each step toward the bed painful. When I let myself look at her face, I couldn't hold in a gasp. There was a deep cut across her nose and one on her chin, both closed with stitches. One cheek was already starting to bruise. She looked like she'd been in a knock-down, drag-out fight and lost.

Oh, my sweet baby girl.

Pulling one of the chairs from the corner next to her bed, I collapsed in it. Emma's hand rested on top of the covers, and I stroked it softly, letting her know I was here.

I started to text David, knowing he was up in the air and might not have cell reception, but called him instead.

"Hello?" he answered.

"I'm with her."

He exhaled heavily. "She awake?"

I told him what the nurse had said, then asked if he wanted to talk to her.

"Please," he said.

I put him on speaker and told him to go ahead.

"Emma? It's Daddy. I'm coming, sweetheart. I'm so sorry I'm not there now. I was in Russia. Remember when I brought you home those stacking dolls when you were seven? I bought those when we played in St. Petersburg. God, I can't believe that was more than half your life ago." He sighed. "I'll be there soon, Emma. You rest up."

"Syl?"

I wiped away a tear. "Yes, David?"

"You doin' okay?"

"Probably as okay as you."

He let out another long, slow exhale. "Which is pretty fuckin' awful. Christ, how did this happen?"

I closed my eyes, rubbing my throbbing temple. "We'll talk when you get here."

"All right. Just...keep me posted."

"Of course."

As I sat there, the doctor came back, telling me all the details of the surgery and potential complications, but it could've been a foreign language for as much as my brain processed the information. After he left, the nurse with kind eyes brought in a tray of...lunch? Dinner? I had no idea what time it was, but it had been many hours since my last meal, so I tried to eat.

I managed to get down a roll before my stomach revolted and I had to run to the bathroom to throw it back up.

Returning to my seat, I sipped some of the apple juice from the tray, and when that stayed down, I laid my head on the bed next to Emma. Maybe I could close my eyes for a minute...

I woke feeling a lot warmer than I had when I fell asleep, and I realized someone had draped a jacket over my shoulders—a hoodie that smelled like smoke mixed with a hint of sweat.

"David?" I said groggily.

"Hey. I'm here," he whispered. "I think she's waking up too."

His voice was closer than expected. I opened my eyes to find him sitting across from me on the other side of Emma.

I hadn't seen David in person in five years, but he never failed to take my breath away. He had a permanent smirk, like he was always on the verge of saying something cruel and it amused him. I should've been repelled by that, but I'd always been drawn to it. Even now, as a thirty-one-year-old mother who should have known better, I wasn't immune.

"Did you just get here?" I asked, my voice raspy, throat dry.

His eyes swept over my face. "Got here a little bit ago."

Emma groaned, drawing my attention. Her brow pinched and her eyes fluttered open. They were glazed and unfocused, but they were open. I'd never been so relieved.

"Mom?" she asked scratchily.

I squeezed her hand. "I'm here, baby."

David grabbed her other hand. "I'm here too, sweetheart."

Emma turned her head slowly to look at her dad. "You're both here? Am I dead? Is this Heaven?"

David laughed mirthlessly. "No, not dead. Although, you scared me half the fuck to death."

She gave him a lopsided, sleepy grin. Seemed like he still hung the stars in her eyes. I hadn't seen the two of them together in years—I'd actively avoided it, avoided him—and bearing witness to their bond was causing a fissure in my chest. I swear, the cracking was almost audible.

"I'm fine, Daddy. Just tired," she said.

He stroked her dark hair, and while he looked at her, I studied him. He was a beautiful man, and thank goodness Emma had gotten his looks. They shared the same dark hair and eyes, but while her features were delicate, his were wholly masculine. The thick stubble on his jaw covered strong, angular bones. His nose was bold—as was mine, but a bold nose was always going to be more attractive on a man. His lips were what captured my attention—always had. Even when his words were crude, his full mouth caressed them, and they sounded sensual.

This was one of the many reasons I hated him and had avoided any interaction for so long.

But now was not the time. I'd deal with my insecurities when my only daughter wasn't lying in a hospital bed.

David and I both reassured her she'd fully recover and feel better soon. She kept up a slurred conversation, but it was clear the effort was wearing her out. A new nurse came in, checking vitals and milling about. She informed us a physical therapist would be by soon to help Emma out of bed.

When Emma drifted back to sleep, I went into the hallway, needing a minute to myself. I didn't get it, though. The scent of weed mixed with cheap women's perfume alerted me to David's presence.

I turned to him stiffly. "Thank you for coming. I'm sure you were...busy."

He rubbed his mouth, looking down at me. "Don't start that

bullshit, Syl. I don't need it right now. You know there's nothing that'd keep me from my kid. *Nothing.*"

I looked away, hating the bitter taste in my mouth. That wasn't me.

"I'm sorry. I *do* know that. I'm tired and worried, but I won't take that out on you."

He leaned against the wall, his eyes closed. "I called my mom. She's at work, but she's coming. Thought you could use a break."

I shook my head. "No, I'm not leaving."

His mouth lifted into a slight smile. "Thought you'd say that. Pretty sure Gwen Wiesel won't take no for an answer." He pushed off the wall. "I need some coffee. Want something? You look like you could eat."

I frowned at his perusal of my body. Even in a loose hoodie and jeans, he made me feel naked. "I tried eating before you got here. Didn't take."

"I'll get'cha something. Hold tight."

He took off down the hall, head down, hands tucked in his pockets. Even from behind, I saw the fatigue and stress weighing on him, curling his shoulders forward. I felt it too—like an anvil had dropped on me and my organs had been smooshed into a cartoon flatness.

I went back into Emma's room and took up my sentry position. I wasn't sure how long I'd slept with my head on her bed, but it wasn't nearly enough. Absently, I wondered how long a person could go without sleep and survive. Then I remembered all those sleepless nights when she was a baby and realized I could last many, many more days.

David pushed back into the room a few minutes later, hands laden with coffee and what looked like the entirety of the hospital cafeteria's breakfast selection. He handed me a coffee and tossed a wrapped muffin into my lap.

"Eat," he ordered.

I didn't want to, since he was demanding it, but I *was* hungry. I nibbled the blueberry muffin and guzzled the coffee.

David interrupted my caffeine fix. "Kinda weird being in the same room, huh?"

Eyes on the black liquid swirling in my Styrofoam cup, I nodded. "You haven't been home for a while now, have you?"

"Almost two months. I think you know that, since Emma stayed with me most of that week."

I nodded again. I had the same love/hate relationship with Emma's visits with David. I missed her like crazy, but I couldn't begrudge him spending time with his daughter.

"Right, I'm sorry. I'm not thinking clearly."

"Don't keep apologizing to me. Makes me feel weird," he said.

It was on the tip of my tongue to say sorry again, but I bit it back.

We sat there for maybe an hour, David scrolling through his phone, tapping out the occasional message, me dozing off and on in the most uncomfortable chair ever made. Emma woke up around the same time Gwen came bursting in with a bouquet of sunflowers and a giant teddy bear.

Emma held her arms out. "Grandma!"

Gwen passed David the flowers and bear before bending down to hug her granddaughter. She was the only grandparent in Emma's life, and she did a bang-up job.

When she straightened, she looked back and forth between David and me, her nose scrunching. "You two, out. Go take a shower, get some rest. You look like shit."

Emma giggled, and the crack in my chest vibrated at the edges. She was much more awake now, and some color had returned to her face.

"Mom...I don't think Emma wants us to go—" David started.

"It's okay. As long as Grandma's here, I'll be fine. I didn't want to bring it up, but you smell awful," Emma said.

David pulled his shirt up to his nose and took a whiff. "Fuck, you're right, I do." She giggled again.

I squeezed her hand. "I'll stay with you and Grandma."

She shook her head. "Nope. You look terrible. You're bringing down the whole vibe of the room."

I gasped playfully. "I'm super offended, daughter of mine."

"At least I didn't say you smell!"

I sniffed my shirt and recoiled dramatically. "I don't smell like roses."

Gwen gave David a quick hug, followed by pushing him toward the door. "Just take a little break. I promise to call if we need anything at all." She reached her hand out to me. "Come here, sweetie."

She pulled me into a tight embrace, and I almost collapsed into her arms. I needed that hug more than I knew.

It felt wrong walking out of that hospital with David, leaving our girl behind, but I wouldn't have gone had I not trusted Gwen implicitly.

As we stood waiting for the elevator, a teenage boy kind of hovered in my peripheral. When I turned to him with an eyebrow raised, he whispered, "Is that the guitarist from Blue is the Color?"

I glanced at David. "Are you?"

He gave the kid a pained smile. "I am. But can we keep this between us?"

The boy nodded. "Of course, man. I was visiting my grandma—she broke her hip. I can't believe you're just standing here!"

He rode down the elevator with us, and David patiently answered his music questions while deftly dodging anything personal. When we got to the lobby, I started to walk off, already dreaming of showers and fresh clothes, but David called my name.

"Just wait a minute, okay?"

"Sure."

I stood by the wall of windows, looking out as he finished talking to the boy. When he laid a hand on my shoulder, I almost jumped out of my skin.

He held his hands up. "Whoa. Did I startle you?"

My shoulder tingled where his hand had been. Not because I desired him so much; more like his skin was laced with acid.

"I guess. What did you need?"

He hitched his duffle bag up on his shoulder. "A ride."

"No, I'm not driving you all the way to Baltimore."

He chuckled. "I'm not asking for that. Mind if I get cleaned up at your place? I wanna get back here as soon as we can."

I couldn't think of any reason to say no, even though I wanted to. Spending more time with David was not healthy for me. But I'd never deny him time with his daughter.

"Let's go."

THREE

DAVID

I'D NEVER BEEN inside Sylvia's house. Emma always ran outside when I picked her up, and I'd certainly never been invited in for tea and cookies.

Sylvia was an enigma, but I knew one thing for sure about her: she'd rather never see me again. I didn't feel the same, but I got it. Our history was mostly little vignettes, bursts of interaction, followed by months of stony silence. The rest of our shared history was a mix of a whole hell of a lot of confusion and disappointment and a few spectacular drops of pain.

This...today, only added to the shared pain. Seeing my kid like that, all banged up and mostly unconscious, carved out a place in my heart I hadn't known existed. Even though I wasn't around most of the time, there was a primal part of myself, maybe leftover from the caveman days, that knew my one job was to protect my family. Em *was* my family, and I'd let her down. It wasn't logical—there was no way I could've stopped a wreck—but knowing that only made it worse. Before now, I'd never had to think about how vulnerable she truly was. The what-ifs had never crossed my mind.

I wanted to get hammered. I'd stopped drinking a few years ago, and I rarely got tempted anymore, but I wanted to grab a bottle and drown out the image of her in that hospital bed.

I wouldn't, though. Bad things happened when I drank. Things I couldn't take back.

Sylvia was quiet as she drove us to her house, giving me a chance to study her profile. She had what a lot of people would politely refer to as an "interesting face." I always thought she was hella pretty. Yeah, her nose and mouth didn't fit her small face, and her deep-set blue eyes were so light, they were almost clear, but I liked it. Usually, I went for the obvious, in-your-face tits and ass, but there was something about Sylvia's unconventional beauty that drew me in.

Not that I ever got to see her in person. She was mostly a mysterious figure at the window when I picked Emma up and dropped her back off. My daughter liked to text me pictures, though, by herself and with Sylvia. I wasn't too proud to admit I saved a lot of them and scrolled through more often than I *was* proud to admit.

She parallel parked in front of her house like a pro, and I hopped out. She and Emma had lived here for the last five years, just a few miles from my mom's house and a half hour from mine. I trekked up the steep, wooden stairs behind her to the front porch. The house was over a hundred years old, and I wished like hell she'd let me pay to have it fixed up, but I knew better than to ask. I was lucky she accepted the meager child support payments I sent each month.

I knew why. It wasn't that she was too proud, it was that she didn't want anything from *me* specifically. I'd fucked up a lot in the early years of Em's life—not being there as often as I should've, missing payments when I got caught up on life on the road. I'd fucked up later too, in other even more staggering ways.

She let me step into the house first, and I was surprised it was a lot nicer than it looked on the outside. Not my taste with its crowded, overstuffed furniture and thick, colorful rugs over the hardwood floors, but I was glad Emma lived in a place like this. Reminded me of my mom's house. Hell, for all I knew, my mom had helped decorate it.

"You want to shower first?" Sylvia asked.

"Uh, there's only one shower?"

"Yes, only the one," she replied tersely.

I contemplated the level of my stench and eagerness to wash off the strange women that had been festering on my skin longer than even I was comfortable with. Smelling like I'd just climbed out of a brothel while spending time with my kid and her mom was pretty much a nightmare.

"You sure it's okay?" I asked.

"I wouldn't have offered if it wasn't."

"All right. Lead the way."

I followed her up a narrow, creaky flight of stairs to a pristine, old fashioned as hell bathroom, complete with a claw foot tub.

"There are towels under the counter. We only have super girly soap, but I imagine you're used to smelling like women." She lifted her chin. "Let me know when you're done."

"That was low, Syl."

She arched a brow. "But not untrue." With that, she walked down the hall and went into a room, closing the door firmly behind her.

In the shower, washing with her *girly soap*, my brain was short circuiting from all the thoughts firing at once. The way Emma had looked so small in that big bed. Sylvia completely wrecked next to her. This house my kid had been growing up in I'd never been inside. The look Syl gave me in the hallway.

Normally, it didn't bother me when someone hated me. In fact, I kinda reveled in it. I loved finding weak spots and poking at them. I didn't know why. Guessed I was an asshole by nature.

But I had trouble knowing Sylvia hated me. I didn't want her looking at me like I was a dirtball. That grated. Possibly because she was this sweet little thing who'd never hated anyone a day in her life, but with me, it seemed to come easy.

I couldn't even hold it against her, 'cause she never held it against me. Never poisoned Emma with her opinion of me. Always went out of her way to share her when I came to town.

She was the good girl who got mixed up with the bad boy. It never should have amounted to anything. Just a memory to think about when she was under her church-going, golden-boy husband, but we were never meant to be tied like this.

I couldn't even be mad about the broken condom, though.

After my shower, I tapped on what I assumed was Sylvia's door, since it was the only one closed, letting her know the bathroom was free, and wandered up another flight of stairs. Emma's room. She occupied the entire top floor—she'd been over the damn moon when Syl let her move up here a couple years ago—with its sloped ceilings and nooks and crannies. I grinned at the window seat covered in pillows, a paperback book still open to the page she'd been reading. I picked it up, planning on taking it to the hospital for her.

I walked around the room, inhaling her Emma scent, and the events of the last twenty-four hours rammed into me like a Mack truck, completely flattening me until I had to sit down on the edge of her bed to catch my breath.

I still didn't know how the accident happened—hell, it felt like I didn't know anything. Just that I could've lost my girl. And then what would I be? My brain refused to even travel down that path. Not an option.

I had to get out of there. Go outside, get some air. Just *breathe.*

I almost stumbled down the stairs, but stopped short when I saw Sylvia, wrapped in a towel, darting across the hall from the bathroom to her room. I followed her path with my eyes, taking mental note of the water dripping down the slope of her neck, the creaminess of her skin, and holy fuck—the flash of ink stretching the width of her shoulders and disappearing under her towel as she shut the door.

That was...a surprise. I didn't need to be thinking about where Sylvia Price's ink ended. But at least it distracted me from the onslaught of a panic attack.

Through her galley kitchen, I found a door leading to a small, rickety deck out back. Sylvia had made it nice with a couple padded chairs, a small, painted table, and umbrella, but it looked like the whole damn thing needed tearing down.

I sat down carefully, knowing I weighed a hell of a lot more than Emma and Sylvia. They could have had so much more than this. So much more. A job in community outreach for a theater didn't exactly compare to playing the guitar for a well-known rock band—at least monetarily. I knew she wasn't rolling in it, but anytime I tried to send more than two thousand bucks a month, Syl would send it right back.

I couldn't complain about the view. Their patch of grass led to a thin layer of trees, the leaves just starting to turn orange and red, and beyond that was a stream. I could hear it babbling from there. I imagined Emma out there with the pink guitar she'd asked for when she'd turned twelve, strumming to the sounds of nature or some shit. Yeah, she'd like that.

I pulled out my phone. I had no idea where my boys were or what time it was there, but so long as they weren't on stage, Nick would answer.

He picked up immediately. "You there?"

I chuckled. "Yeah. Got here a few hours ago. You guys still in Russia?"

"Helsinki, man. You've been gone for a day and already forgotten our tour schedule?"

"Don't think I ever knew it. I just follow you guys everywhere."

In the background, I heard Jas and Tali asking what I was saying. I didn't hear Ian, but that motherfucker was as quiet as a ninja, so he was probably in the room too.

"I'm gonna put you on speaker," Nick said.

"David? Are you there?" Tali asked.

"I'm at Sylvia's house. Em's at the hospital." I filled them on the rest of it. The rod in her leg, the upcoming weeks of physical therapy, and how fucking helpless I felt right now. I wasn't really the type to hold in my feelings, especially around the band. We were together more than we were apart, so if I felt shit, I shared shit.

"How's Em dealing?" Jas asked.

"She actually seemed pretty cheerful when we left. My mom was there, and Em basically kicked Sylvia and me out."

"How's Sylvia?" Nick asked.

"She seems pretty shattered, man."

"Of course she is," said Tali.

"Hey, who you got covering for me?" I asked.

"Fuckin' Laird Jensen," said Jas.

I covered my mouth. "Oh shit. From Airplane Stories?"

"He's the worst," Ian finally spoke up. I *knew* that motherfucker was there.

"He's talented," Nick argued.

"That, he is," I conceded. "But he smells like blue cheese and is a major close talker."

Jasper snorted. "Fucker likes to riff off during the show. Gets right in my face. Dude is ripe."

"We were lucky to get him," Tali said. "And it's only a week. Stop being babies."

"Man, I wouldn't want to be anywhere else, but can't say I'm not missing being on stage with you fools for those last few shows." My fingers were already twitching for my guitar.

"You're missed. But you've gotta take care of your girl," Nick said.

I exhaled heavily. "I am. I will."

"I sent Em some anime. Did you know there's anime Jane Austen?" Ian asked.

"I did not know that. But she's a big reader, so I'm sure she'll appreciate it," I said.

"We're thinking about you, dude. Dalia's in Baltimore, and she said to tell you if you need anything, call her," Nick said.

I nodded, letting my head hang. "Just...send some healing vibes into the universe."

"You've got it," he said.

"Call me if I can do anything, all right?" asked Tali.

"I will."

We said our goodbyes, and I tossed my phone on the table. Goddamn, what I wouldn't give for Em to be fine and me to be back with my boys in fuckin' Finland. I couldn't believe smelly Laird Jensen was taking my place. Bright side: they'd never permanently replace me with him. No one could stand smelling him long-term.

"Hey."

I turned my head to find Sylvia standing in the doorway, a bag of bread in hand. I jerked my chin in response.

"Want a sandwich? I'm making one for myself..."

"That'd be nice," I said.

She nodded curtly. "Give me a minute."

I closed my eyes, listening to the sounds of Sylvia in the kitchen and the slow rush of the water. Being on stage, playing my music, would never get old, but there was something to be said for a little peace now and then.

A clunk on the table in front of me had me opening my eyes again.

"It's peanut butter and jelly." Sylvia gestured to the sandwich now in front of me.

"Cool. Thanks."

She sat down across from me, her eyes on her plate. I took a bite of my sandwich while I watched her. We'd never been together alone like this since...Jesus, the one time we fucked. And that night was clouded in such a haze of cheap liquor, the only thing I really remembered clearly was the horror of pulling out only to find my jizz leaking from a rip in the condom.

Syl was all covered up now, no hint of the ink on her back. Her hair was still damp, piled on top of her head. She looked young. Not like the mom of a teenager.

"This deck's seen better days," I said.

Her eyes met mine, and she slowly blinked at me.

I held my hands up. "I'm just sayin'..."

"I'll get right on that."

"You know, I could have someone out here to rebuild it—" I started. And stopped. Sylvia looked at me like she might stuff her sandwich down my throat.

"Can we not?" she asked.

I cocked my head. "Not what?"

"Talk about anything other than the one thing we have in common. I'm not interested in your opinion of my house or anything else." There wasn't any venom in her voice, only exhaustion. With anyone else, any other time, her words would've ignited me. When someone told me not to do something, it was like waving a red flag in front of a raging bull. I charged head first, even if I saw the brick wall in front of me.

For once in my life, I thought before I acted.

"Sure." Right before I took a bite of my sandwich, I asked, "Whose car was Emma in?"

She cleared her throat. "A friend's."

"Name?"

"Why?"

I wiped my mouth with the back of my hand. "'Cause I'd like to know. Is it a secret?"

"No."

I chuckled. "Yet, you don't seem to want to tell me."

She tossed her sandwich down and rubbed circles on her temples. "His name is Evan. She's known him since they were really little. He was driving her home from school when a mail truck T-boned them on Emma's side. And thank god it was a mail truck. If it had been a faster moving vehicle..." She squeezed her eyes closed.

"Shit, is the kid okay?"

"Fine. I saw him in the ER. He only had a few scratches from the airbag. He was beside himself."

I leaned forward, my brow pinched. "Why didn't you want to tell me that?"

She threw her hands up. "I don't know. It feels like I'm slogging through mud just to talk at all right now."

She did look like she was struggling, and I felt like I was stuck in that same mud, right along with her. "You should get some sleep."

"Not happening. We should get back to the hospital."

I was pretty damn tired myself, so I didn't press the issue. Although, I wanted to. *Who's fuckin' Evan?* There'd be time for that later.

We cleaned up lunch, and I waited by the front door while

Sylvia grabbed some things for Emma. Then, we drove back to the hospital in awkward, awkward silence. I had a thing about silence. I liked to fill it with noise. But in her presence, it was like all my noise died. Not in a peaceful way. More like: *I have a million things I want to say to this woman and know she doesn't want to hear a single one of them.*

So, I shut the hell up and went along for the ride.

FOUR

SYLVIA

WHILE I SAT WITH EMMA, David paced back and forth in the hallway, talking on his phone. I imagined he was updating his band on her condition, but maybe he was talking to a girlfriend.

Then I remembered the smell of cheap perfume wafting off him when we'd been trapped in my car together and thought better of it. Probably not a girlfriend. Unless he referred to groupies as girlfriends.

"How long is Dad staying?" Emma asked.

"No idea. You know he never stays long."

"Actually—" We both jerked our heads in the direction of the door where David hovered. "I'm sticking around for a while. Blue is on a year hiatus."

Emma gasped. "You're going to be in town for a year?"

He sauntered closer, an easy smile playing on his lips. "Don't know about that. A year is a long ass time and your papa is a rolling stone. I'll definitely be home until you're all healed up."

If Gwen hadn't gone back to work, she would have popped him on the back of his head, I was sure of it.

He didn't see light fade from Emma's eyes, but I'd never miss it. After all these years, you'd think she would have given up hope of having a dad who'd do "normal" dad things with her. Who'd be there for milestones and soccer games. But she hadn't. She'd always invite him and get disappointed when he'd turn her down. And then, I'd get the brunt of it. Funny how that worked.

David ended up reading to her for a while, and then a physical therapist named Maria came in to get Emma out of bed. It was horrifically painful to watch. With the support of Maria, she hobbled a few feet to the bathroom, and after she did her business, hobbled back to bed.

Emma was sweaty and glassy-eyed from the effort. David looked completely anguished. And I...I didn't know what I was. Exhausted, sure. But I'd mostly shut down. It was all too much, my girl being hurt and now David here—but not for long—I couldn't deal.

Maria started going over what recovery looked like, and I only took in bits and pieces, although the words "can't climb stairs" zapped my brain.

"Wait, what do you mean about the stairs?" I interrupted.

The smile she gave me was pretty condescending, as if she were talking to an idiot. "Obviously, she won't be able to climb stairs for several weeks."

I sat back in my chair. "This presents a major problem."

"It doesn't have to be a problem. I don't have stairs," David said.

I turned sharply toward him. "Not happening."

"Don't I get a say?" Emma asked.

With my eyes still narrowed on David, I said, "No."

Maria chuckled uncomfortably. "Well, I'll leave that to you folks to figure out. I'll be back in a couple hours to get Emma out of bed again."

I crossed my arms over my chest. "Can we talk in the hall for a moment?"

He followed me out the door, leaning a shoulder against the wall opposite me. "What's your deal?"

"My *deal* is I'm not sending my seriously injured daughter to stay with you for weeks. As brave as she's being, there's no way she won't want me there. And there's no way you can take care of her by herself."

He was quiet for a beat, staring me down, then his lips quirked upward. "You'd stay there too, Syl. You're goddamn right I can't handle her recovery by myself, but then, I doubt you can either."

My hands wrapped tighter around my body. "You have no idea what I can handle by myself."

"Can you carry Emma up those steep stairs? Can you get her in and out of that clawfoot tub?"

I stayed silent, because what could I say?

He softened his stance, shoving his hands in his pockets. "I have three bedrooms. Em has her own room. My condo's big. We wouldn't be in each other's faces. I think I'm going to have to put my foot down right now, for the first time ever, and say this is what's happening. You're staying with me."

I looked away, out of options, out of energy, and out of fight. "Fine. Thank you."

He took a half step closer. "You don't need to thank me."

My eyes lifted to his. "Just promise there won't be any drinking or drugs or parties while we're there."

Any softness on his face disappeared in an instant. He didn't respond, only shook his head as he turned his back to me and walked back into Em's room.

Awesome start.

· · ·

ABSENTLY, I stuffed another T-shirt into my already full duffle bag.

"Are you seriously taking your circa two-thousand-and-four *Rent* shirt? That thing is holey as hell!"

I glanced down at the shirt in my hand, one I'd dug from the very bottom of my drawer, and then at my friend, Suz, who was sitting cross-legged on my bedroom floor. She started laughing, so I tossed it at her.

"Girl, I swear, I've never seen you this nervous!" she said.

"I'm not nervous." I drew an air circle around my face. "This is the face of a woman about to enter an uncomfortable situation for an extended period of time. And I have to be nice because, hello, my kid will be there."

"Evan is dying that Em's going to be so far away."

I sighed, plopping next to Suz on the plush, very faux, Persian rug. "Her physical therapist said she'll be back at school in three weeks. And he can visit. I think. I haven't actually broached the subject of visitors with David."

"Have you broached any subjects with him?"

I laid my head on my friend's shoulder. "Barely. We've been two ships passing in the night these last four days."

Emma spent five nights total in the hospital, and David, Gwen, and I set up a rotation so someone would always be there with her. After five nights of barely any sleep, I hoped the bed in my room at David's was comfortable, because I had big plans of crashing hard.

"Well, you're gonna have trouble keeping Evan away for long. Poor guy feels like shit," Suz said.

"I'll talk to David about it tonight...or tomorrow, or..."

She pushed my shoulder. "Since when are you a wimp?"

"Since never! But it's like one look at his smug, beautiful face and I'm transformed into a little church mouse. It pisses me off like no other."

She snorted out another laugh. "You are the coolest bish in town, and I adore that you've got this dude thinking you're a little lamb."

"I swear to all things holy, around him, I am."

From our limited interactions over the last few days, it was clear David had decided I was a delicate flower who needed careful handling, which was as funny to me as it was Suz. After all this time, he still had no idea who I was.

Suz did, though. We'd shared an apartment when we were both young, broke single moms, basically raising our kids together. Which was why we were both kind of squicked out when her son, Evan, and my Emma declared their love for each other—and not the brother/sister kind. We got over it pretty fast when we witnessed how innocent and sweet they were together. Plus, Evan knew he'd have to deal with my wrath if he ever stepped out of line.

She rubbed the shaved side of her head—something she did whenever she was mulling. "Want me to go with you today?"

I rubbed her head, which *I* did when I needed good luck. "Nah. Let me get settled in and figure out the lay of the land. Hell, for all I know, he'll barely be there. That wouldn't surprise me."

"The offer still stands to stay with me, you know."

I kissed her cheek, then pulled myself off the ground. "And I love you for offering, but you have as many stairs as me. I'm not sure how that would possibly work."

"Mika could carry Em around with one hand."

I laughed. Suz's brand new, muscle-bound husband probably *could* carry Emma around like a little kitten. *He* was the lamb out of the three of us, so soft and sweet to Suz—which she deserved more than anyone. There was no way I'd impose on their newlywed bliss like that.

"Em's already at David's place. If I keep saying it'll be fine, will that make it true?"

She got up too, brushing imaginary lint off her ripped jeans. "The only thing you can do is hope for the best, right?"

I nodded. "And that Emma has extra-human healing abilities."

"Oooh, yeah, right now *would* be a great time to find out she's a fast healing mutant."

I lifted my bag, packed full of who-knows-what, and started down the stairs with Suz on my heels. She lived in a house very similar to mine three doors down. When I met her through a Craigslist ad at eighteen, I never imagined I'd still know her all these years later. Frankly, I thought we'd last a year together, max. But we clicked instantly. And our living arrangement had been symbiotic. She'd worked and gone to school during the day while I watched the kids, and we switched off at night. That left both of us completely exhausted, but in hindsight, those were some of the happiest years of my life.

She helped me load a few essentials into my car, then I ran out of ways to delay any longer. We hugged for a long moment before Suz pushed me away.

"Get outta here. Be the Sylvie I know."

"My spine of steel is on standby." I squeezed her hand. "Tell Ev I don't blame him. If he's beating himself up, he'll have to answer to me."

She hugged me again. "I'll tell him that." Then, she slapped my bum. "No more stalling!"

As I drove away from my little old house, the one I bought on my own five years ago when I'd started my life over for the third or fourth time, I wondered if it would look different when I got home in a few weeks—if *I'd* be different. Then I shook the cobwebs out of my head. These thoughts weren't my own. They were the sheer exhaustion of the last few days creeping in. Of course my house would look the same. Nothing was going to change.

DAVID LIVED IN BALTIMORE, right by the water. His modern condo was surrounded by cobblestone streets and brightly colored row houses. To me, his building was an eyesore. Give me old and full of character any day.

I did have to admit—only to myself—the assigned spot in the parking garage and private elevator to his penthouse was quite convenient. I wouldn't let myself get used to it, but I sure as hell would enjoy it while I had it.

At his door, I didn't know whether I should let myself in or knock. He'd given me the key, but it didn't feel right to use it. So, I stood there, like a doofus, contemplating my options. And that was how he found me when he opened the door, an amused grin on his face.

"You gonna stand there all day?" he asked.

I took a step back, almost stumbling over my duffle bag. "Maybe. I was thinking about it."

He peered out in the hallway, looking left and right. "That's a choice. I gotta say, it's a lot more comfortable in here." He bent down and scooped up my heaviest bag. "I'm taking this inside. You coming?"

I followed him in, not really looking around. I'd been here once, five years ago, and I knew how grand it was, although it had been full of a lot more people then. David had been playing guitar in Blue is the Color for almost two decades, and they'd become pretty damn popular after signing their first record contract thirteen years ago. He was wealthy beyond my capacity of understanding. It made me happy to know Em would always be cared for in that area, but that was as far as my interest in his money went.

It wasn't that I was above needing and wanting more money. If I were ever in a tight spot, I'd have no problem asking David to help. Well, that wasn't true. I'd hate doing it, and I'd exhaust all other options first, but I'd suck it up if I had to. That hadn't happened yet. We were perfectly comfortable—finally. My job was good, paid decently, and I actually had a savings account out of the triple digits.

"Hey, Mom!" Emma was propped on a cream-colored sectional, her pink guitar resting on her lap. Next to her, on the floor, was another guitar. Not pink. The thought of them playing guitar together had that crack in my chest crumbling at the edges.

"Hey, lady," I said. "Are you comfortable?"

"I was thinking about a nap actually."

David hopped into action, grabbing her walker and helping her into a standing position. I followed them down a short hallway into a peacock blue bedroom. She'd described her room to me in detail—David had hired a decorator and let Em go to town—but I never imagined I'd step foot in it. She had a massive canopy bed, with plush, vibrant bedding in magenta, sapphire, and emerald. There was a window seat just like she had at home, but this one was deep enough for two people to share, and the pillows and cushions looked custom made.

It was hard not to develop an inferiority complex seeing all this, but I managed. Em's room in our house was one I would have dreamed of having as a kid, with all its little hiding spots and character. This one was gorgeous, but didn't feel lived in. And it truly wasn't. She probably spent less than a month here total each year.

Once we got Em settled in for a nap, David took me to what

would be my room on the other side of the condo, next to his room. It was a lot smaller than Em's, and more closely resembled a swanky hotel than a guest bedroom.

"It's...nice," I said.

He tossed my bag on the padded bench at the end of the bed and put his hands on his hips. "It's sterile. Sorry about that."

I sat on the edge of the bed, surprised at how soft it was. "I don't mind. It's not like I'm staying forever. It'll do." A wide yawn overtook me.

David chuckled. "You as tired as I am?"

I pointed to my mouth. "Did you see that yawn? My brain is about to shut down and send my body into a coma if I don't get some solid sleep."

He scrubbed a hand over the thick scruff on his jaw. "I'm used to broken sleep, driving around on a tour bus all night. The other guys saw logs. Meanwhile, I'm awake every ten minutes."

"And yet you haven't stopped touring for thirteen years straight." I didn't mean to sound as snarky as I did, but I couldn't take it back.

He cocked his head, his mouth turning down slightly. "Guess I love the music more than sleep."

"More than anything," I mumbled as I went to my bag.

"What the fuck did you say?"

I glanced over my shoulder. "I said I'm tired and ready for a nap too." I took my time finding a tank and shorts to change into. When I turned around, David was still standing there, scowling.

"I'm gonna pretend I didn't hear what you *actually* said. We're all on edge. I get it. But if you say some shit like that to me again, I won't let it slide. We *will* have words."

Pinching my lips together, I stared at him with wide eyes. From the way he immediately backed down, he probably read my expression as fear or intimidation. In reality, I was biting my tongue to stop myself from unleashing all the things I'd wanted to say to him for years.

This was exactly why I shouldn't be around him. He thought very little of me, but I had a million reasons to hate him. And I did.

FIVE

DAVID

I SHOULD'VE BEEN ASLEEP. My kid was back in bed after we shared a quiet dinner. Her mom hadn't emerged from her room since she went in there in the late afternoon. I was dead tired. But it was the kind of tired that left me wired. I knew the crash was coming, but I had to wait until it took me over.

Instead of sleeping, I sat on my balcony, playing my acoustic Gibson. Mostly random notes with a few classic rock riffs thrown in here or there.

I was always the most peaceful when Emma was under my roof. It didn't happen a lot, so my days of peace were few and far between. The kicker was it was my own damn fault.

The balcony door slid open, and I turned to see Sylvia step out wearing a hoodie and microscopic shorts. She hovered just outside the door, staring out at the view.

"I seem to have slept the day away," she said.

"Guess your body did that coma thing you talked about."

She nodded. "Guess so. But now I'm wide awake." She finally turned toward me. "Did Em have dinner?"

"Yep. We had a nice night. I think all the healing her body's doing is wiping her out. She was pretty subdued."

"Okay...well, I guess I'll go scrounge up something to eat."

I pushed a chair toward her with my foot. "Stay a while."

She seemed reluctant, not that I was surprised. I'd been hard as hell with her earlier, and the more I'd thought about it, the more I'd convinced myself I'd misheard her—that she hadn't insinuated I loved music more than Emma. This was *Sylvia*. And if she had said it...well, like I'd said, we were all on edge.

After what looked like a battle waging inside her brain, she sat down, her eyes still glued to the city lights reflecting off the water.

"It's nice up here." Her words floated in the cool air like a feather.

"Wish I had more time to appreciate it."

"Didn't you say the band is taking a year off? Now's your chance."

I plucked at a random string instead of answering right away. "We are, but I can't picture myself not making music in some form. I don't know who I am without it."

She hugged her arms around her stomach. "Maybe it's time to figure that out."

"Yeah, maybe," I muttered.

Sylvia propped her feet up on the balcony railing, and my eyes were automatically drawn to her bare legs. I almost swallowed my tongue when I saw the tattoo running from beneath her tiny shorts all the way to her ankle.

"That's some fuckin' tattoo, Sylvia."

She traced the flower-covered vine on her thigh. "Isn't it pretty? I got this one a couple years ago. My friend Suz's husband owns his own tattoo shop. He did it for me."

"Did he do your back piece?" I asked.

"You saw that?"

"I might'a caught a glimpse a few days ago."

She twisted in her chair, pulling her legs under her...unfortunately. "Yeah, he did my back piece too."

"I'm surprised you have so much ink."

"Why?"

"Ah..." I plucked my guitar again. "I guess I don't know. Doesn't fit the image I have of you."

She let out a short laugh. "Well, as a soccer mom myself, I'll have you know most soccer moms have at least one tattoo these days."

I scoffed. "Like a tramp stamp?"

"Oh, god, I hate that term. Why aren't those swirly, faux-tribal tattoos every bro seems to have called swine signs?"

She had me laughing. "Swine signs? That's amazing."

With an arched brow, she asked, "Do you have one?"

I pushed up the sleeves of my T-shirt, showing her my biceps. "No tribal tats to speak of."

She reached out, stopping herself just short of touching my arm. "Are those clock gears?"

"Yep. Nick has a pocket watch on his neck—he got it when we signed our first deal—and all of us except Jas went out and got a different tattoo of the same theme."

"Aw, that's cute."

"We were twenty. It was pure dumb luck we wound up in a clean, reputable place and didn't contract Hep or some shit. We could have just as easily ended up looking like we'd got our ink in prison."

The corners of her mouth lifted faintly, and she turned her attention back to the view. I plucked at the strings of my guitar while studying her profile. Moonlight lit her pale skin, giving her an otherworldly glow. Yeah, I liked looking at her.

I'd always been curious about her, wondering what she and Emma were up to, what *she* was up to. Sylvia had a wall around her when it came to me. She only let me see what she wanted me to see when she knew I was looking. It was those times when she hadn't known I was looking I caught glimpses of who she really was.

"What were you like at Em's age?" I asked.

Sylvia leaned her head back, turning toward me. "Nothing like her. I was a pretty angry kid." She tapped her fingers on her knee for a moment. "What about you?"

Deflecting, yet her vague answer only had me more interested.

"Pretty chill. Not too different than I am now. I just wanted to play music, fuck around a little, and hang out with my boys."

"The guys from the band?"

"Yeah."

"How's everyone doing since Reinece passed away?" she asked gently, but not gently enough for my heart not to ache at the mention of her name. My stupid heart had no idea what was going on. It'd gone along, thump, thump, thumping to its regular tune for so long, it didn't really know how to deal with all this battering it'd been taking lately.

Reinece was Jasper's mom by birth, and Nick's by choice—hers and his. When I thought about it, she pulled us all into her fold, coming to all our early, shitty shows at tiny, rundown venues. She'd died almost seven months ago from cancer—cancer that took her life faster than any of us had been prepared for.

"I mean, fuck. We're all devastated. Obviously, Jas and Nick are the worst, but there's always gonna be an empty spot in our lives." I smiled. "I can still see baby Em sitting in her lap, watching us practice in Jas's garage."

"Aw, I'd love to have seen that," she said.

I nodded. "I bet I have a picture somewhere. Reinece was our first fan, Emma was our second." I tapped the arm of her chair. "Jas appreciated the note and flowers you sent to her funeral."

"It was nothing. I only met her a handful of times at Gwen's house, but she really was a lovely woman."

"Yeah," I said softly. "She was."

I strummed the bridge of "When It's Gone," the song Nick wrote about Reinece. Sylvia tipped her face up to the sky, listening, and I watched as she mouthed the words. Knowing she was a fan of our music clicked another puzzle piece into place. But there were still a thousand missing. The picture I had of her was scattered and didn't quite make sense.

After a minute, she rubbed her lips together, her eyes skating over my face. "You guys have never fought? Never broken up?"

"Nah. We bicker like an old married couple, but we're tight. Nick wouldn't stand for it if we weren't."

"Nick Fletcher? The lead singer?"

I leaned closer, smirking. "You a big fan, babydoll?"

Her eyeroll was immediate, and so was my regret. God, we'd been having such a...pleasant time, and I had to ruin it. Shit slipped out of my mouth sometimes. Shit that got me in trouble. And I loved it. That look she gave me? The mix of annoyance and disgust? That was my jam. It meant a button had been pressed, which was my intention most of the time.

Not with Syl, though. I couldn't have her thinking I was some slimebag or being pissed at me. She held the keys to the kingdom, our kid. And yeah, I actually cared what she thought of me.

"David..."

"Sorry. I'm being smarmy, huh?"

"Yeah. Let's cool it with the 'babydolls.' I'm not going to be that girl for you. I'm here for Em. When she's healed, I'm gone. If we can be civil, I'll be happy."

"We're not gonna be friends?" I asked.

"No. I really don't think that's in the cards for us."

I inclined my head. "Fair enough."

We slipped back into silence, and I played my guitar, needing noise to fill every space around me. Surprisingly, she stayed for a while, curled up in her chair, watching my hands move over the strings.

And I liked it. I liked having her there as a quiet audience. Her presence reminded me of a cool breeze on a hot night. A brief reprieve from the discomfort. I imagined what it would be like to have this all the time. Late night balcony talks while our kid was snug in her bed. It didn't sound too bad.

When she went back inside without a word, I realized it was better not even knowing how good it could be. Better to stick it out in the boiling heat.

I STUMBLED out of bed in the morning, brain foggy with the five or six hours of sleep I got. Not enough, but it'd do.

Emma was on the couch, tapping away on her phone. "Mornin'. Did you sleep okay?"

She grinned up at me. "Like the dead. I feel a lot better this morning. I managed to get out of bed by myself."

My heart lodged in my throat. "Em, no. You need to call for us. You could hurt yourself worse."

She rolled her eyes. "Look at me! I'm fine. The walker was right next to the bed, and I didn't even come close to falling. I would've peed my pants if I had to wait for you or Mom."

Panic clawed at me. I wasn't equipped to deal with my kid being hurt. If I could've kept her in a bubble, I would've. This worrying wasn't a feeling I was used to.

I hated it.

"Just...be careful," I said. Her attention had already drifted back to her phone, so I went in search of sustenance.

Sylvia was in the kitchen, frowning into the refrigerator.

"What did the fridge ever do to you?"

She jumped, her hands flying to her chest. "Holy crap, David!"

I chuckled, taking her in. Her dark hair was loose around her shoulders. I'd never seen hair so shiny. Didn't know it came that way. It was like a sheet of black glass hanging down her back. I had to shove my hand in my pocket to stop myself from touching it.

She'd ditched the hoodie she'd had on last night, so now her clothes consisted of a tank top and those damn shorts. She'd changed over the years. She was still small, but her arms and shoulders were defined with sleek muscle, and when I lowered my gaze to her legs, I saw they were too. I'd missed that in the dim light of my balcony.

"Damn, Syl, do you work out?"

I knew I shouldn't have said it, so I was relieved when she laughed. "You could say that." She turned back to the fridge. "You have no food. Did you know that?"

"Open the freezer."

Leaning down, she pulled open the freezer drawer, momentarily distracting me with the flex of her biceps.

She held up a plastic, labeled container. "What is this?"

I read the label. "Looks like veggie lasagna."

She lifted another, and another. "Stir fry, turkey meatballs, potstickers...what is all this?"

I rubbed the back of my neck. "I have someone who comes in and cooks for me when I'm home. She makes extra and freezes it. It's good shit."

She peered down in the loaded freezer. "Huh. Anything for breakfast in here?"

"I don't discriminate. I've been known to eat pasta for breakfast."

She put everything back and slid the drawer closed. "Not me. I need eggs, maybe some cereal or oatmeal. You know, actual breakfast food."

"I think there's some bread around here somewhere," I offered.

"I found it. Made Em some toast with jelly." She sighed. "I'll just hit the grocery store today."

"You don't have to. I can call someone to do that."

She shook her head. "That's crazy that you can just call someone. I'll go. I like to cook, so I want to buy my own food." Raising on her tiptoes, she opened a cabinet. "At least you have cookware."

"Pretty sure my chef bought it."

She swiveled around to meet my eyes. "Your chef...?"

"She's not, like, only *my* chef. She works for other people too." I wasn't entirely sure why I felt compelled to explain this. Maybe because I'd been in Sylvia's house, seen the tiny, worn kitchen where she prepared all their meals. The gap between our lifestyles was miles wide.

"My mom's coming over in a bit. She can hang with Em and I'll go shopping with you. See how the little people live."

She started to throw eye daggers at me until I laughed. "I'm fucking with you, Syl."

She cracked a small smile. "I realize that. And sure. Since I have no idea where the store is—" She stopped and studied my contrite expression. "You don't know where it is either, do you?"

"I had big plans of Google mapping it before we left. Way to blow my cover."

She shook her head, but the smile didn't slip. "I'm going to shower. Do you have towels, or should we pick some up at the store too?"

I growled and searched the sink next to me. "If I had a sponge, I'd throw it at you right now. *Yes,* I have towels."

She lifted a shoulder innocently. "Just checking."

I watched her go, and her ass, which I'd somehow never noticed before, was like a gut punch. I had to lean against the counter to catch my breath. Those damn shorts hugged her round ass like a long-lost friend, and with how thin the fabric was, I could almost picture what she'd look like bare.

And fuck me if I didn't have to lock myself in my room at the thought of Sylvia bare. One night—one night living together —and I was already sliding into dangerous territory.

SIX

SYLVIA

I HELD up a bag of spinach. "Yay or nay?"

David grimaced. "What am I? Fuckin' Popeye? Nay forever."

I tossed it in the cart.

"Why ask if you're going to ignore my answer?"

I pushed the cart to the apples, grabbing a bag. "I heard your answer. I just disagree."

"What're you gonna do with the spinach?" he asked.

I piled several Honeycrisp apples into the bag. They were usually out of my price range, but I'd already decided to be generous and let David foot the bill for this shopping trip, so I was splurging.

"Make a salad, add it to my eggs, cook it with pasta...endless possibilities." I pointed to his thick muscles. "I'm surprised you don't make, like, spinach and kale smoothies every morning."

"I get my protein elsewhere. Never been a fan of spinach."

I gave him a pointed look. My mom look. "You've never had my cooking."

He grabbed the cart, forcing me to stop my progress up the pasta aisle. "You gonna cook for me, Syl?"

"I'm going to cook for Em and me. I think it might be a little awkward to have you watching us like a hungry puppy."

He chuckled, picking up a box of spaghetti. "No one's ever called me a puppy before."

I took the spaghetti from him, switching it out for my preferred brand. "Yeah...well, I never pictured us grocery shopping together. I guess it's a day for firsts."

I'd been attempting to pretend I wasn't completely disoriented. That my carefully curated opinion of David hadn't been upended last night. Maybe he wasn't just an asshole who was only decent to his mom and daughter. Maybe he was a decent guy all around. Then I remembered the "babydoll" comment and thought better of it.

When I was short with him at the hospital, I'd had stress and fear as an excuse. Now that Em was home...well, at one of *her* homes, and I'd gotten a more than decent night's sleep, my excuses had run out.

So, there I was, walking through Whole Foods with the man who'd broken my heart on more than one occasion, like we were normal people, living normal lives.

"Why have we never done anything like this together?" David asked.

My head jerked in his direction before I could stop myself. "You're never around. And I'm not sure I realized it was an option."

He'd taken me to buy diapers once after Em was born. I was almost certain Gwen had forced him to knock on my door and ask. At the time, I'd been a little in love with him, which, looking back, was probably due to my raging post-birth hormones. But mostly, I wanted to escape my parents' quiet, but constant, disapproval. So, I'd bundled Emma up and hopped in his car before he could blink twice.

The car ride had been awkward. I'd wanted to ask about his

music, but he'd only wanted to discuss Em. And then, when we'd pulled up in front of Safeway, he hadn't gotten out. He'd shoved a bunch of money in my hand and told me to get what I needed while he watched Emma in the car. So there I'd been, walking the aisles, all alone.

That was when I'd realized that was it. All he'd give me was money and occasionally babysit his daughter. Because that was what he'd done—he'd babysat. He hadn't been a partner. He hadn't been someone I could call for support when Em had cried all night and I didn't think I could stand it for one more second.

I knew he didn't look back on those early days the same way I did. Maybe a dad, even one present for every hiccup and dirty diaper, could never understand the confused desperation a new mom faced—or what I'd faced. I'd loved Em with every fiber of my being. My heart grew ten times its original size, just to make space for that love. But at the same time, I'd wanted out. I'd wanted everything I gave up back. I'd often wondered if I'd had her later, would I have felt the same way, but there was no knowing.

What I *did* know was I'd been completely alone in those feelings. No partner to share with. No one to hold me and tell me I wasn't a horrible person. Not a friend to whisper that this, too, would pass.

David and I had been neighbors since he and his mom moved into a house on the other side of the street when I was fourteen. Sometimes, when I was up in the middle of the night, nursing Emma for the third or fourth time, I'd see him stumbling home, loud and happy. It was on one of those nights I'd decided to hate him too.

I'd held onto that hate like a childhood blankie, but it had always been mixed with love. I couldn't help it. He'd do things for our kid when I'd least expected it. He'd thrown Emma a first birthday party, and not only had he invited all his hard-ass rocker friends, but he'd tracked down the few friends I had as well.

When she was three, Blue is the Color's first album released, and I'd never forget hearing the song that had been so clearly written for Em. He hadn't been the one to sing it, but his voice was all over the words.

When she was five, he went to her kindergarten class and put on a kid-friendly concert. When she was seven, he sang with her at her school talent show. When she was eight, he flew us to Paris so she could spend the day with him before his concert. When she was ten...well, he showed up at my engagement party because she'd begged me to invite him.

It was impossible not to love David, just a little. But I didn't trust him, not with Emma, and certainly not with myself. He'd let us both down in way I was sure he'd never come close to comprehending.

We made it to the bread aisle before I spoke about anything other than the items I'd put in the cart.

"My friend Suz and her son Evan would love to come by and visit Em. Would that be okay?" I asked while studying the English muffins.

"Syl..." He sounded exasperated.

I slowly met his eyes. "If it's not—" My words stopped in their tracks when his hand fell on my arm.

"You don't have to ask."

I tucked my hair behind my ear. "I feel weird inviting people to your house."

"It's Em's house too, and by extension, yours. Especially while you're staying there. Invite who you want."

"Okay. Thank you. I will." I continued walking, throwing a loaf of whole wheat bread into the cart.

"I've been wanting to lay eyes on the kid driving my daughter around anyway."

I let out a short laugh. "I've got the scary parent thing down. Em's friends sometimes think I'm going to be the cool mom because I'm young, but I quickly set them straight. Evan's a good kid. You don't have to thump your chest around him."

"I find it hard to believe you can be scary."

I stopped the cart and gave him my hardest look, throwing the resentment of a year of lonely, sleepless nights behind it.

He took a step back, his eyes flaring as he took me in. "Damn, Syl. I don't know whether I'm scared or turned on."

I poked his chest. "Scared is the answer."

He mock-saluted me. "Consider me duly intimidated." And then, he mumbled, "And a little turned on."

I slapped his arm, even though his flirtation got to me, just a little. "There will be none of that, David."

"Can't help liking it when women are mean to me."

"Probably because it's such a big change," I said.

He lifted a shoulder. "Maybe."

After we checked out and loaded the groceries in his car, I pointed to the liquor store next door. "Mind if I run in there to grab some beer?"

His eyes turned down to his shuffling feet. "Ahhh..."

"Oh. I didn't see any at your place, but if you already have some and I missed it..." I trailed off when he finally lifted his head.

"No, I don't drink. And I've never had to consider it, but I think I'd rather not have it in my house."

My heart thudded in my chest. The last time I'd spent any time with David, he'd been trashed. Since I hadn't seen him in five years, it only made sense I wouldn't know he was now sober. It wasn't like that was something he'd tell Emma, and most of my current knowledge of him was relayed through her.

"That's totally understandable," I said. "I'll have one of those kale and spinach smoothies you love so much."

He released a relieved laugh. "I might not put booze in my body anymore, but I sure as shit don't put that devil's drink in it either."

On the drive back to his place, I had a question. "I couldn't help noticing that first day in the hospital you smelled an awful lot like weed."

He kept his attention on the road, but his hands shifted and tightened on the steering wheel. "Yeah...I've been known to smoke a joint every once in a while. It's never been a problem for me, not like alcohol was."

Because his hands were still tight on the steering wheel, I touched his arm. "I wasn't implying anything. I was more curious than anything."

His eyes slid over to me for a beat. "I don't want you to think I'd do anything to put Emma in danger."

"I don't think that."

"You felt the need to tell me I couldn't drink or do drugs while you guys were staying with me. I know you think I'm a piece of shit, but I hope you also know I try not to be a piece of shit in front of Emma."

I opened my mouth to answer, but all my answers were jumbled. He kept talking anyway.

"I am kind of an asshole. I know it. And alcohol made me into a raging asshole. One who forgot a lot of shit he did when he woke up in the morning. When *I* woke up. But one day, a few years ago, I woke up and remembered. And I fucking disgusted myself. So I was done."

"Just like that?"

"Never touched it again." He pulled into his parking spot and turned off the car. "And now you know more about me than you ever wanted to know."

I snorted. "Why would you think I wouldn't want to know about you?"

With his hand on his door, he glanced over at me. "Come on, Syl. It's been pretty clear."

Meeting him around the back of the car, we both hefted full reusable grocery bags to the elevator.

"Do you know anything about me?" I asked quietly. I wanted the answer, but I didn't.

He sighed. "Not enough, that's for damn sure."

"Well..." I stared stiffly at the swiftly rising numbers as the elevator ascended to the top. "I'm sure by the time I'm back in my raggedy old house, you'll also know more than you ever wanted to know about me."

"I really fuckin' doubt that," he said with a hard edge.

We stepped off the elevator, and David put down his bags to dig his key from his pocket.

"Let's just be here for Em, okay?" I said to his back.

He turned to face me, the key dangling from his finger. "Always. And, Syl, I remember that night like it was yesterday."

Before I could ask which night, he'd slid the key in the lock and walked through the door. And I just stood there, jaw unhinged, face aflame, mind spinning like a top. There were only two nights he could be referring to, and I hoped to god he meant the night we conceived our kid, because the other one, I never wanted to think about again. The only way I'd survived the humiliation and heartbreak of it was knowing David had been too wasted to remember the details.

But now, once again, everything I thought I knew was upended.

"Sylvia! Get your sweet little booty in this house at once," called Gwen.

Pasting on a smile, I pushed through the door, calling out a hello to Emma and finding David and Gwen in the kitchen.

"Hey, baby!" she greeted.

I hoisted my bags onto the counter and gave her a hug. "Hey, Gwen. Emma give you any trouble?"

She waved me off. "Oh, the usual. Robbed a few banks, stole some old ladies' purses."

I nodded. "Cool, cool. You know how much I hate setting boundaries. She has to learn from her mistakes, even if it means jail time."

"My leg is broken! I haven't gone deaf, you know!" yelled Emma from the living room.

Gwen and I laughed together, and already, I felt lighter. She wasn't the typical grandma, at least not in looks. In her mid-fifties, she could've passed for a decade younger. People most likely guessed she was David's older sister rather than his mom. She was a fitness and yoga instructor, so her body was pretty much bangin'.

Once Blue is the Color hit it big, David started supporting her financially, and now she worked for fun. She was a whole different person than she'd been when I'd first had Emma—and, I assumed, when David was growing up.

When Emma was born, Gwen worked two jobs, and to be honest, she hadn't been thrilled to become a grandma at forty. She loved Emma, but she was pretty hands-off those first few years. She'd been a stand-up Grandma for a solid decade now, but from our conversations, I knew she'd thought she'd been a less than stellar mother. A lot had to do with her age when she had David, dealing with a shit husband, and then having to work her tail off to keep their heads above water after he left.

These days, when I asked for help, she was there in a heartbeat. She kept Emma overnight when I needed it, came with me to doctor's appointments and school plays. I think she knew her son's shortcomings and tried to make up for it by being a steady presence for us both.

And, in a way, she had. There was no question we were lucky to have her. Sometimes, I wondered how she'd produced a son like David. Where he was careless, she was measured. Where he could be cruel, she was unfailingly kind.

She wrapped an arm around my shoulder. "You doing okay, sweetheart? Did you get some rest?"

David threw his arms up. "Why didn't you ask *me*, your only son, that?"

She held up her finger, shaking it at him. "Because Sylvia is my girl, and she sometimes thinks she has to carry the weight of the world on her shoulders, when in fact, there are plenty of us to share the load. You, my darling boy, are the love of my life, but you don't carry the burden. I don't worry about you in the same way."

I sighed. "You don't have to worry about me anymore, Gwen. I've got this."

She gasped dramatically. "Me? Not worry? Never!"

From the living room, Emma called out, asking for help to the bathroom, and Gwen rushed out before I could even take a step.

David leaned back against the counter, surveying me with interest as I put away the last of the groceries.

"It's kinda funny my mom never mentioned how close the two of you are," he remarked casually, but there was some kind of accusation behind it.

"I didn't tell her to keep it from you. Are you actually surprised?"

He took a step closer, his hand smoothing down his flat stomach. "I don't know what I am." His mouth twisted as he thought about it. "Yeah, I guess I am surprised. I feel like I've stepped back into a life that's been moving on without me."

I closed the pantry and leaned against it. I probably

wouldn't have said anything had I not been on edge from his admission just before we stepped inside. But I was, so I did.

"It has. We didn't freeze in place the second you looked away. Your daughter grew up, your mom has transformed her life, and I..." I shook my head, "I've been here for all of it. You don't get to just appear and be surprised the people who stayed have learned to lean on each other and love each other. We may be living with you, but you're the interloper in this situation."

It was harsh, harsher than I'd intended, but it wasn't untrue.

He paced back and forth in the kitchen, his shoulders tense and hands balled. Then he stopped a foot away from me, nostrils flared as his eyes raked over me.

"Fuck you, Syl," he whispered harshly.

I pulled myself to my full height, not letting myself shrink in the corner like a scared little lamb.

"When you regret saying that, what's going to be your excuse? Can't use drinking this time, can you?"

His eyes bored into me, the effect visceral. Like he was seeing my insides, sifting them around, looking for the diamond amongst the coal. Crossing my arms over my stomach, I brushed past him, careful not to touch him.

Of course he grabbed me. Stopped me. I whipped around, freeing my arm.

"*What*?" I seethed.

"Why are you always so angry at me?" He had the nerve to sound lost.

"This isn't happening right now. Or ever. Keep your vitriol to yourself, okay? I'm going to check on *our* daughter."

I escaped the kitchen and David, but instead of going to Emma's room, I went to mine. I just needed a minute to stop shaking and will the tears in my eyes to dry up.

It was only day two, and already, our tenuous relationship had gone off the rails.

Did it even matter what kind of dad I thought he was? It shouldn't. Emma could barely remember the times he wasn't there. I was the one with the image of tears rolling down her chubby five-year-old cheeks when her daddy couldn't stay imprinted on my brain. *I* bought her a beret and walked down the *Champs Elysees* with her when David had already moved onto the next city on his tour.

To her, he hung the stars. To me, he was an alien invader disrupting and destroying each time he deigned to land his ship.

SEVEN

DAVID

I WAS A FUCK UP. I couldn't even deny it. But I'd always clung to my "good dad" image like it was a life raft in a stormy sea. I'd been back from the tour for a week, and I was already questioning it all.

I didn't want to question it. If I wasn't a good dad, who the hell was I? *My* dad?

I couldn't even think about it without shuddering.

Sylvia came out of her room composed, like the confrontation in the kitchen hadn't happened. It shouldn't have happened, that was for damn sure. But what she'd said had rung so true, it was like an uppercut to the chin, knocking me on my ass. She'd rocked me in a way I didn't want to be rocked, and I did what I always did when confronted with my failures—I lashed out.

Sylvia spent the rest of the day glued to Emma and my mom, never giving me a chance to apologize or talk to her privately. I was glad for it. There was no excuse for what I'd said. None.

. . .

THE NEXT MORNING, Emma and I were eating eggs and toast when Sylvia came into the dining room dressed for work. She didn't look like a church mouse. She looked like the bitch in charge, with her sky-high heels, skirt, and blazer.

"No classes today?" Emma asked.

Sylvia held up a small duffle bag. "I have a meeting this morning, so I had to look like I know what I'm talking about. I'm asking for a lot of money after all. I'll be back in my yoga pants by noon."

"What for?" I asked.

She blinked at me, her entire face stiff. "What?"

"What will the money be used for?"

Emma straightened, a proud smile on her face. "Let me answer! Mom does community outreach for the Hippodrome. Have you ever been?" she asked.

I shook my head. "Can't say I have. Not a big theater guy."

She rolled her eyes. "Well, you're wrong. When *Hamilton* comes to town, Mom can hook us up with tickets and we'll go."

"Is that the one about history and shit?"

"I feel like you're pulling my leg, and since I already have one broken one, that's cruel."

I laughed. "Okay, okay. I know what *Hamilton* is. You're a real theater nerd, huh?"

"Do you know me at all? Duh. Of course I am. Mom takes me to see a show on Broadway at least once a year. Grandma usually comes with us too."

How the hell did I not know this? What the fuck? When I really racked my brain, I remembered her telling me about seeing *SpongeBob* on Broadway a few months ago. She'd said it had been amazing, and I'd questioned if she'd been pulling *my* leg. No way that shit was real.

"Anyway, on top of all her regular community outreach

stuff, Mom runs a theater program for at-risk kids and teen moms. Sometimes, I get to go help. It's pretty cool."

I looked up at Sylvia, but she avoided my eyes. "Yeah, that does sound pretty cool."

"I hold the babies and play with the little kids while their moms take a break and do something only for themselves. Mom says she would've killed for something like that when I was little. She had to stop her theater classes when she got pregnant."

I couldn't take my eyes off her. And holy hell, was my gut churning. She finally let her eyes stray to mine. It was brief, but I saw the pride mixed with anger there.

She let out a short laugh and ruffled Emma's hair. "That's more than your dad asked to know." She glanced at me again. "I'm meeting with some potential donors. Knock on wood they come with loose pockets."

"Good luck," I said.

"Thanks." She smoothed her jacket and straightened her spine. "The physical therapist will be here at eleven and I won't be home until after five. Are you sure you don't need me to take another day off?"

"We're fine! Get outta here!" Emma said.

Sylvia still hesitated, seeming unconvinced I had it covered, adding a little bit of anger to the self-loathing already churning in my gut.

"We'll call you if anything comes up. But we'll be fine," I said emphatically.

Finally, Emma and I were alone. I smiled at her. She smiled at me. And I realized I had no idea what to do with her. Then, she took out her phone and started texting, filling me with relief.

Which fucking sucked.

I fucking sucked.

I'd watched her and Sylvia together. Saw their shared

mannerisms and inside jokes. We didn't have that. Sure, we had a good time together. But usually, I took her to movies, or parked my ass at Starbucks while she shopped. Our time together was always limited, so we packed in activities. Just hanging out didn't happen a whole hell of a lot.

"Uh...what do you usually do with your day?" I asked.

She tapped on her phone again, then laid it down. "I play soccer after school, so obviously that's not happening. Sometimes Mom and I go running—again, not happening. I hang out with friends—"

"Are you still best friends with Stella?"

She huffed. "Stella thinks she's too cool for me. Avery's my BFF. She's a theater nerd like me *and* she's on the soccer team." Her eyes widened. "Could she come over? Maybe have a sleepover? She's not really into your music, but she thinks it's so cool my dad is famous."

I chuckled. "Uh, let's ask your mom."

We spent the rest of the morning talking about school, and it felt like I learned more about my daughter in those few hours than I had in the last few years of rushed phone calls and busy visits. I knew all about the Stella drama that had consumed the entirety of eighth grade, and how she still wasn't quite over it. I already knew she'd made the varsity soccer team this year as a sophomore, but I hadn't known the ins and outs of the team. She told me about each of her classes—and yeah, during our weekly phone calls, she shared some of that stuff, but never this in-depth. I was mesmerized. Absolutely hooked on the life of this teenage girl I was learning I barely knew but desperately loved. I'd die for her, but until today, I'd had no clue she wanted to be an English teacher when she grew up.

No wonder Sylvia hated me. I was surprised Em didn't feel the same. *Jesus.*

Her physical therapist came, offering me a break to gather

my thoughts and try to figure out how I could have had my head so far up my own ass and not even realized it.

I was twenty when Blue is the Color signed a *big* recording contract with a *huge* record label. I'd always give Nick the credit. He had us practicing like it was our job, day in and day out. We played the shittiest clubs, for the shittiest paychecks, but he never let us lose sight of the goal.

We got lucky, and that first album did better than most. We toured non-stop. Even after we'd kinda cemented our place in rock n' roll, we never stopped. A lot of that had to do with Nick pushing us, but none of us objected. I was the one who should've. But Emma was so young, and Sylvia seemed so on top of everything, I'd convinced myself it was better to be earning money for them than wasting time at home.

I was actually jealous of Sylvia. Jealous of all the memories she had, all the time to appreciate this incredible person we'd made.

I made a promise to myself, even when we went back on the road, I was going to spend more time at home. No more of this week here or there shit. My roots had been dangling for far too long. Time to plant those bitches.

THE NEXT WEEK went pretty much the same. Syl worked, Em and I bonded. Syl came home and made us dinner, while effectively ignoring me. When Emma went to bed, she locked herself in her room. And I...I was getting a little bored. Not with the kid, but with being cooped up, only having a fifteen-year-old to talk to. I needed noise and action. I didn't even know how to live a quiet life anymore.

So when the knock followed by some kicks and scratches came from my front door, I didn't hesitate to run for it, throwing it open so fast, it banged against the wall. Standing there, like a group of ragtag hooligans, were my boys...plus Tali and Dalia.

"*What?*" I laughed.

Nick held up four boxes. "I got you pizza, motherfucker. Let us in!"

I stood back, and they paraded into my place, each one stopping to give me a hug or handshake. They were all a sight for sore eyes.

"What the hell are you doing here?" I asked, incredulous.

"You think our first stop on U.S. soil wouldn't be to see our boy?" Jasper asked.

Nick tossed the boxes of pizza down in the kitchen and wrapped his arm around Dalia's waist. "And to see our mascot."

Tali crossed her arms. "A child is not a mascot."

I chuckled. "She'd probably slay you for calling her a child." I led them into the living room where Emma and I had been hanging out. She blinked up at everyone, clearly even more surprised than I was.

"You've got visitors," I announced.

She waved shyly. "Hi."

Dalia stepped forward first, her hand outstretched to shake. "Hey, I'm Dalia. Your dad has told me *nothing* about you, so I'm going to insist on learning your entire life story."

Emma laughed, instantly charmed.

Nick sat on the ottoman in front of her. "You doin' okay, sweetheart? You had us all worried."

"I'm good, Uncle Nick. Bored to tears and ready to go back to school—God, I never thought I'd hear myself say that—but I'm healing. My physical therapist is impressed with how hard-core I am."

Nick held his hand up for a high-five. "You get that from your uncle."

She high-fived him, but said, "Nope. Definitely from my

mom." She looked up at Ian, who was hovering behind every-one. "Hey, Uncle Ian. Thank you for the *Emma* anime. I made Dad order the anime versions of *Pride and Prejudice* and *Sense and Sensibility*."

That had him coming closer and launching into an in-depth anime discussion with her. She took out her phone to take notes of all the titles he recommended.

Tali patted my shoulder. "She's doing a lot better than I pictured," she said quietly.

I turned away from Emma so she wouldn't hear me, although she was pretty well enthralled with what Ian was saying. "She's got youth on her side, for sure. When I first saw her in that bed..." I shook my head. "Let's just say I didn't imagine she'd come so far in less than two weeks."

"How long is she staying here?" Jas asked.

I lifted a hand. "Honestly, as long as I can keep them."

He raised an eyebrow. "Them?"

"Her. But she's a packaged deal. Syl's not about to leave her here by herself."

"How's that going?" he asked.

"Hell if I know. I messed up pretty quick and she's been ignoring me ever since."

"I'm sure it couldn't have been that bad," Tali said.

"Uh..." I rubbed the back of my neck, "I might've said 'fuck you' to her."

"Shhhit..." Jas hissed.

Tali shook her head sadly. "David...why?"

"'Cause I'm an idiot. That's my only excuse."

Tali crossed her arms. "Do I have to lecture you about how to talk to women the way I did with Nick? You have a teenage daughter for Christ's sake!"

"I get it, Tali. Spare me the lecture. I hate myself enough these days."

Instead of scolding me further, she pulled me in for a fierce hug. "You're a good guy, David. Below all the bullshit is a heart of gold, whether you believe it or not."

I didn't believe it. I knew it wasn't true. Maybe my heart was made of fool's gold. Pretty to look at, but not worth a damn. I thanked her anyway. At least one of us had some faith in me.

BY THE TIME Sylvia came home from work, we were in the middle of a heated game of Uno and had devoured three of the four pizzas. She stutter-stepped, dropping her keys on the floor. I hopped up to help her with her bags.

"Hey."

She wiped a hair off her forehead and looked up at me. "Hi. I didn't know we were having company."

I bent down and grabbed her keys, exchanging them for one of the reusable grocery bags she was carrying.

"I didn't either. They just got back and headed over here," I explained.

We went into the kitchen and unloaded her bags of fruit and veggies. If there was one thing I'd learned about Sylvia over the last week, it was that she was a healthy eater and an amazing cook. True to her word, she made dinner every night—dinners that were so good, I was gonna have trouble going back to my pre-made meals.

She nodded at the pizza boxes. "I'd planned on cooking, but looks like you took care of dinner."

"Yeah, the guys brought it over. We left some for you. I kinda doubt you eat pizza, though."

She scrunched her face. "Are you kidding me? I'd live off pizza if I could."

"There were a few years in my twenties where I *did* live off pizza," I said.

She lifted one of the lids. "This looks delicious, but my pizza's better."

"You make pizza?"

She smiled smugly. "Mmhmm. Everything homemade, down to the sauce."

"You make *sauce*?"

She laughed. "You're repeating yourself. And yes, my mom's Italian. If I didn't know how to make sauce, how could I find myself a husband?" From the way she said it, she'd been told that more than once.

"Can I put in a request?" I asked.

"For pizza?"

"Honestly, I'll eat whatever you make. But yeah, I wanna try this sauce. So, pizza, pasta, meatballs...anything."

She nodded once. "I'll make my Sunday sauce. Em loves it, but I don't usually have enough time to devote to making it."

I leaned against the counter as she put everything away and folded up the bags. "Always on the move?" I asked.

"Well...yeah. We're either at a soccer game, Em's drama stuff, my theater stuff, or just getting errands done I can't do during the week."

I couldn't let myself dwell on the fact I'd never seen a single one of Emma's soccer games. But I felt it—the weight of responsibility I'd passed onto Syl without looking back. It was heavy, but she was still upright. Sure as I took my next breath, I knew I'd have buckled on my own.

Changing the subject, I asked, "Did you get the money you asked for? From the donors?"

"Some, but not enough."

"What will it be used for?"

"It mostly goes toward a big production we do for the community each year. It's a huge deal for the kids. Really gives them something to take pride and ownership in. And it gets people in the theater who normally wouldn't be able to afford it." She sighed. "I'm used to hustling, so I'll figure it out."

"I'll help." The words were out of my mouth before I could think about it, but they felt right. I had money, and I had time—why couldn't I help?

Her brow creased into a frown. "You'd like to be a donor?"

"Yeah, of course. But I could help in other ways too. However you need me."

"Why?"

I stared at her, my mouth open to speak, but nothing came. I wasn't the altruistic sort. I didn't throw my hat in to volunteer for shit. In fact, I was more of the skulk in the back of the group, hoping not to get noticed sort.

I shrugged. "Take it or leave it. It's up to you. I'm goin' back out there."

Exiting the kitchen the way I did was a pussy move if I ever saw one. I finally got her to talk to me for more than a minute, and I couldn't hack it. It was probably for the best that she didn't want my help. We'd end up fighting and probably tearing the entire theater down.

I still wanted my fucking sauce.

EIGHT

SYLVIA

I SNUCK past the living room full of rock stars to change out of my work clothes....and that was a sentence I never thought I'd say.

I'd been conducting a workshop at a city high school, so while my "work clothes" were comfortable yoga pants and a T-shirt, we'd done a lot of rolling around on the dusty floor, so I put on clean yoga pants and a less holey shirt. This one said, "Young, Scrappy, and Hungry," a souvenir from when *Hamilton* played at the Hippodrome. The kids I worked with had a love/hate relationship with my, "My favorite rapper is Alexander Hamilton," T-shirt, but I wore it often to make them laugh.

Needing a few minutes to compose myself, I called Suz.

"What's up?" she answered.

"I'm hiding in my room," I said.

She laughed. "What did he do now?"

"*He* didn't do anything. I walked in to a houseful of rock stars. It's intimidating!"

I could hear her eyeroll over the phone. "Um...honey, you

almost married a dude in a motorcycle club. Don't even try to tell me you're scared of little old rock stars."

"It wasn't like Vince was in Sons of Anarchy. He rode a motorcycle on the weekends with his friends," I argued.

"While looking intimidating as hell," she countered. "I know you. Nothing scares you. Get your ass out there and hang out with your favorite band."

Vince *had* looked intimidating, and truthfully, so had his biker friends when they'd walked into the club I'd been working at. But I'd been twenty-two, a little tipsy, and he gave me more attention than I'd had in years. Pretty soon, intimidating became sexy as hell.

"I'm going, I'm going. How's everything in the neighborhood?"

"The same. Are you coming to our Halloween party?"

I rubbed my forehead. Since the accident, I'd been feeling like I was at one end of a long tunnel, and my normal, comfortable life was at the other. I went to Suz's Halloween party every year. Normally, I looked forward to it, but this year, it was the last thing on my mind.

"It'll have to be a maybe. It all depends on how Emma feels. Which reminds me, do you guys want to come over Sunday? I'm making my Sunday sauce."

"Hell to the yes on the sauce. And boo about the party."

Laughing, like I always did with Suz, we ended the call. It'd be good to see her and Mika, and Em would flip her shit over seeing Evan. Having them here might restore some semblance of normalcy.

Venturing out to the living room, I waited to be noticed, observing the group from the fringes. I recognized all but a younger redhead. Judging by the way Nick Fletcher didn't take his eyes off her, they were together.

Tali, Blue is the Color's manager, was the first to see me and say hi. She was maybe a year or two older than me, and though we'd never met, I recognized her from pictures I'd seen in articles. I wasn't proud, but I did keep track of news about the band...and yes, about David.

He was my version of my, "My favorite rapper is Alexander Hamilton," T-shirt—love/hate.

Tali shook my hand, and I immediately liked her firmness—not just in her handshake, but in her voice and whole demeanor. Like it would take more than a hurricane to knock her down.

"I'm happy to finally meet you," she said.

I smiled. "You too. I read that article in *Rolling Stone* you were featured in. 'The thirty-five most influential women under thirty-five in music today.' You're kind of a badass, aren't you?"

She laughed throatily. "Are you vying for the position of my new best friend? Because you've got it. It's yours."

I tapped my cheek. "I think I still remember how to make some really rad friendship bracelets."

The redhead popped up. "I want in on this!" She pulled me into a hug. "I'm Dalia Brenner."

"Sylvia Price." She wasn't as young as I first thought—probably mid-twenties. Her freckles and apple cheeks would do well for her when she *did* get older. She'd have that eternally youthful look. She was a pretty little thing, and nothing about her screamed "groupie." Then again, I doubted these guys would bring a groupie around Em. At least, I hoped not.

"I'm loving your kid," Dalia said. "Although, I'm starting to suspect she cheats at Uno. How does she keep winning?"

I caught Emma's eye. She looked the happiest I'd seen her since the accident, with rosy cheeks and bright, smiling eyes.

"You've got to watch that one. She's been known to hide cards up her sleeves," I said.

"Don't reveal my tricks!" She held her arms out, so I went to her spot on the couch, bending down to give her a big hug. I knew I was lucky she still requested hugs on occasion. I soaked them up whenever I got the chance. David was next to her, and while I was *very* aware of his presence, I did my damnedest to pretend I wasn't.

When I straightened and turned around, a smiling man with long, beautiful dreadlocks had his arms out too. Jasper Antonio. I laughed, giving him a friendly hug.

"Nice to meet you, Syl," he said.

It was funny hearing David's nickname for me coming out of his mouth. Made me wonder how often, and in what way, I was talked about.

"You too," I replied. I was slightly starstruck. I'd tried to resist, but I loved their music. It was surreal this band I'd been listening to since I was a teenager was casually hanging out with my daughter.

It probably should have been more surreal the father of said daughter was in said band, but in my mind, I'd separated David from Blue is the Color. There was Nick on vocals, Ian on drums, Jasper on bass, and some guy in the shadows playing guitar.

Suz had a field day analyzing my love for their music. She thought it meant more than it did. But it was simple. Their lyrics were poignant, and their melodies rocked.

"I feel like I've met you, since I used to see you guys at David's house back in the day," I added.

Jasper quirked his head. "How did I never see you?"

"Ah, my parents kept me on lockdown. If there were boys nearby, I was to remain in my room, knees together, lest I fall pregnant." I waved toward Emma. "And yet..."

Jasper burst out laughing. "Guess their strictness didn't take."

I laughed too. "Does it ever?"

"Not when I'm around to corrupt you," David said.

I finally looked at him, an eyebrow raised. "You sure that's what happened?"

Emma elbowed him in his ribs. "Mom was a delinquent. Her parents were ready to send her to boarding school. Did you know she was *arrested?*"

The way David's mouth fell open in a perfect O would have been hilarious had there not been so much baggage between us. He saw me in the way he'd imagined me. The person he assumed I was didn't exist.

"I'm not actually proud of that, *Emma.*" She knew my history. I used it as a cautionary tale, and she took it that way, although there was a definite part of her that got a kick out of knowing her mom used to be a troublemaker. Emma was the exact opposite, thank god. If there was a rule, she followed it. I didn't have to keep a tight leash on her. She'd never step outside the boundaries. And if she did, it'd be a half-step, or maybe just a toe.

Ian raised his hand. "I would like to hear this story."

"I second that," said Nick freaking Fletcher.

"Mind your business," Tali scolded.

"It's okay. I don't try to hide it," I said.

Dalia crossed her arms and narrowed her eyes. "What was it? Mail fraud? Did you try to vote before you turned eighteen? Oooh! Was it murder?"

"None of the above! And I was actually arrested three times."

Jasper nodded approvingly. "Look at you, you hardened criminal."

"I left my life of crime in the past." I tipped my chin in Em's direction. "This one made me clean up my rebelliousness."

"What landed you in the slammer?" Dalia asked.

I ticked each arrest off on my fingers. "Let's see. When I was fourteen, I was arrested for underage drinking. I got caught at a party and I was too wasted to run away when the cops came. At fifteen, destruction of property. I threw a brick through my school's window and did some graffitiing with my friends. And then, at sixteen, maybe a month before I got pregnant, I was arrested for shoplifting. I was extremely lucky I only ended up with community service each time. In hindsight, I was lucky I got pregnant with Em when I did. I'm not sure where I'd be now had I not."

"What the fuck, Syl?" David muttered.

Nick snapped his fingers. "I remember seeing you once!"

David kicked at him. "No you don't."

Nick dodged him, laughing. "I do. This story of your misspent youth jogged a memory."

I perched on the arm of the couch, on the opposite side from David. "This, I'd love to hear."

"We were hanging out on David's crumbling front porch. Must've been right after he moved there, 'cause most of the time we were at Jas's house. Reinece stocked the best snacks."

Jasper nodded, smiling softly. "True, true. I swear, my mom singlehandedly kept Entenmann's in business."

"I could put away that pound cake. Gwen had like carrot sticks and shit," Nick said.

Emma laughed. "Like you, Mom!"

I shrugged, smiling. "Guess I learned from the best."

"Enough about snacks. Let's hear about the time you supposedly saw Syl," David demanded.

"I'm getting to it, fucker." He winked at Em. "Excuse the language, sweetheart."

Emma giggled. "I've heard much worse from Dad. It's like he forgets he's supposed to be a good influence on me."

David ruffled her hair ruthlessly, turning her silky strands into a bird's nest. "Hey, kid. I'm a fucking amazing influence."

"Is this story happening, or no?" Tali interjected.

"If everyone would stop interrupting," Nick said.

David held his hand out. "By all means, continue."

I leaned forward, genuinely curious to hear this. I didn't doubt Nick had seen me at some point, but I *was* surprised.

"David and I were sitting on his crumbling porch...were you there, Ian?" Nick asked.

Ian's brows pinched. "Hard to say. I do have a crumbling porch stored somewhere in the memory bank."

"It was definitely David and me. Maybe Ian. Anyway, this girl in a Catholic school get-up comes walking up the opposite side of the street. She looked young, so my only interest in her was curiosity over what she was doing. As she walked, she took off her shoes—those thick-soled boots all the goth chicks used to wear—and she changed into some other flat shoes. Then, she went to the side of a house and came back out empty-handed. No more goth boots."

I smiled wistfully. "I loved those boots."

He clapped. "I knew that was you!"

"It was. I had a hidey hole on the side of my next door neighbor's house where I kept all my contraband. I had to wear a uniform to school, but I rolled my skirt short in defiance. I also used to change my shoes the minute I left for school, then change back right before I got home. Made me feel a little more in control," I said.

The guys stayed for another hour or two, talking about their own high school days. I nabbed a slice of pizza somewhere in there, thoroughly enjoying myself. These weren't my friends, but in another life, if things had gone differently, they could have been. I didn't know if we'd ever spend time like this together again. The realist—Suz would say pessimist—in me said probably not. So, I soaked it all up while I could: Emma's shiny, happy face, Nick Fletcher's gravelly voice and the way he looked at his girlfriend, Jasper's kind eyes, Ian's brimming intensity, the sheer size of Tali's presence, and David...I hated seeing him this way. In his element. Comfortable, relaxed, with his people. I hated it because it made him more attractive to me.

And in between laughter and talking, when the others took over, his eyes strayed to me, and I let him look. I knew he was thrown off balance by what he'd learned about me tonight. But that was only fair—I was always off balance around him.

Once the guys left, with promises to visit once they recovered from jet lag, I helped Emma get ready for bed—although, frankly, she didn't need it. It mostly made me feel better to spot her. She'd adapted to her injury easily—a lot more easily than I had.

I left her there, in her big bed, iPad in hand, going back and forth between texts to Avery and Evan, and headed to the kitchen to clean up, but David was already there, rinsing plates in the sink.

"We have to stop meeting this way," I said from the doorway.

The plate he was holding slipped from his hand, clattering in the stainless-steel sink. "Shit, Syl. Are you related to Ian? Fuckin' ninjas," he mumbled.

Reaching over, I turned the water off. "Listen," I ordered.

He watched, bemused, as I walked a few paces out of the kitchen, then back in. "Have you lost it?" he asked.

"Maybe. But did you hear my footsteps?"

"Not really. Think you should try it again."

I narrowed my eyes at him. "*Listen!*" I walked away and came back. "Hear that?"

"You have a spectacular ass," he said.

Growling, blushing, I-don't-know-what-ing, I picked up the sodden sponge he'd bought on our shopping excursion and lobbed it at him, whacking him square in the cheek.

He laughed, catching the sponge as it fell. "Taken out by my own sponge."

I shook my haughtiest finger at him. "You deserved it."

He tossed the sponge in the sink, wiping his cheek with the hem of his shirt, revealing a wide slash of taut, tan stomach.

"I sure did, Miss Sylvia."

Tearing my eyes from his waist, I met his, and chuckled. "Are you suddenly a southern gentleman?"

"No one's ever accused me of being a gentleman," he said gruffly.

"No, I can't imagine they have." I was tempted to throw the sponge at him again just to see more of his skin.

"Well, I did just check out your ass, so I'm not even gonna be offended," he said.

Laughing softly, I moved around him and grabbed a pizza box to flatten for recycling.

"Did you have a good time tonight?"

I smiled down at the box in my hands. "I did." Shifting my eyes to his, I asked, "So, this is your life? Hang out with friends and make music?"

"Is this a trap?"

"Nope. I'm curious. I have no idea what the life of a professional musician is like."

He leaned on the counter, his hands braced next to him. "I'm not gonna lie. There's a lot of hanging out and making music. That's the shit that keeps me going. Being with my boys, creating with them. It's the endless travel, the press, the appearances, that get old and feel like work."

I stacked the boxes in my arms. "I can see how that would be wearing. I'm surprised you guys haven't taken an extended break before now."

"Let me take those." He reached for the boxes, but I pulled away.

"I'm good." There was a trash chute right down the hall. It was much more convenient than trekking to the trash cans on the side of my house.

"Just let me take them, Syl." He went to grab the boxes again, but I guarded them like they were national treasures.

"I said I'm good." I tried to get by him, but he stood in front of the doorway.

"Can't I be the good guy here?"

I couldn't stop the eyeroll. "You're being the annoying guy."

"You never accept my help."

That blistered. "Are you kidding?" I shoved the boxes at his chest. "Take them. If this makes you feel like the hero, then by all means, take them."

"Syl..."

I stood right in front of him, the pizza boxes the only thing separating our chests. "I'm going to bed. Is that okay, or do you think I need help with that too?"

"I don't get what just happened, but I'm really tired of fighting with you in this fucking kitchen," David growled.

I rubbed my temples. "I'm not fighting with you. I'm tired and cranky and I need to go for a run before I explode."

I had been fighting with him, but I really didn't want to. Contrary to the way I behaved around David, I was a very peaceful, centered person. But here, in this condo, with him everywhere I looked, my center had taken to zigging and zagging all over the place.

He pointed to the ceiling. "Did I not tell you I own the rooftop and there's a gym and pool up there?"

My mouth fell open. "No, you seem to have forgotten that very important information. I'll check it out in the morning."

I turned to head to my room, and from behind me, I heard, "Good night, jailbird." I smiled. He didn't see it, but I had no doubt he knew I was smiling because of him.

By the time I made it to my room, my smile had faded. I was sad for sixteen-year-old me, not having the guy who fought me for pizza boxes in her corner.

No matter how many times David stepped in now, I wasn't sure it would ever make up for the times he stepped away over the years. Not just on Em, but on me.

NINE

SYLVIA

I NEEDED COFFEE.

Lots and lots of coffee.

My office was crazy. I'd spent the entire morning on the phone, setting up workshops and speaking with donors until my throat was raw and my brain was rattling around in my head.

Once I'd gotten through my list of phone calls, I grabbed my jacket and told my assistant I was headed out for sustenance—at this point, I'd take coffee or food, hopefully both. I just needed some fuel to finish my day.

I took a walk, stopping at a food truck for a chicken pita, then stopping at the next truck for a vanilla latte. The food trucks had to be the best part of working in the city. The commute blew, but I could walk outside and have my pick of Korean, Indian, or barbecue on one block.

Being at work was good. Slipping back into my normal life was exactly what I needed. It'd be easy to get caught up in David's life and pretend it was mine.

I knew Em was eating it up. The family dinners and nights of TV watching. She and I had that together, but she loved having her dad around. This was new for her. The longest they'd spent together was the three days he took her between tours at the end of the summer.

I...was having a tougher time with it all. It was hard being angry all the time. Exhausting, really. But I was much more aware of David's patterns of behavior. He'd changed over the last few years—being sober probably had a lot to do with that—but he'd had periods where I'd let myself believe he was going to be more than a once-a-week-phone-call dad. Emma wasn't aware of all the times he'd told me he'd be back in town, then changed his plans at the last minute. I always treated his visits as a surprise for her. She didn't know he was coming until he was at my doorstep.

At sixteen, I hadn't known what I was getting into with him. At thirty-one, I'd wised up, but the fantasy of what he could be was still alive and well.

A man took a seat on the other end of my bench, and I did what many women do in situations like these: kept my eyes to myself and pretended I didn't notice him staring at me. It certainly wasn't the first time a man had sat next to me on a bench to get a rise out of me...or show me his penis.

"Syl."

I whipped my head around to find David smiling at me, a cup of coffee in one hand, the other slung over the back of the bench, as casual as can be.

"What the hell?"

He chuckled. "I could say the same. Last thing I expected to see when I was walking back to my car was you chowing down on a pita." Reaching across the space between us, he swiped his thumb under my lip. "Tzatziki."

The thumb swipe I could handle. The fact that he sucked the sauce off it was another story. He was a bad, bad man.

"Why are you here?" I asked dumbly.

"Jas lives a block over. He kept my favorite guitar when I

bolted from the tour. Brought it home with him on the airplane instead of letting the crew pack it up. I was picking it up from him."

I glanced down, noticing the case at his feet for the first time.

"Where's Em?"

"Home. She's in the middle of writing an English paper. She got annoyed with all my questions and basically kicked me out. When did she get so damn sassy?"

I grinned. "When she started speaking. You're not around enough for her to let her sass flag fly. I guess she's settled in and gotten comfortable with you."

The truth hung heavy between us. There was no denying it.

"You cool if I go out tonight?" he asked.

My gaze sharpened. "Why would you need my permission?"

"Fuck, Syl, I'm just making sure you don't need my help with Em. Jas and Ian are going to a party and I'm gonna go too."

"So, you're actually telling me, not asking."

He exhaled, looking everywhere but me. "Right. I'm telling you I'm going out tonight."

"Have fun."

He still didn't get it. He had no clue. We'd lived with him for a week and a half, but the only thing that had changed in his life was his condo was a little more crowded. To him, we were temporary.

I wasn't a martyr mom who didn't have a life. I dated. I had sex on said dates. I went out without Em. I had my own life. But the fact was, she was my first thought, not an afterthought. My lifestyle was built around her; I didn't slot her in when I had free time.

Going to a party shouldn't have been a big deal. If he were a regular dad. But he wasn't. He was a phone call dad. A *fit you in*

when I can spare the time dad. This week and a half was the first
time he'd spent solid time with Em in years, and he was already
bailing.

Not surprising, but I'd thought maybe something had
changed. Clearly not.

He groaned. "You're frustrating as hell."

"I'm just sitting on a bench, eating my lunch."

"If you don't want me to go, I won't go."

I blinked at him. "Why wouldn't I want you to go?"

He yanked at the sides of his hair like a mad scientist. "I
don't know! Why do I feel like I'm doing something wrong?"

"I'm doing nothing to make you feel that way, David." I held
up my half-eaten pita. "Remember? Bench, lunch."

He stood, took two steps, then came back, sitting down. "I
mean, I have a life. I can't be this pious, do-gooder every second
of the day. I know it comes naturally for you, but it's wearing
on me."

I wrapped my pita neatly in its foil, grabbed my full coffee,
walked calmly to the trash can on the other side of the sidewalk,
and dumped it all. Starving was preferable to listening to this.

Returning to the bench, I slid the strap of my purse over my
shoulder. David was staring up at me like he wasn't sure what to
expect. But this was the David I knew. I'd steeled myself against
him years ago. It was the kind, attentive David that got to me. I
could handle the asshole.

"I'll be home by six. I would appreciate if you would stay
with Emma until then. If you can't, please text me so I can leave
work early." My voice was steady. Some might have said scarily
steady.

I picked up my purse from the bench, and just as calmly,
began walking back to work. He called my name, but there was
no looking back.

.   .   .

DAVID GOT up to leave as soon as I walked in from work. He kissed Em on the head, then paused next to me in the entry. He stood close as I took off my boots and jacket. Finally, when I'd hung up my jacket and placed my boots on the rack—I'd taken my sweet time doing both—I turned to him, facing him fully.

"Should I expect you home tonight?"

He lifted a shoulder. "Maybe."

"Did you need something else?" I crossed my arms to keep from strangling him.

He exhaled, ruffling his hair with his hand. "I won't be out too late."

"Doesn't matter. It would probably be better if you didn't bring anyone back here, though."

He stuffed his hands in the pockets of his worn jeans. "I'm not gonna do that. I don't actually need you telling me that either."

"All right." I brushed by him, but he caught my wrist. We both looked down to where our skin touched, and then, as his hand slowly slipped from mine, we both peered up. I wondered if my face showed the same confused anger as his.

"I'll see you later, Syl."

He left, the door clicking behind him, and I let myself take a moment to catch my breath before I went to Emma.

"Mom, what's for dinner?"

Breath caught. Smile plastered. Time to mom.

"I don't know, honey, what'd you make me?"

She laughed, and everything was okay. We ended up eating paninis on David's pristine white couch while watching *Riverdale*. Then, I helped her to her room, even though she very adamantly proclaimed she didn't need it.

Sitting on the edge of her bed, she asked, "Are you mad at Dad?"

I sighed. "Whatever I feel about Dad shouldn't affect your feelings."

"It doesn't. We have our own thing. I'm good with it."

I stroked the back of her hair, and she leaned into my hand for a moment before pulling away. "I'm glad you guys have your own special relationship," I said.

"But you don't think it's enough."

"It doesn't matter what I think."

She chewed on her lip for a few seconds. "Why didn't you ever ask for more then?"

I rubbed my forehead, not at all prepared for this conversation. "I guess I didn't think I should have had to ask."

She gave me a brief, but fierce hug. "I didn't miss out on anything, mostly just having you. I wish Dad could be around more, but I never felt neglected or anything. I guess what I'm saying is, don't be mad at him for me. If he was a jerk to you, that's another thing."

"Are you trying to make me cry, child of mine?"

She laughed and picked up her chiming phone.

"Evan?" I asked.

She tapped out a message, then looked up, smiling. "Yep. He's checking in."

"I'll leave you to it. Night, Em."

"Good night, Mom."

DAVID CAME HOME WELL before the middle of the night. He'd told me he didn't drink, so I wasn't sure why I'd expected him to come stumbling in, smelling of booze and women. Instead, he walked in and plopped on the couch all casual, like this afternoon hadn't happened.

He leaned his head back, face tilted up at the ceiling.

I continued typing on my laptop, although my carefully

worded document now consisted of random letters and numbers.

"I'm a shithead. I gotta get that out of the way," he said, still staring at the ceiling.

"Okay."

"It's just that...Jasper told me about this party tonight, and my first instinct was to say yes. Then I remembered you and Em, so I turned him down. And I felt like the shittiest person in the world for not thinking of the two of you first. So, when I saw you—and fuck, I can't even explain how utterly delighted I was to see you sitting there, soaking up the sun, lovin' on that pita—and you said the thing about Emma not spending enough time with me to ever really be herself, it was such a truth bomb...I didn't want to hear it." He shoveled his fingers through his hair. "And I guess there was part of me that wanted you to tell me not to go."

I kept typing. I couldn't quite figure out what he wanted from me. Or what I was willing to give to him.

"You clearly didn't think I should go."

I stilled my hands on the keyboard. "Tonight, while you were gone, Emma asked me why I'd never asked for more from you. I told her I felt like I shouldn't have had to ask. But as I've been sitting here, I thought about it more."

David straightened, turning to face me. "Yeah?"

"I grew up on scraps. My parents divvied out affection like they had a finite supply. For a while, that's what I came to expect, and I took whatever I could get. As a mother, I knew from the beginning I didn't want Em to grow up that way. I taught her to expect more than scraps, from her friends, and as she got older, from men."

"Syl..." He sounded anguished.

"It's really hard to instill that lesson when her dad only has scraps for her. I've spent her whole life building you up to her, protecting your image. Not for your sake, but for hers. I never wanted her to think it was okay for her to be second choice for a man. I want her to grow up and find a partner who'll give her the full course, not the leftovers. So, no, I'm not going to beg you for scraps, David. I'll never do that."

He stared at me for a long time, his brows pinched into a tight line, his hands balled at his knees. I only felt relief. I'd wanted to say that to him for a long, long time. And if it hurt, then it hurt. I only regretted not saying it sooner.

"I don't think I've only given her scraps. I love that kid more than my own life." He didn't sound convinced by his own words, though.

"When you're in town for the first time in months and only give her three days out of the week you're here, that's scraps. I know you love her, but you've missed so much."

"How did I wreck this so badly?" His words were muffled behind his hands, but I heard them.

"It's not wrecked. Emma knows you love her. She's not wanting. She doesn't actually know how much more you could've given her."

He let his hands fall, and when he faced me again, I'd never seen him so vulnerable. I hated the part of myself that wanted to comfort him and tell him he'd done nothing wrong and not to worry about it. That part was microscopic. Mostly, I wanted to throttle him and ask him how he'd been so damn stupid.

"Shit, Syl. How are you so good at this?"

I let out a short, bitter laugh. "I'm not sure I had a choice. I was never wanted. My parents were in their mid-forties when I was born. I think they tried to have kids when they were younger, but it never happened. And to this day, I'm surprised they had sex the one time it probably took to conceive me. They had probably just come home from church after the priest gave a sermon about wifely duties and my mom felt obliged." I shuddered. David's lips quirked into a sad smile, but he hung on my every word.

"I never wanted Em to feel that way. She came at the worst possible time in the worst possible circumstance, but that wasn't her fault. I *always* wanted her to know she was wanted. So that's what I did. It wasn't a choice, it was instinct."

He studied me, his eyes locked on my face. "I grew up on scraps too. I feel what you're saying down deep. I don't think about shit like this. I don't, like, examine my actions, you know? I just do."

"I *am* familiar with that part of you."

He scrubbed his jaw, continuing like I hadn't spoken. "I mean, look at my boys. Me, Nick, and Jas all had shit dads who didn't stick around. Ian's dad stuck, but he's just as shitty. Maybe there was a part of me that thought if I was better than those guys, then I was doing pretty damn grand. And my boys never called me on it, 'cause what the hell do they know? Shit, Nick calls Em our band mascot because she came to a few of our practices."

I smiled without really meaning to. He was so damn earnest in his remorse. I truly believed him when he said he'd never stopped to think about the entire situation. Did it make his years of absence okay? No. Not even a little. Did it make me less angry with him? Yeah. It kinda did.

Something in David's face softened. Tension he'd been storing in the twin lines between his eyebrows slipped out.

"The world's a better place when you smile, Syl."

I scoffed. "That's a tad dramatic."

"How about *my* world's a better place when you smile?"

"More believable."

He stared up at the ceiling again while I took in his profile. He really was more handsome than a man like him should have been. David was dangerous enough without the full lips and long eyelashes and jaw so perfect, it looked like Michelangelo himself had come back to life to chisel it.

If he were just an average looking accountant, I'd like to think I wouldn't be so taken in by him. That his beauty had me under some kind of spell. But I knew it was no spell. It had always gone deeper than that. Something in me responded to David Wiesel. Rock star or not, he would always be trouble for me. It was written in the stars. He was the constellation, Orion, stepping out of the heavens, the brilliance of him taking over everything he touched.

Breaking the silence, he said, "I'm sticking this time. I'm fifteen years late, but I hope like hell I'm not *too* late."

"You're not too late," I whispered.

"You hate me?" he asked.

To his profile, I said, "Not right now."

He turned, giving me a lazy smile. "I take that as the highest compliment." His smile fell after a moment, and his eyes grew intense. "Em's really lucky to have you as a mom. And *I* sure as hell am lucky to have you as my kid's mom. I need you to know I realize that. Always have."

A lump formed in my throat, stopping me from speaking, so I nodded.

"I'm gonna keep messing up, Sylvia. A lot. I'm probably going to be an asshole about it too. But I love that kid. I'm gonna be so in her face, she'll beg me to leave, but I won't. I *won't.*"

He had me laughing. It was light, and it didn't last long, but it took me by surprise.

"She begs me to leave her alone all the time, so that sounds like a legit plan to me," I said.

He cocked his head, his lips curling up. "I meant what I said. Everything's right when you smile like that."

I knew the brilliance of his stars was deceiving. He wasn't really this mellow, caring guy he appeared to be tonight. But knowing it didn't stop me from being dazzled. He was David, and I was Sylvia, and that was the way our stars aligned.

I clicked my laptop shut and stood. "This day is the day that never ends. I'm going to bed."

He caught my free hand—really, just the tips of my fingers—and peered up at me. "Are you gonna start hating me again in the morning?"

"Will you be serving asshole alongside my eggs?" I asked.

He laughed, shaking his head. "Night, Syl."

"Good night, David."

TEN

DAVID

I SLID into the booth next to Jasper, Ian and Nick across from us, the three of them already demolishing a plate of loaded nachos.

"Couldn't wait for me?" I asked, grabbing a chip slathered in cheese and sour cream.

"You snooze, you lose, motherfucker," said Nick.

"I thought you'd be nicer now that you have a girlfriend," I said.

"You thought wrong, my friend." He smiled smugly. He might not have been nicer, but he sure as hell was happier. Nick's misery had rubbed off on all of us when we toured over the summer. None of us blamed him—we were a pretty unhappy lot in general. But he was our captain, and if the captain went down, we all sunk right along with him.

Thank god he'd found Dalia. She'd set his ass straight.

Normally, the four of us couldn't go out together. Apart, we could lay low, but together, we were recognizable, especially with Jasper's long locs and Ian's gigantism—slight exaggeration, but dude was six and a half feet tall. But we'd been coming to this diner for years. It was back in our old neighborhood, and the patrons who frequented had been coming here for a half-century. If they knew who we were—which I sincerely doubted—they'd never shown any interest in us besides the occasional grumble about us needing haircuts.

Our regular waitress, Azalea, stopped by the table. "There's my boy!" She patted my cheek, smiling at me. Azalea had to be eighty if she was a day, but she *did* know who we were. Luckily, her silence was bought through autographed CDs and pictures—specifically shirtless pictures of Nick. He had a stash from when we first started out and our label attempted to sex us up. We probably would've gone along with anything they'd asked us to do back then, but our shirtless days were long over.

I grinned up at Azalea's weathered, creased face. "And there's my girl."

She giggled and blushed. Nick was her favorite, but she flirted with us all. "I've missed my boys, but I followed your tour on Facebook. I knew you'd be in soon."

"We can't resist the burgers and excellent service," Jasper said.

She pulled her pen from behind her ear and took out her pad. "Burgers all around? The usual?"

We all nodded as she scribbled down our orders. I didn't particularly want a burger, but once, I'd tried to order something else and Azalea looked like I'd broken her heart, so I never tried that again.

When she left to put in our orders, I took a good look at my boys. They looked good. A lot better than when they'd stopped by my place a few days ago. Personally, I was wrung out from my talk with Syl, but it was like I'd been stripped, hosed raw with ice water, then dressed in the finest of silks. We'd ended our talk on higher ground, and this morning, she'd been friendlier than she'd been in years. But, below the surface, my skin was still pink and tender, and I had a feeling hers was too.

"You guys get some good sleep?" I asked.

"Hell yes," Jasper answered. "There's no place like home."

"You turning into Dorothy on me?" I asked.

He chuckled. "The girl had a point."

Nick nodded slowly. "She did, indeed. I could'a stayed in bed a couple more days."

I smirked. "I'm sure Dalia has nothing to do with that."

"You bet your ass she does. And I'd *still* be in bed with her if she wasn't so damn responsible about her job," Nick said.

I jerked my chin at Ian. "What about you? Glad to be home?"

He turned his hands over, palms up. "Glad to be anywhere. I could sleep on a rock. Don't need a bed."

I had to smile at that. Ian could've been a monk, if not for the no sex thing. He probably would've been fine living silently up on a remote mountain somewhere, as long as he had his sticks, a couple puzzles, and some comic books. I loved the guy like a brother, but after knowing him for nearly twenty years, I wasn't sure who he was, and I kinda thought he liked it that way. He was the definition of self-contained. Except when he played the drums; that's when he unleashed the fire burning just below his surface.

"How about you?" Nick asked, giving me a pointed look. "You still doing good?"

"Yeah, man." I tugged at my hair. "Not drinking, which I know is what you're getting at."

Nick was always checking in, making sure I was okay. Not only with my sobriety, but how I was handling life in general. The boys and I affectionately called him a mother hen. Truth be told, I needed it. Less so these days, but back when I had first stopped drinking, I'd needed Nick pecking at my feet, letting me know I was worth caring about. Back then, I'd felt worthless —hell, I'd felt worthless my whole life.

Nick held his hands up. "Didn't say you were. I just know life went a little crazy for you a couple weeks ago."

"It did. But the truly crazy thing it how normal it already feels. Em's a friggin' rock star, healing like a boss, and Syl..." I shook my head. "I don't know what Syl is. A surprise, that's for damn sure."

"I didn't see that twist coming," Ian said.

I raised an eyebrow. "The juvie twist?"

"Yes. Were you aware of your baby mama's criminal past?" he asked.

"I was definitely not aware. In her years of ignoring me, it never came up," I said.

"I like her," Jasper announced.

I clapped him on the shoulder. "Who don't you like?"

"The list is small, but there's room to add a name or two."

I laughed. "You threatening me, Jasper Antonio?"

"Only if you don't treat Sylvia right," he said.

"Me? Treat *her* right?" I was affronted. "She's probably waiting for the right moment to shiv me. Don't they always do it in the showers?"

"They?" Nick asked.

"Yeah, prisoners."

Nick snorted. "Pretty sure Sylvia isn't a prisoner, unless there's something you're not telling us about your living arrangements."

"Nah, it's more like work release," I said.

Jasper tapped his fingers on the table. "No, but for real, dude, that was a hell of a surprise, huh? I know you always thought she was this sweet little Catholic school girl who happened upon your devil's lair or something."

"Honestly, I can't even say how we ended up in bed together. I remember bits and pieces, but I always assumed it was my idea because...I'm me and she's...well, I *thought* she was this saintly thing. Now, I don't know what's true, and I'm not sure it matters."

"Could make for an interesting conversation," Jasper said.

I spun my fork around on the table. "That, it could. If I don't get shived first."

"Well, if it means anything, I like her too," Nick said. "And Dalia is, like, enthralled by the pair of them—Emma and Sylvia."

I shot him a grin, thinking about my girls. Okay, my girl and her mom. "They *are* pretty enthralling."

Azalea brought our burgers by, carrying all fours plates in her bony hands. She'd once told us she'd started waitressing when she was fourteen, so carrying four plates was probably second nature to her. I always thought I'd write a song about her. Azalea was the kind of woman songs were written about. I wouldn't be surprised if it'd already been done.

She patted our cheeks and left us to our devices.

Lately, my devices were mostly thinking about Sylvia. When I wasn't attempting—and mostly failing—to help Emma with the schoolwork her teachers had emailed her, my mind was on Syl. I'd been curious about her for a long time—really, it had been that way since the first time I caught a glimpse of her getting into her parents' car.

We were at peak levels these days, though. I had to stuff my hands in my pockets to stop from touching her shiny hair. I had to bite my tongue to stop from asking about the guy—the one she was all set to marry five years ago.

I wanted her. Not because I was curious about her, but because I found her so fucking beautiful, I couldn't think straight.

I wasn't a guy who went around wanting women. I was more of a love 'em and leave 'em type, although the women I slept with knew the drill. They weren't surprised at the absence of cuddles and sweet nothings afterwards. None of us were there for that.

A part of me wondered if I even had anything more than a good fuck to give. I couldn't say anyone had ever wanted more from me. Nick, Jas, and even Ian had all done the girlfriend thing here and there over the years, settling down for brief, or sometimes longer, periods, but I'd never come close. I'd never even taken the time to wonder why, or how I'd gotten to almost thirty-four years old without having major, real feelings for a woman.

Sometimes I thought I was missing that chip. Like when my brain was formed, a vital piece was left out. But lately...when I looked at Sylvia, especially when she tuned me out and was unaware of my presence and let her shell soften, I considered the possibility that I was wrong.

A sharp elbow to the ribs brought me back to the present.

"You here?" Jas asked.

I rubbed where his elbow had dug into my side. "Did you think about just saying my name before you dug the knives you call elbows into my ribs?"

Nick grinned across from me. "Dude, you were lost. We all said your name. One minute, you were talking about Sylvia, the next, you were spaced out with a dreamy look on your face."

"Davey's got a crush," Ian said, his eyes on his burger.

My boot met his shin under the table, and the sicko laughed.

"Ouch," he deadpanned.

"One: fuck that Davey shit. Two: I'm not some teeny-bopper—I don't crush."

"Fine, you've got big, beautiful feelings for the mother of your child," Ian offered.

I scowled at him. "I like you better when you're silent."

He smiled at me through closed lips, and I'd never wanted to punch a man more. Well, that wasn't true. It'd been pretty satisfying knocking out a couple racist hicks who'd tried to step to Jasper back in the day.

"I think we've taunted David enough for one day," Nick said.

"Tomorrow is another day," Ian said before biting the end of a french fry.

Nick laughed. "True, true. There'll be plenty of chances to rag on David."

I crossed my arms over my chest, leaning back from the table. "I'm calling Dalia."

"Oooh, he's ratting you out to your girl," Jas said, clearly amused.

Nick pointed at me, jabbing his finger in the air. "You get between me and my girl, I'll go all zombie and bite your nose off."

"Aren't zombies more into brains?" I asked.

"Yeah, but I'm not sure I want to consume your twisted mind," Nick said.

He had me laughing. Jesus, I loved these fools.

"Wasn't there a reason for this lunch? Besides gracing all of you with my charming personality?" I asked.

Nick had texted us yesterday, saying he had an idea he wanted to run by us, but wouldn't get into what it was. He'd piqued my curiosity.

"I've been thinking," Nick started. "I want to start an indie record label. I want to find small, quiet bands that would never get noticed otherwise and cultivate them. I'd like to be as hands on as I can—I'm not sure in what capacity yet. I want you guys on board, if you're into it."

I wasn't surprised. Over the summer, Nick and Jas had seen a Blue is the Color cover band, and their story had stuck with him. He kept talking about all the bands who hadn't had the kinda luck we'd had when he first started out but were hella talented. I knew an idea like this had been playing on his mind for a while now.

"I'm in," Jas sad immediately.

"Me too," I said. Because why the hell not?

All of us turned to Ian. He stayed quiet, glancing at each of us, clearly taking his time to contemplate his words.

"Here's the thing: right now, my attention is on composing for an anime short film. It's been in the works for the last year, but now is the time I need to focus on this." Ian met each of our eyes again. "However, I am very interested in investing in new talent. I can't commit much time at the moment, but I *can* commit dollars, and I *will* have more time in a few months."

"So, you're in?" Nick asked.

Ian tipped his chin down. "In short, yes."

Nick slapped his hand on the table, happy as a clam. "Hell yes. I already have a name in mind."

I leaned forward, my burger long forgotten. "Don't leave us hanging."

"What do you guys think about Rein Records?" Nick was asking all of us, but mostly addressing Jasper.

Jas turned toward the window, nodding, but not looking at any of us. I laid a hand on his shoulder, feeling the muscles tense. "Jas? What do you think?" I repeated.

He sniffed, wiping his eyes with the heel of his hand. "She'd kill you, Nick."

He exhaled a laugh. "Maybe. But she'd secretly love it too."

Jasper finally faced him. "That, she would."

Jas's mom—and Nick's surrogate mom—Reinece, had been a hell of a woman. Her loss would be felt forever. Like I'd told Sylvia, she'd been our first fan, so naming our record label after her was only right.

"Now what?" I asked.

Nick snorted. "Now I get Tali to figure out the logistics.

We'll get the lawyers to draw up whatever paperwork we need. And I have a band I want to check out."

"In Baltimore?" Jasper asked.

"Yep. We don't even have to leave town."

We were all down to go to a concert. It was rare—it damn near never happened—for us to go to a show without playing. Even if we went to see a friend's band, we normally got on stage with them to do a song. But this band we were seeing wouldn't even know we were coming. We could watch anonymously, be like normal people.

The more I thought about it, the more I liked the idea.

After leaving Azalea a handsome tip, the four of us exited the diner. Ian was off to compose, and Nick was practically crawling out of his skin to get home where Dalia was working, leaving Jas and me standing on the sidewalk.

"Crazy, right?" I asked. I didn't have to elaborate. He knew I was talking about starting a label.

"I don't know, seems like a natural progression. Maybe we can get some really dope music made. We've needed some life breathed into our veins for a while now. This could be it."

I smoothed a hand over the back of my hair. "Yeah. Maybe it's sad—I don't know—but I got more excited thinking about watching a new baby band play than getting back into the recording studio ourselves."

"Just proves we're doing the right thing by taking a break."

I jerked my chin in response. "What're you up to for the rest of the day?"

"Hitting the gym, maybe read a book. I'm looking forward to doing a whole lot of nothing for a couple weeks. You?"

"Em's sick of my face. She and my mom are spending the day together and she basically told me not to come back. I was thinking of checking out this theater program Syl runs."

He chuckled, an eyebrow raised. "Were you now?"

I pushed his shoulder. "Shut the fuck up, man. She's looking for donors."

I *did* want to see what the program was like even though I'd already told my accountant days ago to make an anonymous donation. Of course, seeing the program was only part of the reason I was going, and Jasper saw right through me.

"Would it be terrible to be into her?" he asked.

My eyes landed on the cracked sidewalk. "I don't know. The fact that we have Em makes it complicated. The fact that Syl has every reason to hate me makes it pretty impossible."

He laid a hand on my shoulder. "Why would she hate you?"

"Again, complicated."

"You think she hates you because you're not around?"

I exhaled through my nose. "I think I'm only just seeing what I've missed. Believe me when I tell you that's a drop in the bucket."

He squeezed my shoulder before he let his hand drop. "For what it's worth, I didn't get any hate vibes from her. She seems cool as hell."

"She is."

We hugged briefly, then he went his way, and I went mine. And my way was to see Sylvia.

"ELEPHANT!" I yelled.

The three people next to me scrambled into position, one using her arm as a trunk, the others posing as her ears.

"Palm tree!" I called.

Three people on my other side swayed like the wind was blowing through their fronds, and chanted, "Whoosh, whoosh."

I spun around. "Statue of Liberty!"

The next group stood as still as marble. Or copper, as the case may be. I eyed them closely, until one of their mouths started twitching.

I laughed. "Ah, ah! I saw that, Monique!"

The seventeen-year-old sputtered, "I tried, Miss Sylvia. But Omar's going crazy with his trunk."

I turned, and sure enough, Omar was waving his trunk vigorously.

"And scene!" Everyone dropped out of their poses, and we sat in a circle in the middle of the stage.

I worked with a lot of kids, and I wasn't supposed to have favorites, but these ten were, by far. They were theater kids at heart, but until recently, they hadn't gotten to explore that part of themselves. I'd plucked them out of the programs I'd brought to their schools and had asked them to take part in the community showcase I helped produce every year. They all either had a child or were teetering on the edge disaster.

Omar was my angry kid. And from what I'd gleaned about his life, he had every right to be. Absent parents, apathetic grandparents raising him, schools without heat, lead in his water. I was no expert on kids. I had a bachelor's degree in marketing. But I did know something about being an angry teenager walking a fine line between figuring their stuff out and giving up.

He gave me a lot of grief, but each week when we met, I saw some of his rage chip away. And maybe when he left my stage, it built right back up, but at least he had these two hours where he could drop his facade and let some of that twisted turmoil unravel.

I'd had the same thing for a while as a kid. My parents were unimaginably conservative, but they declared theater a suitable activity for a young lady. It wasn't like the nuns at my Catholic school were going to let us put on *Chicago* or anything. My freshman year, we performed *Oklahoma*. My parents didn't show up to watch, but at least they allowed me to participate.

Them not showing up was probably for the best. If they'd seen how happy being on that stage had made me, they would have probably decided musicals were the devil's instrument and forbade me to continue.

Today, we'd worked on their pieces for the showcase they'd be putting on next month. Omar had chosen to sing a solo arrangement of "I'll Cover You" from *Rent*. Every time he sang it, with a baritone that would give Jesse L. Martin a run for his money, I had to wipe away tears.

"Would you like to start today, Monique?" At the end of each rehearsal, we sat in the center of the stage with our eyes closed, humming as each person said something they'd seen or felt over the last week that had filled them with wonder.

"Yeah, I'll go," she said.

My eyes fell closed, and a hum buzzed through my throat and past my lips. I loved this part, hearing how wonderful the everyday could be.

"Dry brown leaves swirling and dancing in the middle of the street." Monique drew out each word. She was dramatic all the way to her bones—not in a bad way, though. Sometimes I wondered if her thoughts were in poetry or paintings instead of words. She was a girl who felt big. When I met her four months ago, she had nowhere to channel all those feelings, no one to tell her there were lots and lots of people like her. But when she started my program, started the acting exercises, I saw a change in her immediately. She felt seen—something most teenagers struggled to find.

We went around the circle, the answers ranging from a surprise piece of chocolate, to the feel of cold tile against a cheek in a hot shower, to a rainbow in a puddle of oil in the street. When it was my turn, I said, "Realizing we're all extremely breakable, but we can also be fixed."

"That's a good one, Miss Sylvia," Monique said.

I laughed, my eyes opening. "Thanks for the vote of confidence."

As everyone grabbed their backpacks to head home, I stopped Monique, pulling her aside. "Are you getting any sleep, honey?"

Her eyes welled up immediately, but not with sadness. She smiled and wiped a relieved tear away. "He slept through the night three nights in a row. The first night, I kept startling awake, checking on him. But the last two nights? I didn't wake up for seven solid hours."

Monique had a six-month-old baby boy named Xavier. To

say he was a bad sleeper was an understatement. She had family support during the day, but her mom worked nights, so she was mostly on her own. I'd given her every tip I remembered from Em's early days. Fifteen years later, and I still remembered what it had been like to stare at my wide-awake baby at two a.m., wondering how I'd possibly keep going.

My smile was as wide as it had ever been. "Amazing what a little sleep can do, huh?"

Her smile softened. "It is. And his daddy came by three times this week. He held Xavier while I did my homework and wrote a paper. Plus, he brought diapers. He didn't even try to get with me. He just wanted to see his son."

I pulled her in for a hug. I couldn't help seeing myself in her, and my heart ached for us both.

"Give Xavier a high five for me, okay, honey?"

She laughed. "I will, Miss Sylvia."

As I packed up my portable speakers, I noticed Omar still lingering.

"What's up?" I asked.

"There's a white dude sitting in the back. I don't know if you saw him or not, but I didn't want to leave you alone with him," he said.

I scanned the dark audience, spotting him immediately. "It's okay. I know him."

Omar seemed dubious. "You sure? Guy gives me the creeps."

I chuckled. I couldn't wait to tell David he gave six-foot-four Omar the creeps.

"I'm sure. Thank you for looking out for me."

He focused on his shoes, his hands stuffed in his baggy pockets. "Ain't nothin'. See you next week, Miss Sylvia."

He hurried out of the theater, and I walked to the edge of

the stage, my hands on my hips. "Are you planning on hiding in the shadows forever?"

David stood, sauntering down the aisle. "I thought it gave me a *Phantom of the Opera* vibe."

"Are you attempting to impress me with your theater reference?"

He stopped at the front row, his head tipped back to look up at me. "Depends. Did it work?"

I held my index finger and thumb an inch apart. "A little. Now, if you belted out some *Cats*, I'd *definitely* be impressed."

His chest inflated as he took a deep breath, then he threw his arms out and scream-sang, "Meeemory...." He stopped, shaking his head. "That's all I got."

I couldn't hold back the grin from taking over my face. I wanted to. I didn't want to be happy David had inexplicably shown up at my rehearsal, but a big part of me was.

I clapped for him. "Encore!"

"I'm not used to the applause coming from that angle," he said.

I sat on the edge of the stage, my feet dangling. He came closer, his face level with my belly button. His hair was so dark and thick, I had to dig my nails into my thighs to stop myself from sliding my fingers through it to see if it was as soft as it looked.

"What are you doing here?" I asked.

"I had a meeting close by, and since my mom and Emma are hanging out, I thought I'd stop by and check out the program I just donated a shitload of money to support."

I sat up straight, my chest tightening. "How much?"

He chuckled. "A lot. But tell me if you need more. These kids are talented as hell."

Before I could stop myself, I grabbed his cheeks and kissed

the top of his head. "David...thank you! Holy wow, thank you! I was panicking we weren't going to be able to do the show and..." I choked up, a knot too big to swallow blocking my throat. I'd been trying not to let myself worry about the money I still needed to raise, but I had been. I'd been dreading having to tell the kids we'd either have to postpone or cancel the show. I knew they wouldn't take it well. A disappointment like that could be a life changer.

He grabbed my hands, squeezing them. "Don't cry, Syl. Please, you're gonna make me cry, then I'll feel like a real asshole."

Freeing my hands, I wiped my eyes. "I'm so relieved. Thank you again. I know I was a jerk when you offered—"

He caught my hand again, and this time, I was very aware of the feel of his long, callused fingers holding mine captive. And I just...let him. "It's nothing. I wish I'd known you were running this program years ago. I'd have been donating all along."

I didn't know what to say to that. We hadn't been on speaking terms until now. There was never a point in our curt texts and short emails where I could have dropped in "oh, by the way, I run a theater program and we're looking for donors..." It never would've occurred to me he'd be interested anyway.

"I'm glad you got to see them rehearse today," I said, acutely aware of the way his thumb brushed back and forth over my wrist.

"Me too. Are you gonna perform at the showcase?"

I nodded. "I usually do a number with the kids. I haven't chosen what I'm going to do yet."

"What's your favorite musical?" he asked.

I patted the stage next to me. "I'm tired of looking down at you. Come up here."

I would've had to walk to the side of the stage to climb the steps, but David's biceps were the size of my thighs, so he pushed himself up and swung around to a seated position like it took no effort at all.

He smiled at me, and it was different than his usual smile. It didn't feel like he was on the verge of snarking at me. His eyes were warm, and if I was a fool—and far too often I was with him —I'd have said full of affection. Warm sounded safer. Warm didn't mean anything. It was neutral, not hot with burning passion, not cold with icy hatred. Just a comfortable warm.

So comfortable.

I smiled back. Despite all my confused feelings, I was happy to be sitting next to him on the stage of a Baltimore performing arts high school, talking musicals.

"That's better." If my voice came out thicker than normal, it was only because I was thirsty. It had nothing to do with how good David smelled, or the way his leather jacket fit him like it had been made for him. Actually, it probably *had* been.

"A lot," he murmured. His eyes skated over my face, and I regretted that my hair was pulled to the side in a braid instead of down. During an art unit in middle school, we studied Pablo Picasso. When our teacher showed us Woman with a Blue Hat, one of my kind classmates pointed out our resemblance. And to tell the truth, she hadn't been that far off. My features seemed to have been picked out of a hat and plopped haphazardly on my face.

I'd grown into my nose somewhat, but I was never going to be a beauty. I had character, and most days that was enough for me. Plus, I knew my ass was bangin' from years of running and working out with Gwen, and my hair and eyes were enviable.

But back then, during my teenage years, my self-esteem had been nil. In retrospect, that probably had something to do with why I'd snuck out to parties and had drunken sex with boys I barely knew.

When David looked at me like this, though, I wished I was

prettier—and I *hated* myself for it. Whether he found me attractive or not was irrelevant.

Taking a deep breath, I forced a smile back on my face. "Do you actually want to know my favorite musical?"

"That's why I asked."

I tried to regain some of the lovely warmth I'd been feeling a minute ago. "Well, I have my sophisticated, theater-approved answer, and my *real* answer."

He laughed. "Lay it on me."

"I always say it's *Les Mis*, and while I do love it, it's not my favorite."

"I bet I know what it is," he said.

I cocked my head. "Do you?"

He tugged the end of my braid. "*Rent*."

I let out a surprised laugh. "How'd you guess that?"

"Pretty easily. You wear that ratty-ass T-shirt every other day, and when you cook, you sing "La Vie Boheme." I had to Google it to find out where it's from."

I rubbed my burning cheeks. "Holy hell, you hear me singing when I'm cooking?"

He smiled smugly this time. "I do indeed. And I enjoy the hell out of it, especially when you twerk."

I pushed his shoulder. "I don't twerk!" Sometimes, I *did* twerk.

"You do."

I shook my head. "I think I've gotten too used to it only being Em and me. She doesn't judge my twerking."

He held his hands up. "Not judging! I told you I enjoy the hell out of it. I never took you for a twerker."

"I'm sure there's a lot about me that'd surprise you."

"Oh, I have no fuckin' doubt about that." He tugged my braid again. "Tell me more about theater."

"What do you want to know?"

"Why do you love it?" he asked.

"I've never really thought about it." My eyes drifted toward the maroon curtains as I contemplated my answer. "I love how big everything is. Even if it's a quieter show, there's something powerful about expressing the story through music and movement."

"I get the hell out of that," he said.

I met his dark eyes. "I know you do. Music transforms the simplest thoughts into art. I've sobbed my way through more musicals than anything else. I defy you to listen to Collins singing "I'll Cover You" after Angel dies and not cry your face off. And don't get me started on "It's Quiet Uptown" from *Hamilton* after his son is killed."

David's eyes widened. "Uh, spoiler alert!"

I laughed and bumped his shoulder with mine. "I don't believe you have any plans of ever seeing a musical."

"I didn't, but I can't say I'd object to going with you or Em. Although, fuck that *SpongeBob* shit!"

"*SpongeBob* was amazing! John freaking Legend wrote some of the music."

He nodded and rubbed the scruff on his chin. "He's cool. But I'll still pass."

David helped me up and grabbed my bags, then we walked outside to the parking lot. We were both dragging our feet. This was the first time we'd had a semblance of a normal conversation that hadn't devolved into fighting, and it felt like neither of us were in a hurry to end it.

"What was your meeting about?" I asked.

We stopped by the trunk of my car, and he turned to me, holding my bags in both his hands. "Right. So, my meeting was more like a shooting the shit session with Blue. I dunno. We tossed around the idea of starting an indie label."

I popped my trunk, and he set the bags inside. "You'd produce records?"

He rubbed the back of his neck. "That's the idea. We've talked about it for a long time, you know, but this feels like the right time...if we're gonna do it."

All I could think was something like that would keep him here...for Em, obviously.

"That seems like it could be really fulfilling."

"Yeah, it'd be rad to kinda hand-pick new bands and guide them. We just have to figure out the logistics of it all. And rope Tali in."

I leaned against the side of my car, searching his face. It really wasn't fair for one man to be so damn beautiful. It had only gotten worse with age, too. The shallow lines etched around his mouth and the corners of his eyes made me think of nights full of laughter and days spent concentrating on writing music. He'd lived, and it showed.

I'd lived too. Oh, I'd lived. But my lines were mostly contained within the four chambers of my heart, in the cracks and chips from each and every heartbreak, several of which had been given to me by David.

"I hope it works out."

A faint smile played on his lips. "Me too."

I had to continually remind myself we were playing house right now, but none of this was for keeps—not for me anyway.

TWELVE

DAVID

LYING IN BED, I slid my thumb across my phone screen, pulling up my Spotify app. A few taps, and a moment later, "It's Quiet Uptown" began playing. I had the volume low, since there was no way I wanted Sylvia or Emma to hear what I was listening to.

But I was curious.

If this was what my daughter loved, I should have been familiar with it, right?

No need to bring up the fact her mother had been the one to mention this song.

I listened to the lyrics, and damn if my eyes didn't get wet. I knew nothing about this show, but hearing two grieving parents singing about trying to get on with their lives pulled at my old, rusty heartstrings.

I had to shut it off. It hit too close to home so soon after Em's accident.

I needed a smoke, so I hopped out of bed, stuffed my pack of cigs in my sweatpants pocket, and headed for the balcony. Since it was after eleven, I figured Syl and Emma were asleep, so neither of them would have to witness me poisoning myself.

I didn't smoke too often anymore, but sometimes, the occasion called for it.

As I walked by Syl's room, I saw her light was still on through the cracked door. When I paused, I heard her tapping away on her computer. I should've figured she was up working. More often than not, she pulled out her laptop when Emma went to her room for the night. At first, I thought she did it to avoid talking to me, and maybe that *was* part of it, but it didn't take me long to realize she was legit working.

The crisp, fall night air hit me in the face when I slid the balcony door open and stepped outside. My view was the shit, but on nights like tonight, a part of me wished for the smell of firepits and dried leaves. Syl and Em probably had that. Their neighborhood, with its well-loved old houses, seemed like the type where people knew each other. They probably had potlucks and street parties.

I'd never had anything like that. It'd been my mom and me since my addict dad took off when I was eight. He stuck around in my life just long enough to leave a deep, lasting wound. Nothin' like walking into the kitchen to find your dad passed out in a chair with a needle hanging out of his arm.

Later, in a lucid moment, he'd hugged me and told me the needles gave him his medicine for his headaches, but even at eight, I wasn't an idiot. I knew what those needles contained had nothing to do with healing.

My mom had been relieved as hell when he took off. Broke, but relieved.

Her brokeness dictated we move a lot—always looking for lower rent, a better deal. We'd lived in a lot of grungy apartments and windowless, basement rooms. Through it all, I stayed in the same schools. My mom had my school district mapped out, and she'd only move us to places within those borders. She couldn't offer me the stability of sleeping in the same place year to year, or even month to month, and she'd even admit she hadn't been the most attentive parent, but she gave me what she could.

Turned out, it was everything. School was where I met Nick, followed by Jasper and Ian. It was where I learned to read music and picked up a guitar for the first time.

Inhaling the wicked beast, nicotine, into my lungs, I leaned my elbows on the balcony railing, letting my shoulders relax and memories fade. I didn't have firepits and street parties, but I was in a pretty damn good place. And I was grateful as hell my kid had that life. As much as I loved having her here in my condo, she wasn't a condo girl.

Neither was Syl.

I knew where she grew up: the last pristine house in a steadily declining neighborhood— the only reason we were able to afford living there. Her parents were decrepit. At first, I'd assumed they were her grandparents. When we moved in, my mom had forced me to go around with her to all the neighbors' houses to introduce ourselves. Mr. and Mrs. Price hadn't been impressed by either of us. They'd only cracked the door long enough to tell us their daughter wasn't allowed to talk to boys and they didn't abide by loud music or wild parties.

Before The Night Of The Broken Condom, I'd only ever caught glimpses of Syl floating past cracked curtains or through the window of her parents' station wagon as they drove down the street—I had zero recollection of the story Nick told us the other day, but I'd probably been high as hell, so that wasn't surprising. I'd started thinking of her as a ghost, and with one big exception, she'd pretty much maintained her status as a specter on the fringe of my vision ever since.

Not now, though. Now, she was front and center—and so fucking real. Seeing her with those kids, witnessing the way they hung on her words and she built them up, had done something to me. It set off an ache in my chest I couldn't soothe.

It pissed me off too. It felt like the Sylvia Price I thought I knew didn't exist. And I guess she didn't. She'd been as much a screw up as me when she was a teenager—maybe more. I'd spent all this time thinking I'd been her downfall, but nah.

More like we'd been each other's.

I wondered who'd been raising my kid all these years. Not a lamb, that was for damn sure. More like a raven-haired, silver-tongued lioness. Her cubs were all that mattered, and she'd gnaw through the windpipe of any lion who got in between them.

The door behind me slid open, and out stepped the lioness, her hair spilling around her shoulders and face. She frowned at the glowing cigarette in my hand.

"Really?"

I took a long drag, my eyes locked on hers, exhaling slowly when my lungs were at capacity. "Really."

"I'm surprised I haven't smelled it on you," she said.

I shrugged lazily. "I haven't smoked since you started staying here."

She leaned against the railing next to me, facing away from the view. "What brought on your sudden need to poison your lungs?"

I was hardly gonna admit listening to showtunes had brought me to tears.

"Just needed to relax. I didn't think you'd want me blazing with Em inside."

She let out a surprised laugh and shook her head. "No, I really don't. Not that I think you would." She met my eyes and must've seen the mess behind them. "What's up, David?"

I stubbed out the cigarette and tossed it on the glass table behind me. Already, I regretted smoking. I didn't want Syl to smell it on me. I didn't want her to have another excuse to keep away from me.

"Just stuck in my head."

"You look a little sad."

"Yeah, maybe."

"Why?" she asked softly.

"Lotta things I'm realizing."

"Like what?"

I studied her face. Her soft blue eyes held only kindness and concern. She should hate me, and she might've, but she cared about me too. I had my boys and my mom, and they cared, but they were obligated. The way she looked at me had me unraveling. All my protective coating was disappearing under her concerned expression.

I wasn't ready for it. So, I went for the safer answer.

"Like I shouldn't listen to showtunes at bedtime."

She gasped, turning to face me fully. Maybe this wasn't safer. She was too close. It took all my strength to hold onto the railing instead of burying my hands in her impossibly shiny hair.

"You were? Which ones?" she asked.

The smart thing would've been to step away. Add some distance between us. But I'd never been smart, and we'd spent years with too much distance between us.

I turned to face her, and we were close enough to feel each other's body heat.

She inhaled quickly, but didn't move. She kept her eyes on mine, waiting for me to answer.

"The song from *Hamilton*. The one you told me about," I admitted.

She laid her hand on my arm, squeezing lightly. "Oh, honey, that's not a song for beginners."

I chuckled. "What can I say? I like to dive in head first."

"Did you cry?"

"I kinda did, yeah. How 'bout we never tell anyone else about this?"

"Did it make you think of Em?"

Sighing, I let my head fall forward, so close to Syl, my hair brushed her forehead. "Yeah. It did."

"I'm not sure if I'll be able to listen to it anytime soon. When I got the call from the hospital, I thought—" her voice thickened, "I thought she was gone."

"That was my first thought when I saw your name on my phone."

"She's okay." Syl sounded like she was reassuring herself as much as she was trying to reassure me.

"She is."

And then, I was no longer just close to her, I was wrapped in her arms and she was wrapped in mine. It was hard to say who initiated the hug, but both of us stiffened when we realized we were in the middle of it.

I wasn't letting go, though. Not yet. It wasn't every day I got to hold a ghost, to feel the solid warmth of her, so I'd keep her in my arms until she disappeared again.

The stiffness left her limbs slowly, and she laid her head on my chest. I curled around her, my cheek resting on the silk of her midnight hair, my hands spanning the small of her back and between her shoulder blades. She was small, but not the wisp she used to be.

Sylvia was solid, and even now, when she let herself be held, I could feel the strength contained within her.

I didn't speak. I was self-aware enough to know my mouth got me in trouble more often than not, and I didn't want this to end—didn't want for her to raise the barrier she kept between us. I could've held her like this forever.

Which was crazy. But that's how it felt. Like all I needed was this woman in my arms to sustain me for the rest of my life.

The need wasn't sexual, although my cock was as hard as it had ever been pressed against Syl's belly.

She smelled fresh, like a cool breeze, and she felt like a glass of water in the desert. Like maybe she wouldn't save my life in the long run, but I couldn't have lived another second without having her.

I didn't move. Didn't try to kiss her or rock my hips into her. I didn't want her thinking that was what this was about. Not tonight.

It hurt to hold her, just as much as it felt imperative. We should've done this years ago. When our daughter was born. At her first birthday. When they flew to Paris. So many fuckin' opportunities passed us by. We'd done this big, amazing thing together, but we'd remained as separate as two people could be.

I didn't want that anymore. I didn't know what the hell I wanted, except for this to go on and on.

Syl *did* move. Her hands roamed my back, slowly stroking up and down, like she was both soothing me and taking her own comfort.

She whimpered quietly, her body trembling, like maybe she was hurting in the same way I was.

"David…" she whispered my name, but nothing else came.

I stroked her hair, my shaky fingers getting lost in the glassy strands. I couldn't think of a thing to say. Not one damn thing.

We stayed like that for a long time. Could've been minutes, could've been hours. Finally, we separated, but she twined her fingers with mine as we walked inside. At her bedroom, she squeezed my hand before letting go, and then drifted inside, quietly shutting the door behind her.

I stood there in the dark hallway, wondering if that had actually happened. Had Sylvia Price really let herself relax in my arms?

When I got into bed, I asked myself if I'd been dreaming all along.

The stiffness of my cock said I hadn't been. When I took it in my fist and pumped, I thought of what Sylvia had felt like pressed against me. The slope of her back just above her ass. The give of her breasts against my chest. Her whimper. Silky hair sliding through my fingers. Her hands exploring. The scent of her. The ache in my heart, just beneath where she'd laid her head.

I came hard, gritting my teeth to keep myself from growling out the name of the one woman who'd haunted me for years. Knowing there was only a wall between us made it that much more intense. I wondered if she knew what I was doing. There was no way she hadn't felt the effect she'd had on me.

There was no way I'd be forgetting it for a long time.

THIRTEEN
SYLVIA

I WIPED my forehead with the back of my hand, my breath coming in heavy pants, feet slapping on the treadmill. I woke up this morning needing to run hard and fast. I went to bed with the same feeling, but I forced myself to lie there and try to forget the feel of David's...just David.

It wasn't working. No matter how steep the incline or how far I ran, he still surrounded me.

I went to bed so wet last night, my thighs were coated. It took a few short minutes and a few soft touches to find release, my face pressed into my pillow to stifle my sounds. And thank god for that, since I couldn't stop his name from tumbling from my lips.

It wasn't that being held by David was sexual. It wasn't. But it had pulled at this thread in me, one I'd begun wrapping around myself the first time he disappointed me. Over the years, I'd twisted and twisted that thread until I was lost in a sweater of it. One hug, one long overdue moment of tenderness, and I was undone. My twisted thread of a sweater had me unraveling and my insides were knotted to the point of pain. Touching myself and making myself come was necessary to breathe again

I still hated David, but a lot of it had unraveled last night too. I'd lived with the feeling for so long, I couldn't quite figure out how to go on without it.

I'd woken up early, much earlier than Emma and David, hoping running and sweating would clear my mind enough to function.

The door opened, and I almost stumbled off the treadmill. David stood in the doorway, letting in the morning chill, rays of orange sun around him like a halo.

He smiled, and I held onto the handles to keep my footing.

"I wondered if you were up here," he said.

I waved and pointed to the earbuds in my ears. He nodded, but instead of taking the hint that I wasn't into talking right now, he moved to stand in front of the treadmill.

"What're you listening to?"

"Music," I replied.

He shot me a heart-stopping grin. "Are you grumpy this morning? Need a hug?"

My stomach squeezed at him making light of what had happened last night, but I really shouldn't have been surprised. I kept making the same mistake with him—thinking things meant more to him than they did, just because they meant the world to me.

"I'm good. Just in the zone."

He watched me for another minute, but I kept my eyes from him. The rooftop gym was attached to an indoor pool, which I hadn't taken advantage of yet, but I had big plans. The walls were all windows, and the treadmill faced a view of the harbor. I usually ran outside, which I loved, but with this view, I didn't mind the treadmill at all.

David finally moved away, but not far. He perched on the row machine next to me, and it took all my willpower not to watch him. I could see enough of his reflection in the glass in front of me to know exactly what he was doing, but my mind wanted to watch his sinewy muscles work with each push and pull, to count the beads of sweat on his forehead, to see the way his abs tightened and relaxed. He wasn't shirtless, but that didn't matter in my fantasies.

I slowed my pace, until I was walking, then I did chance a glance at David. His eyes were locked on my ass, and I didn't mind at all. This ass was hard earned through years of running, theatrical dancing, and Gwen's yoga classes. Not to mention the endless squats and lunges.

I liked being bigger and feeling physically stronger than the slight girl I once was. I'd always felt like I had to stay small so I didn't take up too much room. I'd thought if I was barely there, I wouldn't be such a burden to my parents, especially after Emma came along.

It took a while, but I learned to claim my space.

I moved through the circuit machines, starting with shoulder presses. I felt David's eyes on me, but I steadfastly ignored him. I was being immature, but I was much too raw from last night to engage in playful banter. And playful, snarky banter was David's signature.

When I moved to the leg presses, David took up on the treadmill, running at a steady clip. I faced him now, but I studied my feet as I pushed the weights away from me.

"Hey," he called.

I looked up. "Yeah?"

"What's the deal?"

I took an earbud out, but I didn't pause my leg presses. "I told you, I'm in the zone. I'm not super chatty when I work out."

His eyebrows drew together, hooding his eyes. "I don't buy that your feet are as interesting as you're pretending they are."

I wiped my forehead. "I'm just working out. I can go if I'm bothering you, but I'd rather not."

He hopped off the moving treadmill, letting it run without him, and came to kneel next to me. He picked up my discarded earbud and tucked it in his ear. When he heard what I was listening to, his smile grew broad, and his eyes brightened.

"I didn't know you were such a fan," he said.

Who knew it'd be this embarrassing to listen to my favorite band in front of one of the members? Oh, yeah, me. I should've turned it off the second he'd walked in the door, but I'd been so distracted by him, I hadn't thought of it.

Now, David knew I listened to Blue is the Color when I worked out.

I licked my lips. "I like Nick's voice. And Ian's drums."

His grin grew even wider. "Same."

"The bassist rocks too," I continued. "I always felt the guitarist could use some practice."

By now, my legs had stopped moving, and I was basically folded in half, my knees at my chest. It wasn't exactly a position of strength, so I swung myself around until my legs dangled right in front of David.

His hands landed on the outside of my knees. "Oh, burn. Way harsh, Syl."

With him on his knees, his face was at a similar height as when I was on the stage above him. "I could get used to this angle, with you down there, and me up here."

He held my eyes and did that thing he liked to do where it felt like he was seeing inside of me. His hands flexed on my knees, the tips of his fingers pressing into the soft undersides. "I really don't mind it either. I'm used to seeing people from the opposite side, but this works for me in a lot of ways." His voice was soft and smoky, all hints of joking gone.

My hand moved before my mind sent a signal, wiping his damp brow, fingers combing through the side of his thick hair.

He leaned his face against my wrist, closing his eyes for a moment.

"I like having you here, Syl. Did I tell you that?"

My hand stayed in the side of his hair, his breath hot on my wrist. With his eyes closed, it was easier to say what I wanted to. "I like being here. I never imagined I would, but I do. It'll be hard going back to our normal life in a couple weeks."

David's eyes flew open and he leaned back, leaving my hand floating in mid-air until I let it drop.

"Right. Can't forget this isn't your normal life."

"Well…it's not. This isn't really your normal life either, is it? Having Em and me around?"

His eyes were so deep and dark, when he looked at me like this, it was disorienting, like I'd found myself at the bottom of the ocean with no sense of which way was up.

"Nah, it isn't. Can't say I'm complaining, though."

"Luckily, you're sticking around for a while. You can have Em more often—if that's what you want," I said.

He pressed his lips together into a hard line, and the fingers behind my knees tightened, riding the border of pleasant and painful. If he only knew how much I liked that exact feeling…

"Of course I want that."

I laid my hands on his thick wrists. "Can I finish my work out now?"

"Are you going to keep ignoring me?"

"Maybe. But not as studiously."

His grin was back, but not quite as wide. "That sounds like progress."

He hopped back on the treadmill while I moved around the circuit machine, keeping my earbuds out of my ears. I couldn't bring myself to listen to *any* music, knowing he'd think I was listening to his. Instead, I got to hear the treat that was David Wiesel breathing heavily as he ran.

I'd be adding that sound to the things I hated about him. One man shouldn't sound that sexy while working out. I should have been able to do bicep curls without getting turned on by the sweaty beast working out next to me.

Should, but I couldn't. David had always affected me, no matter how much I loathed him. And seeing him now, sweat trickling down the planes of his hard chest, the ropey veins running up his forearms and muscles in his powerful legs flexing with each stride, I couldn't look away.

"When did you get all buff?" he asked, nodding to my arms.

I dropped the dumbbell in front of me and wind-milled my arms a few times, stretching them. "In my twenties. My...uh, ex, was a trainer. He got me into doing more than just running."

He frowned. "Vince?"

"Yeah, Vince." The man I almost married.

"I thought he was some kinda athlete," David said.

"He was a pro-rugby player."

"Dude was giant."

I sighed. "Yeah, he was." David knew firsthand what Vince looked like. The two had met five years ago at our engagement party—the one Emma had begged me to invite him to. I never actually believed he'd show up, but showed up he had.

David slowed the treadmill until he was barely walking. "Did you break his heart, Syl?"

"Yes. I think I did."

I had. I'd broken his heart—and mine. Despite Suz's joking about Vince being in a biker gang, he truly had been a good guy. A great guy. I could've met anyone where I worked, doing what I did, but I met and fell for the real deal. A man who worshipped me and never looked at another woman from day one, even when I'd tried to keep him at arm's length because of Emma.

He'd asked me to marry him twice before I'd said yes, and

even then, Em and I didn't move in with him. I'd said it would be an easier transition for her if we waited until after the wedding, but the truth was, I'd needed an escape route.

I'd loved Vince. I could've been happy with him. I couldn't convince myself he was my forever.

"Why?" David asked. "Why didn't you get married?"

I shrugged. "He didn't love Emma the way I wanted him to, and I didn't love him the way he needed."

David tensed. "What the fuck? What do you mean he didn't love Emma the way you wanted him to?"

I stood, wanting to soothe him, but stopping myself short. "Nothing bad, I swear. He *did* love her. She loved him too. But he'd always talked about wanting his own kids, and I could tell Emma was always going to be an 'other' to him. It's hard to explain, I guess. But that's how I felt."

"He was good to her?" David asked.

"Yes. Always. I would have murdered him if he'd ever thought about not being good to her."

He let out a short laugh. "I know you would've. You've got your prison shiv tucked under your pillow."

"Have you been snooping in my room?"

"Just in your underwear drawer."

Instead of going to him like I really wanted to, I turned and went to the spot I'd left my water and a towel. Bending over, I grabbed them both and took a long drink of water.

"Damn, Syl."

I peered over my shoulder at my ass. The leggings I had on did wonders for my backside. A little thrill went through me at David appreciating the view.

"I always did look better from behind," I quipped.

One moment I was standing there at the window, wiping my forehead with a towel, the next, I was being spun around by strong hands on my shoulders.

David gripped my chin between two fingers. He scanned my face, not missing one freckle or line. I wanted to shrink away, to remove myself from his eyes that saw way too much.

"Look at you," he whispered. "This face..." His thumb brushed my lip.

"What?"

"You already know I think your ass is spectacular, but you gotta know I think you're pretty as hell. Don't you see me always looking at you?" His words sounded like smoke, and I could barely grasp them. What he said didn't make sense.

"Never. I've never noticed."

He dropped his hand and took a step back. "Start noticing."

I licked my lip where his thumb had been. "I will."

He held his hand out. "Come on. The kid is probably thinking her parents ran out on her."

I slid my hand in his, and he gripped it firmly. "The kid is probably still fast asleep."

He shook his head. "Oh, yeah, sleep. I could'a used a little more of that."

"Why'd you wake up so early?"

"Maybe I wanted to spend some time with you, just the two of us."

"Maybe you're full of it."

He squeezed my hand. "I am, a lot of the time. But not right now. Doesn't it feel different?"

"After last night?" I asked.

"Yeah. After last night."

"To me, yeah. It does."

"I don't know what it means," he said, "and I sure as hell know I'll screw it all up, but while I have you, I want to get to know you. And I don't want to fight with you. I want to hold your hand and watch your ass while you run on my treadmill. Is that okay?"

He sounded so earnest, so sincere, and yeah, a little puzzled by it all, that I couldn't possibly say no. And I felt it, that thread being tugged, and a little more of the hate I carried unraveled.

"That's okay with me. I don't want to fight either." I kept my voice and gaze steady.

"And the ass watching and hand holding?"

I shifted my hand so our fingers wove together. "That's okay too. Just...not in front of Emma."

His shoulders dropped, but he nodded. "Got it. Wouldn't want to weird the kid out."

I released a little laugh. "I'm kinda weirded out."

He reached up and swiped my chin with his thumb again. "Get used to it, Syl. Life is always a little bit weird with me around."

"Of that, I have no doubt."

FOURTEEN

DAVID

"DESCRIBE YOUR MOM'S sauce in detail."

Emma rolled her eyes. "You're going to be eating it in a couple hours. Just wait!"

I pointed to her face. "You're gonna break your eyeballs too if you keep rolling them."

She rolled her eyes again. "Oh please. I'm well-practiced. My eyerolling game is strong. There's no chance of breakage."

I laughed, slowing my grocery cart at the flower section. "You sure you don't need one of those motorized cart things?"

Em held up one of her crutches. "I'd rather be dead. And I'm making crutches cool again."

I rubbed my chin, contemplating her crutches. "Nah, I think you need a lightning bolt or some racing stripes."

She laughed. "I was thinking pink."

"I'm down for pink crutches." I turned back to the flowers. "Think your mom would want some?"

Em laid her head on my shoulder. "That'd be sweet. No one ever buys her flowers."

I kissed the top of her head. "You know me. My nickname in school was Sweetie Pie."

She cackled. "No it wasn't!"

I grinned. "Nah, it wasn't. Mostly, it was 'Hey asshole!' Anyway, what kind of flowers?"

"Depends. What's the message you're sending? Is it *thanks for cooking for me*, or *I think you're the prettiest woman I've ever seen*, or *let's be friends*?"

"Uh...somewhere in between those three?"

She nodded at what looked like a bouquet of wildflowers. They probably all had names, but I was no flower expert. I couldn't remember ever buying flowers before. On occasion, my chef would bring a bouquet with her, arranging them in a vase I apparently owned, and they'd disappear again a few days later when my maid came to clean.

Jesus, that made me sound like an asshole.

I picked up the flowers Emma suggested, laying them in the seat of the cart.

"What else do we need?"

"Mom said to get ingredients for salad, fresh, crusty bread, and something for dessert."

Sylvia was at home cooking and had sent Emma and me out to the store. To be honest, before Syl and I went shopping together, I couldn't remember the last time I'd set foot in a grocery store. I had people who did this for me, but I was digging the domestic shit lately.

I wouldn't chance being out with Emma if I thought paparazzi would be around, but the good thing about living out of the main scene of New York or LA? There wasn't a whole lot of that around here. I got recognized, but it was usually by fans of the band who wanted a picture and an autograph, and sometimes to shoot the breeze. They didn't give two fucks about my personal life, usually. From time to time, I ran into a fan who'd probably boil my bunnies, but I tended to steer clear when I spotted crazy eyes.

"You good with hobbling the rest of the way around the store?"

"Yep. I've got to get used to it. I start back at school in a week."

"I've never heard a kid so excited to go to school," I said.

"You hung out with the wrong kind of kids. I'm out for the rest of soccer season, which blows, but auditions for *Beauty and the Beast* are coming up—I'm clearly not landing the part of Belle with my gimpy leg, but I figure I can be one of the towns-people, even on crutches—and then there's HoCo in two weeks."

I threw a loaf of french bread into the cart. "What the hell is HoCo?"

She snorted. "Homecoming. You know, big football game, followed by a dance."

"I'm familiar with the ritual. Didn't know it had a nick-name." I side-eyed her. "Do kids these days go as big groups or...?"

She rolled her eyes yet again. "Dad, obviously I have a date. But we'll go with a group too."

My stomach rolled at the thought of some dickwad touching my daughter. It hadn't even occurred to me to be worried about that yet, but damn. Worry officially activated.

We picked out brownies for dessert and moved through the produce section swiftly, throwing in romaine lettuce, peppers, and carrots.

"Do we need dressing?" I asked.

"Nope. Mom makes her own."

"Of course she does. Is there anything that woman can't do?"

She laughed. "I haven't witnessed it. I guess that's what happens when you have a kid when you're sixteen and have to make it on your own. You figure it out."

I wanted to protest that Sylvia hadn't been entirely on her own, but I couldn't. I sure as hell hadn't been there. I'd taken Em for a couple hours at a time every week in those early days, but that was a drop in the damn bucket. A drop in the ocean, really.

I wrapped my arm around Em's shoulders and kissed her head noisily. "I love you, kid. You know that?"

"Yeah, Dad, I know." She tried to play it cool, but I saw the smile on her face. I didn't get a lot of "I love yous" in my life, so sometimes I forgot to say it, but I had to do better. I had to do better about a lot of things.

WHEN WE GOT HOME, we were welcomed by showtunes blasting and the smell of garlic and oregano. Emma bypassed the kitchen to go to her room to get ready for her friends who were coming over later. I stood in the doorway, grocery bags and flowers in my hands, but I had no intention of interrupting Sylvia's show to set them down.

Her back was to me, and she was chopping something up, all while swaying her hips and singing. Her voice wasn't rock n' roll, but it was clear and strong. Pretty. She sang about needing her candle lit, and right then, I'd light all the fuckin' candles in the world if she'd rock her little ass against me and—

"I know you're there," she said, interrupting my filthy, filthy mind.

She peered over her shoulder at me. "Unlike me, you're not a ninja. It's those giant boots you always wear."

Grinning, I toed off my *giant boots* before I moved into the kitchen behind her and set down the bags on the counter.

"I like your moves, Syl."

She turned the rest of the way around, her arms crossed over her chest, grinning like the Cheshire cat. "You missed the twerking portion of the show."

"As long as I get to eat the sauce, I'll make any sacrifices I need to. But I'm gonna have to be notified well in advance the next time twerking occurs."

Her eyes strayed to the flowers, but she didn't say anything. I offered them up to her, suddenly feeling like a shy kid asking his crush on a date. The hell of it was, I'd never actually asked a girl on a date, and based on my knotted intestines, I'd rather this not become a habit.

"I didn't know what you liked, so Em helped me picked these out."

She took them from me, cradling them like they were precious. She looked pretty damn pleased with my choice, setting off an unfamiliar warmth in my chest.

"You did good," she said. "I like to buy myself flowers once a month or so, and I always go for the colorful ones. I couldn't tell you the names of most of them." She fingered a flower. "Except these. These are Alstroemeria."

I snorted. "*That's* the name you remember?"

"That was almost Emma's name."

My lip curled. "Nooo…"

She laughed, shaking her head. "No, not really. I like saying it, so it stuck in my head." She held them up to her face, inhaling. "Smells like a garden. Thanks. That was really sweet of you to think of me."

I glanced around the kitchen, still feeling ridiculous about the whole thing, but also so damn warm. "There's gotta be a vase around here somewhere."

"I've decided to find it charming that you have no idea where anything in your kitchen is."

I huffed a laugh. "Why don't you stick around and see what other areas of my incompetence you find charming. Grown man, barely able to fold his own clothes! Thirty-three-year-old can't find his neighborhood grocery store without research."

She took a step, closing the space between us. "Don't do that."

"What?"

"You did something nice for me, and maybe you don't know why, so you're deflecting. You're turning it, and yourself, into a joke."

I sighed, looking down into her clear blue eyes. "The flowers seemed like a good idea at the time, but now I feel like an idiot."

"Why?"

I picked up a piece of her long hair, rubbing the silk of it between my fingers.

"Doesn't matter. I'm glad you like the flowers, Syl."

She stepped closer and circled her arms around my neck. "I do. Thank you for thinking of me."

It took me a second to react before I pulled her against me, hugging her back.

The me from five seconds before I got the call from Syl about Em's accident would have been hysterical at getting hard from hugging a woman. It was like I was in one of those cheesy-ass, made-for-TV, wholesome Christmas movies where the couple was made for each other, but barely kissed until the end.

Yet I wasn't trying to hump her or bite her neck or suck her tongue. I just wanted to hug this fucking sweet, beautiful woman.

Her face turned, and I felt her hot breath next to my neck before she inhaled deeply.

"I'll buy you flowers everyday if you're gonna be this friendly," I said.

Her hands slid from behind my neck to my chest, where she let them rest for a moment.

"I'm easily bought. You could just pick me a dandelion and

I'd be happy. It's the thought."

"Damn. I saw a dandelion growing in a crack in the sidewalk. I should've picked it and saved my money."

She laughed, patting my chest before she stepped back. "Stop distracting me. I've got to get everything in the pot. Suz and family will be here soon, and this has to cook for two hours."

I pushed up the sleeves of my Henley. "Anything I can do?"

She gestured with her knife. "Find the elusive vase for the flowers. Other than that, we'll wait until it's closer to dinnertime to do everything else."

I had to stand there for a second to admire how utterly competent and in-charge she was. If my dick hadn't been hard already, it sure as hell would have surged to life then, Sylvia in her tight little jeans and theater T-shirt, in complete control of the situation.

I would've liked her to take control of my situation. I pictured her with a crop in her hand and thigh high boots on her feet telling me exactly how she wanted me to lick her pussy.

"Dad! The remote needs new batteries!"

My boner wilted, and I was brought right back to reality the second I heard my daughter's voice. *Right. Sylvia is not a dominatrix, and I'm a fuckin' dad.*

I might've been the worst dad in existence, making up dirty fantasies about my kid's mom in the kitchen.

"Em! Dad's looking for a vase, he'll help you in a minute," Sylvia called back, once again taking control when I failed to.

She looked at me, amused. "Did you get lost?"

I released a breath. "A little bit, yeah."

She bent down and opened a cabinet under the sink. "A-ha! I had a feeling it would be here!" She straightened, holding up a vase so clear and blue, it reminded me of her eyes.

"Why am I not surprised you found that without even really looking?"

She shrugged. "Because it's where I'd put a vase if it were my kitchen."

She gasped and turned the volume up on her phone. "La Vie Boheme" poured out of the speakers, and Sylvia danced a little jig, throwing ingredients into the pot on the stove. Then she turned, using her spoon to lip sync the words as she stalked toward me.

This was the one time in my life I wished I knew the words to a showtune. Her enthusiasm was so infectious, I would've been singing right along with her. When she reached me, I curled my arm around her waist, and grabbed the hand holding a spoon, dancing with her. She laughed, but never broke part, mouthing all the words to the song.

"You're amazing," I said quietly under the music.

Her eyebrows raised. "Hmm? I didn't hear you."

I smiled and shook my head. "Not important. I'm gonna go help Em with the remote."

She laughed and danced her way back to the pot, swishing her hips as she went.

I actually did know where the batteries were, and I brought them to Em, sitting next to her on the couch.

This entire day had been the picture of domesticity so far, and if I let myself, I could settle into it like a cozy sweater. In an alternate timeline, where I wasn't an asshole, this could be my life. The pretty wife who danced while she cooked Sunday dinner. The talented daughter who had endless patience for her uncool dad.

But this was reality, and I had to face facts. There was a time limit on this. I'd be back on the road eventually, playing the rock star, and Em and Syl would be a pair again instead of a trio. I *was* the interloper in this story, and soon, I'd be on my own again, where I belonged. I'd always been okay with that, but these days, my real life had lost some of its luster.

I WAS ODDLY NERVOUS.

Suz, Mika, Evan, and Em's friend Avery would be here any minute, and my stomach was churning with anticipation. I felt a little bit like a fifties newlywed about to entertain my husband's boss at our new home. I'd even dressed the part, slipping on a retro-style royal blue A-line dress with sweet little cap sleeves. Never mind the fact that it was a stretchy cotton and more comfortable than my jeans.

Before heading out to the living room, I swiped on my favorite red lipstick. When I opened my bedroom door, David was leaving his room too. He'd changed into a charcoal button-down and slightly less tattered jeans.

I smiled at him, and his mouth fell open for a moment. "You clean up nice," I said.

"You clean up gorgeous," he rasped, coming closer.

I looked down at my dress, swaying so it swished around my legs. "Oh, this old thing?"

"Red lipstick should be illegal on mouths like yours. That's enough to bring a man to his knees." He rubbed his thumb under my bottom lip. "Come on, Syl. This isn't fair."

I tipped my chin up, wanting to capture his thumb with my teeth. My breathing shallowed, standing so close to him in the shadowy hallway.

"Why?" My voice dropped, coming out much more sultry than I'd intended.

"'Cause you make me think about doing things I shouldn't be thinking about." His rough fingertips traced the contours of my jaw, from under my ear to my chin.

"Why shouldn't you be thinking about those things?"

He opened his mouth to answer at the same time the doorbell rang. We both exhaled heavily, and I smiled up at him. "They're here!"

He pressed against the front of his jeans. "I'll be out in a minute. Don't eat all my sauce." With that, he went back into his room, shutting his door quickly behind him.

Emma was already headed to the door on her crutches when I got out there. She'd changed into her own dress and curled her long, mahogany hair.

"You look pretty," I said.

"I'm nervous. I haven't seen Evan since the accident..."

I gave her a quick hug and kissed her temple. "He's going to be so happy to see you. I guarantee it. Can we lay low with the PDA? I'm not sure how Dad will react if you're all smoochy-smoochy with Ev."

Emma groaned. "*Mom!*"

"Sorry, dude! I had to say it!"

"You really didn't."

I opened the door to my best friend and crew. Suz held up two wine bottles, grinning broadly. "I have the vino!"

"Come in here, you fool," I said.

Suz came inside, pressing a kiss to my cheek. Evan followed her, giving me a barely-there hug before heading straight for Emma. Avery trailed him, waving shyly at me. I wholly approved of her as Em's BFF. She wasn't one of those cool Instagram teenagers. She was an average, soccer-playing, drama-loving fifteen-year-old.

Mika came in last, closing the door behind him.

"Welcome to my temporary home," I said.

He nodded, surveying the vast, open space. "Nice digs. The neighborhood's not the same without you and Em, though."

"We'll be back soon. Don't you worry."

He held his arms out. "C'mere."

Laughing, I hugged him. Or attempted to. Mika was a mountain of a man, with a shiny bald head and tree trunk arms. He lifted me off the ground with all the care of a gentle giant. When I first met him a few years ago, I'd been a little intimidated, and I'd spent time with rough characters. Mika had a resting mean face, like he was seconds away from ripping someone's throat out. But the second he smiled, I realized he was more likely to give the shirt off his back to anyone who needed it.

From behind me, I heard the distinct sound of a throat being cleared. Mika set me down, and I turned to find David standing a few feet away, scowling at the scene. Emma, Evan, and Avery had disappeared to her room, and Suz was somewhere in the kitchen, so it was just me and Mika, hugging like long-lost friends.

Of course, David might not have seen the same picture, from the dark look in his eyes.

I patted Mika's arm. "Mika, this is David, Emma's dad. David, this is Mika, my friend and husband to the best woman I know."

David stepped forward, and Mika held a hand out. "Thanks for having us," he said.

David shook his hand. "No problem. I know Sylvia and Emma are ready to get out of here and back to their home, so

I'm just happy I can make their stay a little more comfortable."

The hurt behind his words was clear. He must've heard me calling this my temporary home, but that was what it was. We'd be going back home in a couple weeks. This palatial condo in the sky would never feel like home, but I'd miss the hell out of living with David.

Suz came out of the kitchen. "Well, that's a cook's wet dream, isn't it? How are you gonna give that up, Sylvie?"

I laughed. "I might sneak the stove home in my suitcase. Suz, meet David."

She covered her mouth with her hand. "Oh shit. I didn't see you there. What a wonderful first impression."

David chuckled. "I'm actually quite charmed."

Mika beamed at his wife. "She has that effect."

Suz curtsied in her ripped skinny jeans and metal studded ankle boots. "I charmed Mika right down the aisle, didn't I?" She turned to David. "It's nice to meet you. I have to warn you, we're a family of huggers."

David's eyebrows shot up. "I'm into that."

She launched herself at him, giving him one of her tight Suz hugs with a less-than-gentle thump on the back. She'd been around since almost the beginning. She knew everything. *Everything.* I had a feeling that thump was in my honor.

We ventured into the living room where Mika studied the art hanging on the walls and Suz inspected every corner. She ran her finger along a glass shelf housing David's various awards, including three Grammys, then moved to the Lucite coffee and end tables. I saw her mind working, adding up the decor of the place, coming to a conclusion.

She nudged the Lucite coffee table with her toe. "This place was obviously not designed with a child in mind. It's pretty much a death trap."

David tucked his hands in his pockets, his eyes straying from Suz to me, clearly uncomfortable.

I tried to laugh it off. "I don't think Em is going to knock her head on the coffee table, Suz."

She crossed her arms, brow arched. "No, not now. But she *is* known for spilling things, and this place is so white, *I'm* kind of afraid to touch anything. Definitely not a kid house."

I grabbed her arm. "Didn't you say you wanted a glass of wine?" Pulling her toward the kitchen, I called over my shoulder, "We'll be right back!"

In the privacy of the kitchen, I grated, "What the hell?"

"This place pisses me off," she stated simply.

"It's none of your business how he chooses to decorate."

"Are you kidding me? You didn't walk in, see all the glass and white, and think this is not a guy who's made space in his life for his kid? This is a guy who expects his kid to bend to his life. Because that's all I see."

I yanked open a drawer, finding a corkscrew, and set about uncorking the first chilled bottle of wine.

"What was with the hug when you walked in then?" I asked as I pulled out the cork.

She pushed a wine glass across the counter. "Hugs are instinctual for me. And I'd planned on being nice. But god, I walked into the living room, saw the million-dollar view, the pristine, shiny surfaces, and it set me off. All I could think of was the moldy, run down little two bedroom we shared."

I poured a generous portion of wine into each of our glasses. "He wasn't living like this back then."

She picked up her glass, leveling me with her sharp gaze. "Come on. You know he was living the high life while you were changing shitty diapers and working your ass off."

I held up my hand, trying to silence her. "Let me fight my own battles. We declared a truce, and I don't need you coming in here and tearing down the white flag. I can't keep being angry with him. Where is that going to get me?"

"He should know what a shithead he is," she said bluntly.

"All I care about is him being good to Emma. He's really come through for her."

She clinked her glass on mine. "Cheers to your low standards."

I flipped her off. "He's not my boyfriend. How he's treated me is irrelevant."

She clinked her glass on mine again. "Cheers to denial."

I narrowed my eyes at her. "If you do that one more time, I'm taking your wine."

She gasped and huddled protectively around her glass. "You wouldn't."

"You're the one always saying what a badass I am." I picked up the corkscrew, threatening her with it. "I'll take your wine with no remorse."

David ambled into the kitchen, taking a step back when he saw me with my weapon.

"Damn. I got rid of your shivs, but I never even thought about how dangerous the kitchen was."

I laughed, tossing the corkscrew on the counter. Then I realized I was drinking, in David's home, when he'd expressly asked me not to.

"David, I'm sorry. I wasn't thinking." I set my glass down, feeling guilty.

His eyes darted to my wine glass, then back up to meet mine. "Don't worry about it, Syl. I'm not gonna go nuts and start guzzling your Riesling. Wine was never my drink of choice. If you were drinking vodka or a Corona, I might not be able to control myself."

He sounded so disgusted with himself, even though he'd been aiming for humor, I wanted to hug him and pet his hair and tell him how proud I was he'd given up drinking when he'd needed to.

Instead, I picked my wine glass back up and took a sip, holding his gaze the entire time.

"Suz was saying how nice this place is," I said.

He snorted. "I got the message out there. And you're right. When I bought this place, I was twenty-five. I was picturing parties and a place to chill. I'm just gonna come out and admit I didn't have it designed with Emma in mind. Yeah, the designer went balls to the wall with her room, but for me, the rest of it was always intended as a bachelor pad."

I glanced at my friend. Her mouth was hard as she stared David down. "I appreciate the honesty, but whatever self-reflection you're doing now is too little, too late. When you have a child, you make sacrifices from the very beginning. It sucked to be home alone on my twenty-first birthday nursing my brand-new baby, but tough shit, you know? I see this condo, and it's a slap in the face to all Sylvie went through. She's too nice to say it, but I'm not."

I wrapped my arm around her shoulders, pressing my head to hers. "Honey, it's okay. I'm all good."

David looked like he'd been punched in the gut. He leaned against the doorway, his eyes on me.

"Suz, go find Mika. I'll be out in a minute."

She left, brushing by David. Suz wasn't a mean person, but she loved me just as fiercely as I loved her. Evan's dad died when he was a newborn from a drug overdose, so she'd never gotten a chance to tell him what a piece of shit he was for leaving her with a baby at twenty-one. She'd had it even rougher than me, but she'd put herself through school to become a dental hygienist with only me to lean on. We'd lived apart for a while now, but we were still as close as sisters.

I leaned my back against the other side of the doorway, facing him. "I don't think any of that."

"You should." His gaze was intense, burning into me. "What'd you do on your twenty-first birthday?"

"I went to my college classes during the day, then worked until three a.m." I could remember that day clearly. The owner of the club I'd worked at had bought a round of shots for all the employees in honor of my birthday, then he'd cornered me in his office, telling me to give him a blowjob before I went home as thanks. Luckily, he'd taken no for an answer and never asked again, but I left that night with the knowledge it could have easily turned out much differently and became even more determined to get my degree.

"Three a.m.?" he asked.

"Yeah, I worked at a nightclub. Picture me holding glow sticks." I waved my hands around wildly. "It was the early two-thousands. I go-go danced and served drinks."

"God, I hate that you had to do that." He squeezed his eyes shut. "I can't even remember my twenty-first birthday. I probably played a show, got high, and fucked around. I love Emma more than anything in this world, but I've been so selfish for so fucking long, I don't even know how to stop."

Reaching out, I squeezed his hand. "Start by helping me make a salad."

His eyes opened, and he stared down at our joined hands. "Why are you so good?"

"I've messed up too. On a grand scale. I just try not to keep making the same mistake." Except for you, I wanted to say. *I keep making the same mistake when it comes to you.*

He sucked in air, then quickly let it out. Standing straight, he glanced around at the walls and counters. "I think I'm going to tear this fucking kitchen down."

I chuckled softly. "We do seem to keep having some intense moments in here, don't we?"

Instead of answering, he gathered me into a hug, laying his head on top of mine. "I'm sorry, Syl. For all of it."

"I know you are." I wasn't quite up to offering forgiveness. Not yet.

We worked together for a while, chopping up veggies and boiling pasta. Mika and Suz floated in and out of the kitchen, offering to help and stopping to chat. Emma checked in once, letting us know the teens were "literally starving" and their deaths from hunger were imminent.

I dished the food out family style, and David carried everything to the long, concrete and metal table in his dining room. Now that I thought about it, nothing in this condo was kid-proof. I had to laugh how *un*-kid friendly it was.

When David took his first bite of my sauce and pasta, I watched his face, and he did not disappoint. His eyes rolled back as he chewed. "That's it," he said. "You're never leaving. I demand you stay and cook this for me every day."

"How about I send some over with Em when she visits?"

"Not the same."

No, it wouldn't be the same. How were we going to go back to just being vague presences in each other's lives? It seemed impossible right now, but I was experienced enough with David to know the second we were gone, he'd move right on. Out of sight, out of mind.

Emma was happy as a clam, with Evan on one side and Avery on the other. David had a lot of questions for the three of them. He asked Avery all about the soccer team and wanted her opinion on the Stella situation.

I caught Suz's eye during his inquiry, and she offered up a half smile. It was better than nothing.

Mika and I got into a conversation about my next tattoo. I

had a lot of empty skin to be filled. I didn't want to be covered head to toe, but I also didn't feel my ink was complete.

"What about something geometric?" I asked.

He set down his fork. "I'm digging on the geometric trend, but that's what it is, a trend. You're softer than that. We should do watercolor."

I raised an eyebrow. "Geometric is trendy, but watercolor isn't?"

"Maybe. But it's also really pretty."

David tuned into our conversation, leaving the teens to their own devices. "You getting more ink?"

"That's the plan. Mika knows what I like, so we're debating what I should do next."

"You don't know what you want?" he asked.

"Not really. When I got my back piece done, I had a very clear vision. Now, I want *something*," I said.

"What *is* your back piece?"

"Aw, man, you haven't seen it? It's sick," said Mika.

I patted his hand. "I feel like you shouldn't say that about your own work. Even though it *is* sick."

"Mom has a *Rent* tattoo," Emma said.

David smirked. "Oh yeah?"

"What's with the tone?" I asked.

He shook his head. "Nothing. You must *really* love *Rent*, that's all."

"I do. And it's not like the characters' faces or anything. It's a subtle homage."

David snorted.

"It's kinda rad, man. I think you should reserve judgement," Mika said.

Suz scraped her fork on her plate, making me cringe. "I highly doubt he's going to be seeing Sylvie's bare back," she muttered.

That kind of ended the conversation, but David kept trying.

"So, Evan, do you play soccer too?" he asked.

Evan looked like he might faint. I wasn't sure if it was because David was famous, or if it was just the fact that he was Emma's father. "N-No. I'm not very athletic."

"You into music?" David asked.

"Yes, I am."

"What're you listening to these days?"

"Um...I like Post Malone, Kendrick Lamar, Chance...and some oldies, like Weezer."

"Oh, my dude. Oldies? You're breaking my heart." David clutched his chest like he was dying.

I turned back to Suz and Mika while they talked music. I mouthed, "Be nice," to Suz, and she mouthed back, "Never."

"Do you have a costume picked out for the party?" I asked.

"I thought about going as an angel, but then I realized I wouldn't even have to dress up to be that, and that's not fun," Suz said.

I snorted. "You mean devil."

Mika cupped his wife's cheek. "She might be the devil, but she's *my* devil."

"What's your actual costume?" I asked.

"We're doing the couple thing. Mika's going to be Hagrid and I'm going to be his dragon, Norbert," she said.

"Totally makes sense," I said. If you knew Suz, it totally did. She'd been milking Harry Potter for costume ideas for years. She never went obvious, like Harry and Ginny. A couple years ago, she and Mika had been Tonks and Lupin, and the year after that, they'd been Ron and his rat, Scabbers—Suz the rat, Mika was Ron. I figured they had a good twenty or thirty years of costumes from the seven books.

"How about you, Sylvie? Any costume ideas?" Mika asked.

"You can't be Morticia Adams again," Suz said.

I laughed. "But it's so easy! Throw on some red lipstick and a black dress, and I'm Morticia."

She pointed her finger at me. "That's exactly why. Plus, you don't even do a sexy Morticia. You wear your funeral dress. Mika invited some cute boys from the shop. You should be prepared." She clapped. "Oh! You should be seventies Cher. You've got the hair, and I bet you still have your go-go boots."

The teens and David had stopped discussing music and were now hanging on every word Suz said.

"I could do Cher. It would be lame without a Sonny, though," I said. I wasn't touching the go-go boots comment.

"I'll be Sonny," David said.

I scrunched my nose at him. "Do you even know what you're signing up for?"

"I heard something about a party, you being sexy, and go-go boots. I'm there."

Emma groaned. "Dad, that's gross."

He held his hands up. "Can't help it."

"Did you hear the part about cute boys?" Suz asked sharply.

David leaned back in his chair, his arm slung casually over the back of mine. I didn't miss the way he toyed with a strand of my hair. "I did, but that's not really my thing. Thanks for thinking of me, though."

She stared him down for a moment. "I'm not sure if I really hate you or really like you."

"Yeah, I get that a lot," he said.

"You'll be my Sonny?" I asked.

David tugged on my hair. "Hell yes."

Right then, I really, *really* liked him.

SIXTEEN

DAVID

SYLVIA'S FRIEND SUZ WAS...INTENSE.

The crazy part of it was, I was glad she held my feet to the fire. She had every reason to be wary of me. Sylvia and Emma deserved to have someone like that in their corner—I was pretty sure she'd throw down if she needed to.

To be honest, she reminded me of myself.

Em took her friends back to her room—I was gonna keep an eye on that Evan character. He was on the nerdy side, but I saw how he looked at my girl. If her other friend hadn't been there as a buffer, no way I'd be letting them hang out in her room alone. He'd be in the living room where I could stare him down.

I had no clue how Syl dealt with this. Did she let Em have boys in her room? She said I didn't need to beat my chest around this kid, but I don't know, I was feeling kinda thumpy.

Once Syl and Suz finished their bottle of wine, and Mika and I demolished the brownies, our five visitors started getting ready to go. I shook Mika's hand, and after a brief hesitation where she shot laser beams out of her eyes, Suz hugged me fiercely.

When she pulled away, her eyes blazed into mine. 'Course,

her eyes were slightly glassy from the wine, but the intensity still came through. "I want you to turn out to be a good guy, David. This is your chance, you know? You have to get it right."

"I got it, Suz. I'm glad Sylvia's had you all these years."

"We've had each other," she said.

I felt good about it all, meeting Syl and Emma's friends, having them in my home. It was just another part of the fantasy. I could pretend I had a real part in their lives for a little while longer.

Emma was saying goodbye to her friends, and I was about to turn away and head into the kitchen to clean up when a fuckin' horror show unfolded in front of me. This motherfucking kid, Evan—stupidest name I'd ever heard—leaned down and kissed my daughter. On. The. Lips.

I glanced at Syl, but she was laughing at something Mika had said, like some kid wasn't mauling our daughter's mouth.

Luckily, the kid kept his tongue inside his mouth, or I wasn't sure I would've been able to control myself. I was about two seconds from punching a hole in the wall as it was.

When they finally left, I took myself right out to the balcony, grabbing my pack of smokes on the way, not really caring if Emma or Sylvia saw me smoking. I needed a few minutes to myself to get my head on straight.

Em and Syl left me alone to sulk. Not that they knew I was sulking. I got through two smokes when I admitted to myself staying on the balcony, smoking my lungs crispy, was not a viable option.

Emma was on what had become her spot on the couch, already immersed in one of the mangas Ian had recommended. I sat next to her, studying her face. She'd lost some of the roundness I swore had just been there the last time I saw her. Her eyebrows, which had always bordered on Frida Kahlo-esque—poor girl had inherited that from me—had been plucked or waxed into a perfect arch. Her hair, which had always been dark brown, like mine, now had lighter brown highlights streaming through it. She didn't look like a full-grown woman, but she sure as shit wasn't a little girl anymore.

From behind her book, she asked, "Why are you staring at me?"

"Is Evan your boyfriend?"

She dropped her book into her lap. "Duh. Mom thought it was weird at first because we grew up together, but whatevs. It's not like he's my *actual* brother."

"How come I never knew about this little romance?"

"Dad, don't be condescending."

I rubbed my sweaty palms on the legs of my jeans. "Sorry, kid."

"I'm sure I told you about Evan and me. We just had our three-month anniversary."

"What do two teenagers do for such an important anniversary?"

Emma held up two fingers. "Number one, you're *still* being condescending, and number two, I feel like you're belittling our three months, but have *you* ever had a three-month anniversary?"

She had me. My fifteen-year-old was more experienced in relationships than her dear old dad. I didn't know how to feel about that.

I mimed grabbing my condescension out of the air and tucking it in my pocket. "No more talking down to you. Tell me what you did for your anniversary, please."

She launched into a description of the picnic Evan had set up next to the stream that ran behind both their houses. I had to give the boy props; he knew his romance. From the hearts bursting out of Em's eyes, she agreed.

Sylvia had come into the living room during Em's story, perching on the chaise section of the couch.

"Did you tell your dad about the painting Evan made you?" Syl asked.

Em's hands covered her cheeks, and her eyes brightened. "He's a terrible painter. The absolute worst. But he tried so hard."

I chuckled. "What'd he paint?"

"A picture of a tree with our initials carved into it. It's adorbs, Dad."

"Did you ever do anything like that when you were sixteen?" Sylvia asked.

I scoffed. "I think I did the exact opposite of that when I was sixteen. This Evan kid might be my literal foil."

Sylvia smiled. "Me too. Suz and I made a pact to raise our kids as nerdy as possible, and I think we did a pretty bang-up job."

Emma flopped back on the cushions. "*Mom*! Just because we're not juvenile delinquents doesn't mean we're nerdy."

It didn't escape me that Syl's pact on how to raise *our* kid was made with someone else. Not at all.

"Fine," Syl conceded. "But you're very wholesome and sweet."

Emma groaned. "I can't argue with that without setting myself up for trouble. Can we actually end this conversation?"

I still had about nine dozen questions, but probably none of them were appropriate. And truthfully, I didn't know if I wanted all the answers.

THE CONDO WAS QUIET. Emma had long since gone to bed, and from the darkness seeping from under Syl's door, I assumed she had too. I couldn't sleep, but what was new? Seemed to be happening a lot lately.

I headed up to the roof, intending to run myself into a coma. Now that I didn't drink, and I tried to limit getting stoned to once or twice a week, running was my sleeping pill of choice.

When the elevator door slid open, I saw the lights were on. The gym was empty, but the pool was occupied. I stood at the window separating the gym from the pool and creeped on Syl swimming laps. She wasn't going full out. Her strokes were long and leisurely.

I couldn't make her out with the distance between us, and I'd be damned if I gave up a chance to see her in a bathing suit. I'd probably be damned if I saw her in a bathing suit too. I already thought about her far too much. Knowing what the curve of her waist and the bare slope of her back looked like would only send me farther into hell.

It was mighty toasty here, though.

Pushing through the glass door, I stepped to the edge of the pool. If she noticed my presence, I couldn't tell. Her stride continued as I kicked off my shoes and socks and sat down, hanging my feet and legs in the water.

Minutes went by, and I fell into a trance, watching her cut back and forth through the pool. I had to blink and blink again when she finally stopped in front of me, water dripping down her cheeks, her hair floating around her on the surface of the pool.

"Hey. Why are you still awake?" she asked.

"Hey, Pot. Nice to meet you. I'm Kettle," I replied.

She smiled and wiped away some of the liquid trickling down the side of her face. "Did you answer my question?"

"Nah. The answer's obvious. Can't sleep," I said.

She slid through the pool until she was in front of me, the

tips of her fingers barely resting on my knees. "Why not?" she asked.

I tugged her hands more firmly in place on my legs. "Are your feet tired? 'Cause, girl, you've been runnin' through my mind all day and all damn night." It was a line, but not a lie.

Sylvia groaned. "Seriously?"

I cocked a brow and smirked.

She licked her top lip and curled her finger. "Come here." Her voice had dropped an octave, and her lids had suddenly gone heavy.

I should've seen it coming. It was so obvious. But Syl tells me to come in that voice, I damn well was gonna come.

I leaned forward until my face was almost level with hers. "What do you need?"

She gripped the front of my shirt, stared right into my eyes, and yanked.

I went flopping into the pool, taking in a mouthful of water and flailing before I found my feet. I shook my head, making it rain on Syl. She looked way too pleased with herself.

"I should dunk you," I said.

She jerked her chin. "You like it."

I prowled toward her through the water, and she backed against the wall, feigning fear. "No, no. I have a child. I want to live!" she pleaded.

The distance between us disappeared until I was only inches from her. "Did you ever stop to wonder if I could swim? I could've drowned, Sylvia."

She pushed at my chest. "It's four feet deep! And I probably would've saved you if you needed it."

"Probably?"

She bit her plump, pouty lip. "Most likely."

"You're a cruel, cruel woman."

She leaned her elbows back on the edge of the pool,

bringing her chest out of the water. Sylvia was a bikini girl. Her tits were little, but I'd never needed more than a handful to satisfy me. I had no doubt I'd be picturing her like this the next dozen times I jacked off, all dripping wet and happy, wearing that red string bikini.

"I don't know why you ever thought I was a nice girl."

I shook my head. "Honestly, I don't know either."

"Did you know I went to that party with the intention of sleeping with you?"

I jerked back. "What?"

"Mmhmm. Months before we were together, I saw you guys play at another party."

"I'm confused. You saw Blue playing? How did I never see you?"

"Don't know. I'm good at blending. But I..." she trailed off, shaking her head.

"What were you going to say?"

"I found out where you were going to be playing and showed up."

Even in the dim lighting, I could see the embarrassment in her cheeks. It was endlessly sexy.

"And you wanted me? Not Nick? Every chick was, and still is, into that fucker."

Her answering smile was small. "No. It was always you. From the second you moved into the house across the street."

My heart hammered in my chest. "You had a crush? That's cute."

Her smile fell a fraction. "More like a minor obsession. Especially after I saw you play. I think I was your first groupie."

"Don't say that."

"It's true. The way you played and strutted around the stage like you were already famous..." She fanned her face, sending droplets of water flying. "Is it wrong I still think about that sometimes and swoon?"

I chuckled. "Maybe, considering I was only, like, seventeen at the time. Tell me more about you going to the party to sleep with me."

Her hand settled on the surface of the pool, skimming back and forth. "It's not complicated. I wasn't...choosy about who I had sex with back then. I did what I wanted, consequences be damned. I wanted you, so I made it happen. I think...I guess I didn't realize you were as drunk as you were."

I rubbed my wet hands over my face. "Syl...I've gone all these years thinking I was the asshole who took your virginity and forgot about it in the morning."

Her lips pressed into a tight smile. "No. The virginity ship sailed away when I was fourteen."

"Holy shit. *Fourteen?*"

She shrugged, like it was no big deal. "I guess I went looking for love in all the wrong places."

"I guess..." I muttered. "And here I was, not even thinking about Emma dating yet."

"Yeah...well, she's not me. Or you."

"Thank god for that. I'm kinda perplexed I didn't get a heads-up email about it, though."

Her brows pinched. "I've had to make a lot of decisions on the fly that I don't email you about. It never even occurred to me I should."

I huffed out a long breath. "And I fuckin' hate that. I hate that my kid is old enough to date, and I hate that I haven't been around enough to earn a say in the matter."

She came closer, her eyes on mine. "If it's any consolation, dating isn't required to get pregnant. I got knocked up without ever having a boyfriend."

"I don't feel all that consoled." My eyes followed the trail of water dripping down her neck. "Tell me more about that night."

Her chest skimmed mine with each breath she took. "I put myself in your path."

"I remember you had on the tiniest skirt. And I remember your hair. I thought you looked sweet."

She smiled. "Even with the tiny skirt?"

"Yep. I recognized you, you know. I always thought you were a ghost, but then, there you were, right in front of me," I said.

"A ghost? Yeah, I think I was a ghost back then. Sounds like you remember more than you realize," she said.

"I wish I remembered more. When did we kiss?"

"We skipped that part."

With my eyes on her lips, I asked, "How? How could I have not kissed you when I had the chance?"

"Everything was rushed. I think we were both interested in the main event."

"I wanna go back and kick my own ass." I shook my head. "What happened next?"

"Your poured me a beer. I told you I liked your music. You told me you liked my hair—"

"I was a smooth bastard, even then," I said.

"You could have told me you were an axe murderer who ate his boogers and I *still* would've been into you."

"Damn, Syl. Boogers? Gross."

She laughed. "You have no problem with me having a thing for axe murderers?"

"Didn't realize it was plural. I kind of thought it was specific to me. I'm offended."

"Oh, it was very specific to you."

It was probably sick, but my cock was achingly hard from

this conversation. Having it alone in a pool with Syl in a sexy red bikini probably didn't help things.

"How'd I get you upstairs?" I asked.

"You didn't. I got *you* upstairs."

Reaching out, I ran my knuckles along her jaw. "Always knew you were a seductress."

Her eyes fluttered closed for a moment as I touched her face. "You didn't. You thought I was a good girl virgin."

"A good girl virgin seductress."

She spun around, leaning against the side of the pool, then turned her head, meeting my eyes. "We did it standing up, with you behind me."

I moved through the water, recreating the position. "Like this?"

"Mmhmm. But you were a lot closer."

It was a mistake. A huge, red-flag-waving mistake, but I'd never been wise, and Syl looked so damn pretty, her pink lips telling me stories and midnight hair floating like a waterfall down her back.

I pressed my hips to her ass, my arms caging her in. "Is this right?" I said low against her ear.

Her head fell back on my shoulder. "Yeah. This feels right." It did. Holy hell, it did.

Letting go of the pool wall, I brought my hand to her throat, trailing it down between her breasts. "What happened next?"

"What do you think?"

I pressed my cock against her, finding a spot in the valley of her ass. "I think, even if I didn't kiss your lips, my mouth was on you." Pushing her hair aside, I licked a line up the side of her neck, stopping at her ear. "Did I do something like that?"

"I think you did a lot of that." Her voice was sexier than I'd ever heard it, and she was fucking limp in my arms. I couldn't keep my mouth off her if I tried, and I was well past trying.

Between licking and sucking her neck, I asked her what I did next. She shakily told me I'd taken off her shirt and touched her tits. I pushed the flimsy bathing suit aside, for historical accuracy, and kneaded her perfect little tits. Sylvia moaned and rocked against me.

"You keep doing that, I'm gonna be like a real teenager and come all over your back," I gritted out.

She rocked again and again. It was ridiculous, but dry humping Sylvia had to be the hottest thing I'd done in a long time.

"Did I touch you, Syl? Did I finger your clit until you were screaming?"

"Maybe not. But you should've," she said.

"Yeah, I definitely should've."

With one hand gripping the curve of her hip, the other smoothed down her flat belly, slipping easily beneath her bathing suit. I could hardly believe this was happening, that my fingers were sliding through the wetness between her legs, but Jesus Christ, it was so real. Her hips rotated in tight circles on my cock while I teased her, touching her everywhere but the place she really wanted me.

"David...don't be a bastard," she panted.

I bit down on her shoulder to keep from laughing at her bossy tone. I didn't want to make her mad, because then she might stop moving her ass like that, and if she did, I wouldn't be long for this world.

I found her swollen clit, and she gave a full body shudder when I finally circled it.

"Did you come that night, Sylvia?"

She shook her head wildly. "No. No, I didn't."

"Are you gonna come for me tonight, pretty girl?" I thrust two fingers inside her, keeping the heel of my hand pressing against her clit.

"Oh...oh, yes! I'm..." She stopped speaking, stopped moving, and tightened all over. I pushed my fingers in deep and hard, wishing like hell it was my cock being squeezed by her slick pussy. God, I hadn't really seen any of her body, but I knew without a shadow of a doubt she was the hottest woman I'd even been with.

Sylvia's limbs quaked, and her head thrashed as she came. She wasn't a quiet orgasmer. Her moans were loud and reckless, like she gave no fucks who heard her while she was getting hers. I loved it. Next time I made her come, I needed to be looking at her, to see what she looked like when she fell apart.

SEVENTEEN

SYLVIA

I SHOULD'VE BEEN WORRIED. Getting fingered by David in his pool certainly hadn't been part of tonight's plans. But my brain had turned to mush, and my body had been electrified. Regrets might come later, but I wanted to ride one of the best orgasms of my life all the way into the sunset.

I came down slowly, but his hands lingered on me, his breath hot against me neck.

"Sylvia..." he whispered into my ear.

"I know," I said, my voice just as soft. I didn't know exactly what I knew, but oh, did I know.

We stayed there for a while, David hard and pressed against me, his arms wrapped around my middle. My head lolled on his shoulder, my fingers playing with the hair on his arms.

"We should probably get out," I said.

"Yeah, probably."

But we stayed and stayed, until I almost drifted off. David's lips on the space behind my ear pulled me back to the present.

I tugged free from his grasp and moved to the ladder to climb out of the water. By the time I got out, David had already pushed himself up the side and was in the process of removing his dripping shirt.

"I forgot a towel," I said.

He jerked a thumb over his shoulder. "There's a cabinet full of them over there."

Shivering, I went to the cabinet and wrapped myself in one of the fluffy, oversized white beach towels. I grabbed one for David too, but when I turned around, I almost dropped it.

He stood there, on the edge of the pool, stark naked. I already knew he was beautiful, but bearing witness to the sinews of his taut muscles all at once was staggering. I followed the trail of colorful ink on his arms and chest to his cock, standing thick and proud.

Oh, Jesus, he was so hard.

My feet were moving before I was even aware of the plan. David held his hand out for his towel, but I didn't give it to him. Instead, I tossed it on the floor, then dropped to my knees in front of him.

He stared down at me with confused lust darkening his eyes.

I couldn't have him confused.

I wrapped a hand around the base of him and slid my mouth down his length. I'd never wanted to give a blow job this badly. My mouth watered for him.

His hands dug into my hair, and for a second, I thought he'd push me away or try to be gentle with me, but he didn't disappoint. His fingers tugged at my hair, and his hips rocked into my mouth. The groans I worked out of him told me how much he appreciated how far I took him.

With my free hand, I reached between my legs and swirled my fingers around my clit. I'd been sated a few minutes ago, but this moment was so hot, I was already on the edge again, desperate to come.

I held his cock, but David directed the pace. He was demanding, pushing in to the back of my throat and lingering there while I swirled my tongue around his length. I looked up at him, surprised to find him watching me. In his eyes, I saw desire, but also adoration, and I hoped he saw the same thing in mine.

"Oh, Jesus, Syl, I'm gonna come," David gritted out in warning.

He said it like he was giving me an out in case I didn't want to swallow, but he held either side of my head and thrust his cock down my throat. I loved it. The way he rutted into my mouth, like I'd sapped every ounce of his self-control, had me coming on my fingers. I moaned around his length, making him thrust even deeper.

I swallowed every drop of it. Not because I particularly loved the taste, but because it was only mine. I'd done it to him, and I wouldn't waste one drop.

He was gentle when he pulled out of my mouth, and even more gentle when he helped me up from the floor. I wrapped the towel I'd brought him around his waist, giving his cock one last squeeze before I covered it. I started to go for my own towel, but David pulled me into his arms.

"I don't know what just happened, but I'm not ending this night without kissing you," he said.

My mouth tasted like him, but that didn't stop him. His lips pressed to mine, chaste for a moment, while I got used to the feel of him and he got used to the feel of me. Then, he cupped my jaw with both hands, tilting my face exactly how he wanted me, and he pulled back for a second, meeting my eyes. I stared back at him, my breathing shallow pants, waiting.

He captured my lips with his, kissing me like there was no tomorrow, no five minutes from now. Everything disappeared. The only thing that existed was David's mouth and mine. I curled my arms around his neck, my breasts pressing against his chest, my belly taut against his, but it still wasn't close enough. I needed more—needed to feel all his skin, the weight of him on top of me, his body surrounding me.

He bent down, and without unlatching his mouth from mine, slid a hand under my ass, lifting me. My legs wrapped around his waist automatically, and from this angle, our kiss happened on an even playing field.

His mouth finally broke away from my lips after long minutes, and he buried his face in my neck, panting. My fingers tangled in his thick, damp hair, my thoughts fuzzy around the edges.

"I should get you to bed. You have to go to work in the morning," he said.

I expected him to set me on my feet, but he carried me to the elevator while I stayed wrapped around him. And David was just as wrapped in me. His hands caressed and explored, charting the terrain of my curves and plains. The ride was brief, but he kept me pressed against the wall, hot breath on my neck, low, rumbly growls tumbling unrestrained from him.

At the door to his condo, my brain finally started working again. My legs let go of his waist, and though his arms were slow to let me go, he eventually let me drop to the floor.

We stood there at the door, eyes locked. I didn't know what he was seeing in me, but there was an intensity about him I wasn't used to.

It took me shivering to snap us both out of the spell. There I stood in my bikini, wet and freezing, but I probably would've stayed for a while longer had David not nudged me inside.

The condo was quiet, and I didn't stop him from following me into my room. He went to my dresser and pulled out a T-shirt and shorts. How the man knew where I kept my pajamas, I didn't want to know. Well, I *did* want to know, but I wouldn't ask.

He handed the clothes to me, then sat on the edge of my bed, watching me.

"We can't...with Em here..." I protested, but there wasn't much strength behind it. Truthfully, if David dropped his towel right now, I'd be on the bed, welcoming him inside me.

Thankfully, one of us had sense. "I know. I just got the life sucked out of my cock. I'm feelin' pretty satisfied right now. I just wanna look at you, then I'll tuck you in."

I walked over to him and dropped my pajamas on the bed next to him. Turning away from him, I lifted my hair, and over my shoulder, I asked him to untie the strings of my bikini.

His fingers traced over my spine and up to my shoulders, checking out my tattoo. The string tugged around my ribs, then fell loose, leaving my top hanging around my neck. Then he untied that too, letting it fall to the floor.

Gripping my hips, he placed a warm kiss on the center of my back. "This is really pretty."

"My tattoo?"

"All of you." He tugged at the strings on the sides of my bottoms until they untied too. I gave my hips a wiggle, and they fell to the floor along with my top. He cupped my ass, spreading me, then his lips pressed against the very base of my spine, leaving another warm kiss. "Turn around, Syl."

Slowly, I spun around to face him. His eyes were all over me, darting around like he couldn't take me in fast enough. His hands slid up my ribs to my breasts, cupping them for just a moment before sliding back down to my hips. He leaned in and pressed a kiss to my belly button, making me shiver.

"Cold?" he asked.

I rested my hands on his strong shoulders. "No, not even a little."

He picked up my shorts and shook them out, then bent forward. "Step in," he ordered.

Using his shoulders for stability, I stepped into my shorts and he took his time sliding them up my legs and hips. He stood, his bare chest pressed to mine.

"Arms up," he said.

I raised my arms, expecting him to pull my T-shirt over my head. Instead, he ran his hands from my wrists, down my arms, and over my sides, pausing when he got to my ribs. I wondered when he'd see the words tattooed on my side.

He traced each letter carefully, as though he was reading them with his fingertip.

"*Rule with an iron fist*
Rule with a gentle mind."

"When did you get this?" he asked.

"When I heard the song."

He bent down to kiss the words, then straightened, cupping my face. "You knew I wrote it for Emma?"

"There was no question."

"You don't have any idea what it does to me to see my words on your skin. My heart is thumping so hard, I feel like it's gonna do an *Alien* and claw its way out of my chest."

He pressed his forehead against mine, and I laid my hand on his chest, feeling the beat of his heart.

"You *do* have a way with words," I said.

Shaking his head, he dropped his hands and backed up a step. I thought he was about to bolt. His eyes held a world of panic—and mine might have mirrored his.

But then he tugged on my hand and crushed my lips with his, kissing me hard and fast.

"I got a little distracted from my job." He picked up my T-shirt and slid it over my head, covering me. I was torn between being disappointed and relieved.

"Thanks," I said.

"This was, uh..." He rubbed the back of his neck, looking anywhere but me.

"Fun, right?"

"Don't do that." He exhaled heavily, scrubbing his face with both hands. "Jesus, I'm kinda overwhelmed here."

I laughed. "Yeah, me too."

His eyes searched my face. "You tired?"

I sighed. "I actually am." I glanced at the digital clock next to my bed. "I have to be up in five hours."

Moving around me, David pulled back the covers, dropped his towel, and slid his bare ass between my sheets, making himself comfortable. He patted the spot next to him. "Come sleep."

"You're sleeping...in my room?"

He yawned. "Yep."

"Are we...?"

He closed his eyes. "I don't know, Sylvia. I'm tired. You're tired. You have this big, comfy bed, and I don't really feel like leaving it. Hop in." I stood there for another moment, staring down at his relaxed face until he cracked one eye. "Stop thinking and get in bed with me."

"Just sleep, correct?"

His smile was sleepy. "Yeah, pretty. Just sleep."

I climbed in bed next to him, pulling the comforter up to my chin. I hadn't slept in a bed with a man since Vince. And I never imagined the next man filling my bed would be David.

But here I was, with a big, naked, tattooed rock star sleeping next to me.

"Sleep, Syl," he mumbled.

I snuggled down in the bed. Sleep sounded amazing right now.

· · ·

IF FALLING asleep next to a big, naked rock star had been disconcerting, waking up completely wrapped in one was ever more so. When I tried to move out of his arms, they tightened around me.

"You're keepin' me warm. Don't move," he said, his head above mine.

"You're making me hot," I said. Although, he wasn't. His body was emitting just the right amount of heat.

"You're already hot, Syl. You don't need me." He bit my shoulder, making me squeal.

"Is this what waking up with you is like? You hog the bed and bite me?"

"You like it."

"It's not the worst."

He slung his leg over mine. "I'm keeping you here all day."

"Our child might have questions."

He sighed. "True. Guess I'll have to tiptoe when I sneak in here tonight."

He didn't let me escape, but he *did* let me turn to face him. "Why would you think this is happening again?"

He gripped my chin and the laughter left his voice. "Because I don't think either of us are done after last night. Because sleeping next to you was the best sleep I've had in a long ass time. Because I wanna be around you more." He kissed me softly. "Because you're even prettier and softer in the morning."

I didn't know who this David was, but he was making it impossible to hate him.

Who am I kidding? Hating David had become impossible since he showed up at the theater.

"And you're uncharacteristically sweet," I said.

"Your fault."

I laughed, pushing off his chest. "I really do have to get up. But you're welcome to stay."

"Nah, I better go back to my room. Don't wanna traumatize Em." He tapped his lips. "Give me something to remember you by."

"You won't remember me if I don't kiss you?"

He gripped the back of my hair, sending a thrill all the way to my belly. "Just fuckin' kiss me."

When he put it like that, how could I say no?

EIGHTEEN

DAVID

THE HOT CHOCOLATE burned the roof of my mouth, and Sylvia laughed at my wince.

"I told you it was too hot. You should've waited."

"I'm not the waiting type," I growled.

"And look where that got you. A burned tongue. What use are you to me now?" she asked.

"You have no idea what I can do with my tongue, burned or not," I said quietly.

The crowd surrounding us in the bleachers stood and cheered. Sylvia clapped too, letting out a loud whistle.

Nodding toward the field, I asked, "Do you know what happened?"

She laughed. "No idea. Someone keeps distracting me."

I'd spent the last four nights in Sylvia's bed. Mostly sleeping, mixed with a heavy dose of fooling around. I barely recognized myself. I'd turned into this puppy, following the pretty lady around—the pretty lady with the mouth of a vixen.

Tonight, I followed her to Em's soccer game. 'Course, Emma wasn't playing. She'd ditched us as soon as we got to the field. A few of her teammates helped her find a spot on their bench so she could cheer them on from the sidelines. Sylvia and I were on our own, and after buying cups of hot chocolate, I pulled her to the top bleachers, telling her that was where the bad kids sat.

Back when I was one of those bad kids, I spiked my hot chocolate with vodka and never came prepared with a thick flannel blanket to keep me warm. I sure as shit never had a girl as pretty as Sylvia by my side.

Whatever we were doing, we were keeping it strictly to the bedroom—after Emma went to sleep. As many times as I wanted to touch Sylvia or kiss her or make a dirty joke, I kept my hands tucked firmly in my pockets and my mouth zipped. It wasn't easy. It was something to get used to. But the nights made it worth it.

We were like teenagers, kissing until our lips ached. Hand jobs had never been hotter. Hell, I probably hadn't had one since I *was* a teenager. But with Sylvia, I came all over myself within minutes of her wrapping her hand around my dick. It would've been embarrassing if it wasn't so fucking hot. And I don't know, it kind of felt like we were starting over. Starting out where we should've fifteen years ago.

Not that I wouldn't have taken her behind the bleachers right this second and plowed into her if she gave me the slightest signal.

Sylvia had a good, pragmatic head on her shoulders. She was more of an adult than I'd ever dream of being. Probably had been since the second Emma was born. I found it both sexy and frustrating as hell. Sexy because she had her shit under control. She walked around all self-assured and in charge. How I'd never noticed that about her was beyond me. She wasn't some meek little thing. Her strength was quiet, but it was gorgeously fierce.

Her pragmatism was frustrating because I felt the distance she was keeping between us. I wanted to King Kong her up the side of a building so everyone could see she was mine and no one else could reach her, but she was having none of that. She let me touch her and kiss her and sleep with her, but she was still very much like the girl I only saw through the crack of her curtains. She gave me herself, but only a glimpse.

"You come to a lot of these things?" I asked.

"Yeah. I love watching her play," she said.

I watched the action on the field as the heat from the paper cup in my hands seeped through the thick calluses on my fingertips, just this side of bearable. Her team was good. Really good. It seemed like they didn't stop moving up and down the length of the field...which, hell, I guess that was what they were supposed to be doing. I could picture Emma out there, ponytail flying as she bumped hips with the opposing players, fighting for control of the ball. I could picture it, but I wouldn't be seeing it.

"I'm sitting here kinda gutted that I never came to see her play," I said.

"I sent you videos."

"And I watched them all. But it's not the same, is it?"

"No. But she knew you saw the videos. She knew you were cheering her on."

I shook my head. "Don't make it easy on me."

She tugged on my scarf. "I think at this point you're beating yourself up enough for both of us, you know? I'm not really interested in rehashing everything you missed over and over. We can't change it."

"I need to learn from you, oh wise one. Teach me the art of letting shit go."

Her eyes moved to the field, and she stood and cheered. I should've stood too, but I was too busy checking out her ass.

"I'm not the greatest at letting things go. I'm still a work in progress." She played with the fringe on the bottom of the scarf she'd given me to wear. I felt like a tool in it, but damn was I warm. "But I think if you and I are going to be friends, or whatever—"

"I choose the 'whatever' option," I interrupted.

Her mouth curved into a smile, and she looked up at me from beneath her thick lashes. "If we're going to be *whatever*, we both have to let things go."

This unfamiliar surge of absolute need spilled over me. Not in the *whatever* way, but in a need to care for her and keep her warm and happy way. My heart galloped in my chest, and all I wanted to do was wrap her up and cart her off to my cave.

I decided it was her eyes. No one else had eyes like Sylvia. The clearness of the blue made me feel like I could see right through them and peer into her. They were tricky, making me feel things I shouldn't have been feeling—making me think I could really have her.

I cupped her cheek, and she jumped. "Your hand is hot."

"This fucking scorching hot chocolate. Who makes it this hot?" I shook my head. "I was trying to have a sweet moment with you."

She snorted. "I don't need sweet moments. Just real ones. Don't get all soft with me just because I made you come a few times. I'm not a moonbeams and poetry kind of girl. Pull my hair and tell me I'm pretty, and I'll be happy."

She blinked at me, like she had no idea what she'd said had reversed my flow of blood, sending it all straight to my cock. I was speechless. I was never without speech.

"I know you might not like me now that you know I'm not a good girl," she teased.

I gripped the back of her neck, jerking her close. "Holy shit, Sylvia, shut up before I have to fuck you right here in the bleachers."

She laughed, pushing me away. "That might make for an awkward PTA meeting next month."

Absently, I took a drink of my scalding hot chocolate, never taking my eyes off her.

"Where the hell have you been all my life?" I asked stupidly.

She arched a brow. "Just here, raising your kid."

I opened my mouth to speak, but again, speechless. She pushed my jaw up.

"Can we watch the game, drink our boiling hot chocolate, and pretend we're just two regular parents?"

"I'm a regular parent!"

"You're not a regular anything, David. But we can pretend."

She laid her head on my shoulder, and I kissed her hair. I told myself it was all part of the make-believe.

I LAY in bed after the game, filling a notebook with lyrics. They weren't really songs, more like fragments of thoughts that popped into my head.

Tender, burning kisses
Drowning in black glass fantasies
Holding a ghost, but just for today
Fool's gold promises
Broken feet traveling down careless roads
Cracked, but not ruined. Chipped, but not damaged

There was a tap on my door, then Sylvia peeked her head in. "Still awake?"

I set my notebook down with more enthusiasm than was called for. "Just waiting for you."

She came in, closing the door behind her. I loved this part, when she came to me. She didn't even try to feign reluctance since that night in the pool.

She crossed the room, looking too fuckin' sexy in a long T-shirt and nothing else. When she reached the bed, she climbed up and straddled my waist. My hands went to her hips, gripping them, then slid over her ribs, getting a feel for her.

"Were you writing?" she asked.

"Yeah." I pushed her shirt up so I could get my hands on her soft skin. "Don't know if it'll amount to anything, but it feels good to get the words out of my head."

Sylvia drew figure eights on my chest with her fingernail. "Would it be presumptuous to ask if you were writing about me?"

I grinned, tugging the ends of her hair to pull her closer. "You're all I can think about, so no, not presumptuous."

"Tell me what you think about me."

Cupping the back of her neck, I captured her lips, kissing her slowly and thoroughly. She wasn't the least bit shy in her reactions, meeting my tongue boldly and moaning into my mouth when I squeezed her ass.

Against her lips, I said, "I think about how powerful you are. How I want to make you feel."

I bit her bottom lip, giving it a gentle tug. "I think about you dancing in my kitchen and how your scent is everywhere in my house. I think about how I never want you to leave. I want to tie you up and keep you here with me."

I pushed her hair aside and pulled her earlobe between my lips. She moaned. "I think about your pussy. How good it feels on my fingers, and how much I want to taste it."

Sylvia shuddered in my arms. "I think about you too. So many things."

Fisting Sylvia's hair, I tugged her head to the side to devour her neck. Whimpering, she dug her nails into my chest and rocked her hot core against me. My cock throbbed, aching to slide inside her.

"David..."

"Mmm?"

"I want your mouth between my legs."

I almost came in my damn pants. Pulling back from her neck, I met her heavy-lidded eyes and tapped my lips. "Climb on, sweetheart."

Sylvia slid off me for a second to pull her panties and T-shirt off, then, to my complete fucking astonishment and delight, she straddled my face backward, freed my cock from my sweatpants, and leaned forward to take it between her lips. It took me a moment to catch on. I'd been half serious when I'd told her to sit on my face, but I sure as hell hadn't expected *this*.

She popped my cock out of her mouth, squeezing my length while she waited for me to catch up.

"You ready to ride my tongue, sweetheart?"

She swirled her tongue around the head of my dick. "Mmhmm."

Gripping her hips, I lowered her to my face and pulled her swollen clit between my lips. She tightened all over, including her grip on my length. It was impossible to concentrate with her scent and taste invading my senses and her warm lips closing around me. So I didn't think, I only felt.

This was sloppy, messy mouth fucking...truly the best kind. My face was coated in her, and I was minutes away from coating her too. She never let up on my cock, sucking me off like she'd been waiting her whole life to do it. I'd found heaven between her thighs, licking her *everywhere*.

When I worked two fingers inside her, her legs tightened around my head and she mewled around my cock. Curling those fingers just right, Sylvia came apart on my mouth, and the feel of her walls squeezing my fingers set me off. With a muffled bellow, I followed her over the edge, pumping into her mouth with abandon.

Sylvia took all I had to give, then laid her head on my stomach, warming my flesh with her panting breaths. She tasted too good for me to stop licking her, and she gave no indication she wanted me to stop. I could've kept at it all night, sliding my tongue through her slick folds, curling around her hard clit.

I gave her another orgasm, this one languid, going on and on until she finally rolled off me, declaring no more.

Pulling her limp body onto my chest, I was overcome for a minute. Not only from how scorching hot that was, but from the flood of tenderness that came after. With a languid touch, I stroked the ink on Sylvia's back while she snuggled against me.

"Am I sleeping here tonight?" she murmured.

My hands skated down to her ass, kneading the soft swell. "Yep."

"Are you going to actually let me sleep?"

"I'll think about it. As much as I enjoy you awake, I adore the way you stay right next to me when you sleep. You really burrow in...like a naked, sexy bunny."

I felt her smile against my chest.

"Who knew you could be sweet?" she asked.

"I sure as shit didn't. Am I sweet?"

She propped her chin on her hands to look at me. "You are."

"I can honestly say I've never been told that before."

She laid a finger on my bottom lip. "I'm fairly certain you've never given anyone a chance to see this side of you."

I nipped at her finger, and she pulled it away, giggling. "What side?"

"Are you fishing for compliments?"

"Nah. I'm curious. But that's okay. I probably wouldn't believe you anyway."

"Where's that rock star ego?"

"My ego pretty much starts and stops at my guitar skills. I'm just a dude—a dude who somehow got lucky as hell to have you in my bed."

"That!" She tapped my lip. "That was sweet."

I smiled at her like I was puzzled. "Was it?"

"It was. And I think because we share a child, I get to see this side of you more than anyone. But I also see the way your bandmates care about you. That doesn't happen by accident."

"I'm an asshole," I grumbled.

"A loveable asshole with a magic tongue," she corrected.

I chuckled. "Yeah, my bandmates don't get to experience that part of me."

"David," she sighed, "I think you might be trouble for me."

Of that, I had no doubt. I was a fucked-up man only just beginning to see past my own nose. I wanted to be good enough for Sylvia. *Damn*, did I want that. I wasn't, though. That wouldn't stop me from taking what she offered, then asking for more. 'Cause now that I'd had a taste, I had no doubt there'd never be anything sweeter. Sylvia was the end of one road and beginning of a new one. Whether that road led to Hell or Heaven was yet to be seen. For either of us.

But this wasn't a time for deep thoughts. I had a beautiful, naked, sated women in my arms.

"I might be. But not tonight. Tonight, it's time for sleeping. We'll see about trouble in the morning."

She laid her head on my chest, and I wrapped my limbs around her, keeping her trapped against me. I thought, not for the first time, not for the hundredth time either, this might have been the only way I'd get to keep her.

NINETEEN

SYLVIA

I FELT him looking at me as I bent down to zip up my boots. I knew what I was doing. My skirt barely covered my ass when I was standing, so bent over like this, David had a pretty clear shot of my lacy boy-shorts. Using some of my go-go dancing skills from long ago, I trailed my fingers up my legs, stopping at my knees, then rolled my hips in sensual circles.

David groaned, and I straightened, turning to laugh at him.

"You can't go out like that. I'm gonna be walking around with a hard-on all night. You want your neighbors to see the outline of my dick in these tight ass pants?" He adjusted the bulge behind his zipper as he sat on the high-back chair in the corner of my room.

"I love your tight ass pants. You do Sonny proud."

His eyes raked over me as I slipped on my furry vest. "And I never knew I found Cher attractive, but damn, you've stunned me. I think the only thing capable of moving right now is my dick."

I walked across the room until I was in front of him and straddled his legs, my knees on either side of his. He held my hips, and I circled my arms loosely around his neck.

"This isn't possibly going to help my dick go down."

I smiled, straightening his oversized collar. He looked both ridiculous and delicious in his sixty's paisley shirt and white bell bottoms. He'd gone all out at a thrift store, while I'd scrounged in my closet for my costume. I had a bad habit of never throwing anything away, and my gold lame bikini top, tiny white skirt, white go-go boots, and furry vest were vestiges of my dancing days.

"I can't help it. You look so cute," I said.

He growled and yanked me against his chest. "Don't call me cute. I'm extremely manly and potent."

I laughed, squirming in his arms, but not really trying to get away. After almost a week of spending every night in bed together, having everything *but* sex, I was one big ball of want. And god, did I want him. Once I let go and admitted that to myself, life sure was a lot more fun. I'd drawn an arbitrary line in the sand though, and said no sex while Emma was in the house. It didn't make sense given we were getting each other off in other ways every night, but it slowed whatever was happening between us down. Sort of.

However, I'd dropped Emma off to spend the night with her friend Avery a couple hours ago, so there wasn't anything to stop *whatever* from happening tonight.

I ran a finger along his exposed chest—he'd only buttoned his shirt halfway. "I'm sorry. You're very, *very* manly. I think I'm spontaneously ovulating from being near you."

He squeezed my ass and chuckled. "I guess I've gotta accept the state of my dick, huh?"

"I guess so. I'm not changing. I think I look good," I said.

"You look like Aphrodite rising out of the sea. Honestly, you take my breath away."

His eyes moved around my face as he stroked his fingers down my cheeks and over my shoulders. He touched my hair and the beaded headband I wore over my forehead before traveling down to my bare thighs and under my skirt, cupping my ass again.

I was barely breathing by the time his hands stopped. The man knew how to touch me. He didn't go straight for my clit or breasts. He worshipped my belly button and back and ankles. When we were alone, his hands were everywhere, like being able to feel me reassured him. I hadn't expected that from him, but I wasn't complaining.

The way he touched me made me feel wanted. Not just sexually, although that was a big part of it. He touched me like my physical presence was the one thing he'd always wanted, but never expected to have.

It was funny how that worked, because in truth, it was the exact opposite. *I* was the one who'd pined over him for so long. *I* was the one who'd fantasized about having him as a real partner.

And now that we were here, I couldn't quite let myself go. David was so damn honest in his affection for me, sometimes I had to look away. Like now. The way he looked at me, like I really was his Aphrodite...I couldn't take it.

So, I kissed him. I kissed and kissed and kissed him until I could stand to meet his eyes again.

"We have to go," I panted.

"You expect me to walk after that?"

I climbed off him, feeling a little weak-limbed myself, and held out my hand. "Come on, Sonny. I got you, babe."

He groaned. "Oh shit. Am I gonna be hearing Sonny and Cher references all night?"

"Put your little hand in mine," I said.

He laughed and stood up without my help. "You managed to kill my erection. Good job."

I hit his chest. "I thought you were attracted to Cher? You've sold me a mountain of lies!"

He swooped me off the ground and over his shoulder, giving my ass three hard smacks.

"If you really want to go to this party, we'd better get out of here or we're never going to leave."

It was tempting, but Suz would kill me if we missed her party, so off we went.

We parked in front of my house and walked down the cracked sidewalk to their place, David keeping me warm with his arm around me.

"All your neighbors are gonna be here?" he asked.

"It's a mix of neighbors and friends. It's kind of funny to see Mrs. Wilson from down the road mingling with Mika's tattoo buddies. She's sixty-five and never leaves home without her pearls, but she always manages to find her way into their group every year."

His arm around me tightened. "Maybe Mrs. Wilson's like you, a bad girl in disguise."

"Oh, I was never in disguise. You just didn't see."

Suz and Mika's house was almost an exact copy of mine, but since Mika could basically do anything with his hands, he'd completely remodeled the place. Their main floor was open and airy, leading to a huge deck and brick patio. It was absolutely perfect for parties.

The house was buzzing with music and voices and laughter. Costumes ranged from zombies to sexy nurses. Over the years, this party had evolved from families to just adults. Evan was off with friends as well.

Normally, I'd partake in some spiked cider, but I didn't know what the protocol was with David being sober, so I bypassed the drinks all together, pulling David outside with me to find Suz. She usually hung around the firepit, and tonight was no different.

"Sylvie!" she called when she caught sight of us.

I held out my arms. "Suz!"

We hugged, and when I pulled back, I held onto her arms to get a look at her costume. Her mini dress was made of iridescent scales and she had patches of black scales painted on her arms and legs. She had horns coming out of her forehead, scales on her cheeks, and shiny black lips.

"You look amazing," I squealed.

"Look at you, mama! I can't wait for you to meet Mika's friend, Eben. Did you see a sexy Axl Rose on your way out here?" Suz asked.

From behind me, David cleared his throat. "Hey," he said, slipping his hand around my waist.

Suz's eyebrows shot up to her horns. "Oh, hi, David. I didn't know..." she pointed between the two of us, "this was a thing."

My eyes went wide, and I stammered. "It's not really—"

"It is," he said simply. "We are."

Suz stared at me like she was checking to see if I'd gone mad. "Well, damn. This is a surprise. Was this a thing when we came over last week?"

"No," I said.

"It was starting then," David said.

I looked up at him. "It was?"

He quirked a brow. "Wasn't it?"

I smiled and looked back at Suz. "Yeah, I guess it was."

"Aren't you just the cutest." She didn't sound like she meant that. There was no chance we wouldn't be having words the second she could get me alone. I made a mental note not to let her get me alone any time soon. I wasn't ready for her inquisition.

Mika joined us, holding a red Solo cup. He made an amazing Hagrid, even without hair. He said he drew the line at wigs, so he was always the bald version of whatever character Suz talked him into.

He held the cup out to me. "Cider? I know it's your favorite."

I took it, reluctantly. "Thanks."

He and David shook hands. "Good to see you again. Sorry I didn't get you a drink." He lowered his voice. "There's bourbon in it, and I know that's not your thing." God, Mika was such a gem of a human.

David patted his shoulder. "Thanks for looking out, man. Nice place you got here." He turned to me. "You should do something like this with your backyard."

I stiffened, because I loved my rickety old house, but Mika laughed. "I've been trying to talk Sylvie into letting me build her a new deck, but she won't have any of it."

"You built this?" David asked.

"Yep," Mika said proudly. "A couple guys from the shop helped, but it's kind of my hobby. I've built decks for a lot of our neighbors."

"Well, damn. I'm feeling completely inadequate. My only skill is playing the guitar, and that won't get me far in a zombie apocalypse," David said.

"I wasn't aware we should be preparing for one," Suz said sardonically. "But now that you mention it, cleaning teeth doesn't seem like a useful skill either."

I laughed. "I'll distract them with showtunes."

David's fingers lowered to my ass for a second. "And your twerking skills. That would distract anyone, brainless or not."

Mika pointed between us. "So, this is a thing?"

Suz stood on her tiptoes and kissed his cheek. "Catch up, honey. It's a thing, but Sylvie doesn't want to talk about it."

"Hey! I never said that."

She scoffed. "We've met. I know you."

She and Mika turned to greet some guests, and I exhaled. I

hadn't really thought about answering questions tonight. I just wanted to drink, enjoy David, and hang out with my friends.

David pushed my hair away from my ear, rubbing my earlobe between his fingers. "You can drink that, you know. I'll be your designated driver."

I glanced from him to my cup of cider, then yanked on his shirt, bringing him in for a kiss. A long, hard kiss.

He leaned his forehead on mine, smiling. "What'd I do to deserve that?"

"I just like you. I like who you are right this second."

He planted kiss after kiss on my mouth. "You're so fucking great. You know that? Makes me want to be great too."

"We need to dance together. Come dance with me."

"I'd love to."

As we made our way back inside, we were stopped by a few neighbors. I drank my cider while I updated them on Emma's recovery and David was...well, he was charming. He asked questions, and I could tell my neighbors were burning with questions of their own. But I didn't supply David's identity, beyond that he was my friend.

When we finally made it to the makeshift dance floor, my cup was empty, and I was feeling happier than I had in a long time. David spun me into his arms, one hand low on my back, the other holding my hand, and we rocked to the beat.

"I like it here. This neighborhood. It's got a cool vibe," David said next to my ear.

"Not as cool as your condo," I said.

"Nah, it's different. There's life here. It seems like a place you'd never feel alone."

"Do you? I mean, do you feel alone a lot?" I asked.

He nibbled the shell of my ear, making me whimper. "Not right now."

I dug my fingers into the back of his shirt, my hips swaying with his. "But sometimes you do?"

"Yeah. Sometimes I do. I try not to let it happen. I keep busy, surround myself with people. But it still happens."

"Sometimes I get lonely too," I admitted.

"But you have Emma."

I toyed with a button on his shirt. "It's not the same. She's my kid, the person I take care of. Sometimes I want someone to walk next to."

He spun me out, then pulled me in until my back was flush to his front. David led and I followed, rolling hips and rocking thighs, dancing to a slow, sensual version of "Wicked Game." His hands were splayed on my stomach, and he sang the words of the song, low and rough, just for me.

"I love your voice. You should sing more," I said.

"I'll sing to you whenever you want."

He continued singing to me until my eyes were rolling back in my head.

I spun in his arms to kiss him again. The lights were dim, but I was afraid if we didn't pump the brakes, I'd be climbing David like a tree and wouldn't be able to look any of my neighbors in the eye again.

I broke from the kiss, breathing heavy. "Can we press pause? I need a drink."

"Want me to get you one?" David asked.

I shook my head. "I'll grab a drink and meet you by the firepit." I ran my fingers up the bare skin of his chest. "We can hang out a little while, then go home, okay?"

He nipped at my bottom lip before growling. "I'll give you two minutes. If you're not in my lap at the firepit by then, I'll hunt you down."

I laughed. "Go, be social. I'll see you in a couple minutes."

TWENTY

SYLVIA

THE KITCHEN WAS SURPRISINGLY EMPTY, so I poured myself a cup of cider, then checked Suz's fridge for un-spiked punch for David. I found an unopened bottle and poured a cup for him. When I turned with both cups in my hands, I almost ran into a wall of man.

"Vince?"

Leaning his shoulder against the wall, my ex-fiancé smiled down at me. "Happy Halloween, Sylvie."

"Wow, I didn't expect to see you here." I set the cups on the counter and gave him a hug. He held on a little longer than I did, but eventually let go.

"I saw Mika at the shop last week and he mentioned it. I figured you'd be here." His eyes skated over me. "You look gorgeous, baby."

I let the "baby" slide. He'd been calling me that for nearly a decade; some habits were hard to break.

I gave him a once-over. If possible, he was even more pumped than the last time I saw him. His Henley strained over his chest and his biceps looked like they were going to burst through the fabric.

"Thanks. Would you believe all this was in my closet?"

"Hell yeah. I think I remember that bikini," Vince said.

His New Zealand accent used to drive me wild, but it didn't do a lot right now. Just made me think of the good times we had. And we did have a *lot* of good times.

"How are you?" I asked.

"I'm okay. Melissa and I broke up. Been thinkin' about you."

I winced. "Oh, Vince..."

He stepped closer. "Been missin' you, baby."

Vince and I had been broken up for five years, but it hadn't been a clean break. The feelings I'd had for him hadn't magically disappeared when I'd realized I couldn't marry him, and neither had his. That first year, we clung to each other, having desperate, sad sex whenever we had the chance. We both started dating other people after that, but we couldn't quit each other. It had been a year and a half since I last saw him. He'd met a nice girl, fell in love, and faded from my life. And thank god for that; it had been well past time.

"I've missed you too, Vince, but not like that," I said.

He took another step, and I held my hand up, trying to halt him. "Come on, baby. It's always like that with us."

"I'm seeing someone," I said.

"Oh."

The thing about Vince was, as passionate as we'd once been about each other, ever since we broke up, he'd never, not once, asked about Emma. And that's how I knew, without a doubt, I'd made the right decision.

"Emma was in a car accident a month ago. Had to have surgery," I said.

Vince blinked, the sudden change of subject throwing him. "Shit. She okay?"

"She will be. She's finally going back to school on Monday, but it'll be a long recovery."

He rubbed my arm, and it took everything in me not to cringe. "Forgive me, I'm caught off guard. Poor Em."

"Your two minutes are up," David said as he walked into the kitchen. The smile dropped from his face like a lead balloon when he saw me standing there with Vince, his hand on my arm. The look he gave me made me feel guilty, even though I'd done nothing wrong.

"I ran into Vince," I said.

David sidled up next to me, claiming me with an arm around my waist. "Hello, Vince," he said.

Vince's gaze locked on David's hand on my bare skin. "Really, Sylvie. This guy?"

"Yeah," David answered. "This guy."

Vince's eyes met mine. He was hurt, but beyond that, he was pissed. "Are you fuckin' kidding me? You're with the guy who showed up at our engagement party, fucked out of his head, and told you he was in love with you? We were getting married —then boom, he loved you. Fuck that. I can't believe you."

I held my hand out, trying to move closer, but David held me firmly. "That's not what happened and—"

"Don't you dare defend him to me," Vince gritted. I'd never seen him so angry. His face was flushed, and a vein pulsed in his forehead. It was like he'd put on a mask...or maybe his mask had finally slipped. "Does he know how we met? That you wore those cute little boots of yours when you danced in a cage? He couldn't be bothered to support his kid, so her mom had to go-go dance at a seedy nightclub."

"Vince..." I pleaded. "Come on."

David's grip on me tightened as he stared at the side of my face. I wasn't ashamed of my dancing days, and it sure as hell hadn't been anything like he was implying. As a patron of said "seedy" nightclub, he shouldn't have been casting stones, that was for damn sure.

"Don't do this, man. We don't need to go down this road," David warned.

"I took care of your daughter for years. We've been going down this road for a long ass time, rock star," Vince sneered.

"Vince, stop. *I* took care of Emma, not you. And what I do now is none of your business." I pushed at him, trying to get him out of David's face.

Vince looked right over my head. "Bet you didn't know I've been warming her bed for the last five years, even after you fucked up our engagement. We're never gonna be done, you fucking cunt."

I pushed at his rock-hard chest. "We're *so* done. If I never see you again, it'll be too soon."

David nudged me aside, getting in Vince's face. "There's a reason my appearance at your engagement party made Syl call off the wedding, and it ain't me, mate. I could give a fuck about whatever else you have to say to me. Sylvia and Emma are *my* family, and nothing's gonna change that."

Vince shoved David's shoulders, knocking him into me. I hissed in pain when my hip hit the counter behind me.

David shoved Vince back, but he barely budged. The man had played rugby for a living and was built like a tank. It would take a bomb to knock him down. Then again, David looked ready to explode.

Vince poked at David's chest. "You'll never keep her. Pretty damn sure she isn't capable of loving anyone but that kid."

I would've slapped him, but David was blocking me. All I saw was his elbow rear back, then a loud pop. Vince growled and charged at David, ramming his head into David's chest. I was lucky to jump out of the way before I got crushed against the counter.

I probably screamed. I'd worked in a club long enough to have seen plenty of bar fights; they didn't faze me. But seeing the man I'd once loved plowing his fist into the face of the father of my child wasn't something I was prepared for.

David wasn't small, but Vince was massive...and he was angry. He pushed David against the wall, and the way his head bobbled on his neck made me sick. They shifted places, David pushing Vince into a cabinet. Glasses shattered inside, and in the back of my mind, I knew Suz was going to be out for blood when she found out.

Vince slammed his fist into David's cheekbone, but David held onto him, shaking him by the collar of his shirt. Then Vince popped him again, sending David careening into the fridge.

I was about to jump on Vince's back and claw his eyes out when Mika came running in, taking charge of the situation. He brought with him a couple guys from the shop, and they had David and Vince split up in seconds.

I was pushed behind them, completely unable to see over the crowd of giant men. Suz pulled me back even farther.

"Let Mika handle it," she said.

"But...I need to know he's okay." My voice was weak, and so were my attempts to escape. She held me next to her while I quietly cried.

"Which one?" she asked.

I stared her down. "David."

She shook her head. "I can't believe Vince showed up here. And Mika is in crazy big trouble for inviting him." She'd never really liked him for me, and she especially hadn't liked that I'd gone back to him over and over.

No chance of that ever happening again.

There was another commotion in the kitchen, and at first, I thought David and Vince were going at it again, but when I heard my name being called frantically, I realized David was trying to get to me.

I pushed at the backs of the men blocking him from me. "David!" I groaned. Why was every man at this party a brick wall? "Let him through!"

Finally, they parted, and a bloodied, frenzied David came into view. When he saw me, his eyes were wide, like a caged animal. I held my hand out to him, pulling him through the crowd.

His hands went to my face immediately, checking me over. "Sylvia, Sylvia, are you okay?"

I choked back a sob. "I'm okay. I'm fine. Are you?"

A trickle of blood fell from his eyebrow. "I'm fine, as long as you are."

"Let's get out of here. I need to fix you up."

Once I had him, his hand wrapped around mine, everything else fell away. My body was moving on instinct, leading him to a place safe from prying eyes and crazy exes. I was sure the neighbors would have a field day with this bit of drama, but right now, all I cared about was taking care of David.

We went to my house, and when I tried to unlock my door, my hands were shaking so badly, I couldn't stop fumbling with the keys. David laid his hand on mine, stilling them just long enough to get the door open.

Inside, David pulled me against him. We were in the same position we'd been dancing in, my back to his front, but it felt like a lifetime had happened since then.

"I'm sorry," I said.

"You didn't do anything wrong. I thought you were hurt. When I couldn't see you, I thought I was gonna go crazy."

"I know, I know. Me too." I sucked in a deep breath. "Let me take care of you."

He sighed. "Okay."

I took him to my kitchen, where I kept a first aid kit. I busied myself gathering ice and bandages, but when I finally faced him, letting myself get a good look at the damage that had been inflicted because of me, I had to bite my lip to keep from wailing.

"C'mere," he beckoned.

Full of emotion, I made my way to him, carrying my supplies like a shield in front of me. I set everything down on the counter next to him and reached up to touch his face, but stopped myself. This was my fault. I might as well have been the one who punched him.

"You gonna fix me, Syl?" David's voice was rough as he watched me.

"Yeah, I'm just a little shaky here. Sorry," I said.

David grabbed my hands, cradling them in his. He was being so gentle, it almost broke me.

"Me too, me too, sweetheart."

Our eyes met and held. The air was thick between us. Even with blood dripping from his cheek and eyebrow, I'd never seen a more beautiful man.

He pushed the headband off my forehead and tangled his fingers on the sides of my hair, bringing his face down to mine. "I'd knock every last person down to get to you. Do you know that?"

"I'd do the same," I said.

His mouth came down on mine hard, and I tasted blood. Whether it was mine or his, I didn't care. I needed him.

Without taking my mouth from his, I yanked his shirt out of the waistband of his pants and slid my hands underneath, needing to feel his skin. I dug my fingers into his chest and back. I would have burrowed inside him if I could have, just to reassure myself he was okay.

Spinning us around, David picked me up and dropped me on the Formica counter. My legs circled around him, locking behind his back.

His hands were all over me, cupping my jaw, then pushing my vest off, sliding up my legs and under my skirt, skimming my belly. He pulled me to the edge so the center of me aligned with the hardness of him.

I writhed against him, completely out of my mind with want and frenzy. I'd lost whatever semblance of control I'd maintained over the last week, and the only thing I knew for sure was I'd die without David inside me.

"Please..." I moaned.

"I'm gonna fuck you right here unless you object. You gotta tell me if you don't want this." David's voice sounded pained, like he was verging on death right along with me.

"I want you. *Please.*"

He shifted, fumbling with his wallet. He pulled out a condom, tossing it on the counter next to me, then backed up a step and yanked my panties down my legs, leaving me open and bare. He plunged a finger inside me, then another, all while he had my hair wrapped around his hand. I had no choice but to watch his face as he felt me from the inside.

"So damn pretty. You know you're mine, don't you?" David's brow was furrowed as he waited for me to answer. But there was no question. I'd always been his, even when he didn't want me—even when *I* didn't want to be.

"Mmhmm."

"Say it, Sylvia. Say you're mine." He circled my clit with his thumb until I saw stars.

"Yes, David. I'm yours. I'm whatever you want me to be."

"Take my cock out."

I freed him from his pants, then slid the condom down his length, all while he pumped his fingers inside me.

"Tell me you're mine again." His mouth was at my throat, biting and licking.

"I'm yours," I breathed.

He pulled his fingers out and gripped my hips, then pushed his cock inside me in one hard thrust. It smashed the air from my lungs, but he kept going, pushing into me like there was a time limit, and if he passed it, I'd disappear forever.

I clung to him, kissing whatever skin I could reach, his cheeks, his neck, the triangle of exposed chest. It wasn't enough, but having him inside me for the first time in fifteen years had sent me to another plane. We were the one bright spot in a sea of darkness. All the stars had burned out except for the one above us, shining on this moment.

"No one's ever gonna touch you. Never," he murmured against my skin.

"No one," I agreed.

He was wild in his thrusts, but his hands were careful and protective, touching me with reverence. He draped my legs over his arms, tilting my hips so he could drive even deeper. It felt like he'd found a place inside me I hadn't realize existed. Like he'd discovered and conquered me.

I tried to hold onto something, my fingernails scrabbling on the counter, but nothing was working, so I clawed at my chest, freeing my breasts. I rolled my nipples between my fingers, making my inner walls clench around the thick cock stretching me. David grunted, and I moaned.

"Jesus, Sylvia."

I did it again and again, until I couldn't hold back. I touched my clit in fast, tight circles, sending myself flying into space. The stars behind my eyelids danced and twinkled until I was dizzy and utterly wrecked.

I didn't crash, though. David lifted me from the counter and pressed me against the closest wall, driving into me with a brutal force. My orgasm never stopped. From this angle, he hit my clit each time. My limbs and belly were both tight and shaky, vibrating from the overwhelming pleasure mixed with just the right amount of pain.

"God, you feel too good." David bit down on the side of my neck, sending another wave of bliss crashing through me. My pussy squeezed him, making him grunt and take me even harder.

His mouth was all over my neck and chest, leaving smears of blood on my skin. Seeing the slashes of red coloring me only heightened what was happening between us. This was primal. A need that had laid dormant between us for years, but now that it had been awakened, it wouldn't stop until everything in its path had been decimated.

"I need you, David. I really need you." I talked, said some things that made sense, but a lot of it was incoherent. He seemed to understand, though. He answered back in grunts and moans, which my body responded to like he was speaking its language.

Pushing away from the wall, he carried me to the couch. He laid us down like it took no strength at all, and from above me, he worked his hips against mine.

David's eyes never left mine. This time, he was seeing my diamonds, finding each location and marking them for later. He knew my secrets and knew where the treasure was buried. Right then, I would have told him anything he'd asked—I would have *done* anything he'd asked.

"Sylvia..." he whispered.

I arched my back, lifting my hips off the couch. Cupping my ass, he held me there, taking me deeper than ever. Even with my eyes wide open, the stars were taking over again, filling the edges of my vision.

David plunged into me one final time, his face contorted in agony, my name filling the room. Instead of flopping onto me and holding me, he pulled out quickly and flipped me over onto my stomach. From behind me, he pushed my knees apart and under me. The room's cool air shocked my heated core.

The air was quickly replaced by a hot mouth licking me from top to bottom. My toes curled, and my fingers gripped the pillow in front of me. David's lips surrounded my clit, pulling at it until I would have rocketed off the couch had he not been holding me down. I mewled, grinding my pussy into his face as I came on his lips. One orgasm wasn't enough for him, though. He licked and sucked until I was so overwhelmed and sensitive, I had to nudge him away.

Finally, he collapsed on top of me, both of us breathing hard. He rolled us so we were side by side, me the little spoon to his much bigger one. He kept kissing my neck and shoulders, his hands touching me like he always did, moving all over my body, checking to be sure I was really there.

I twined my fingers with his roving hand, stopping him at my belly.

"I'm here," I said.

He laid his forehead on the back of my head, slowly exhaling. "I love the way you feel. So hard and soft."

I sighed in his arms. A tear fell from my eye, dripping onto the couch. I wasn't sure I could form a coherent thought, but I knew the talking was coming. I just wanted to stay here a while longer, with my savagely gentle beast of a lover.

I HISSED. "I'm not trying to be a baby, but damn, that hurts."

Sylvia dabbed more antiseptic on my eyebrow. "More than getting punched by a giant?"

I closed my eyes. "Gotta admit, that getting punched shit is for the birds. In my twenties, I could throw down, but I think my fighting days are over."

"Good. I really didn't like that."

I opened my eyes and rubbed my thumb along her smooth cheek. "No, sweetheart, I didn't like it either. I'm sorry your night ended like that."

"*You're* sorry? You have nothing to be sorry for." She bit her lip. "And I kind of liked the ending."

I started to grin, but the pain in my lip quickly reminded it had been split only a couple hours ago. "Kind of?" I asked.

She hooked an arm around my neck. "Kind of a lot."

"Wasn't too crazy?"

"David, that was the exact kind of crazy I get off on. I told you, pull my hair and tell me I'm pretty. I like it rough and intense."

My cock swelled, completely oblivious to the busted,

painful state of my face. "Shit, Syl, I'm gonna have to have you again if you keep talking like that."

"You just stopped bleeding. Maybe let's talk for a few minutes. Want some coffee or cocoa?"

This time, it was my heart that swelled. Sylvia might've liked it rough and intense, but she also had this hugely sweet and nurturing side to her I found inexplicably attractive.

"Cocoa sounds good. Maybe not scalding, though?"

She grinned. "I'll put an ice cube in yours like I used to do for Emma."

"Smart ass."

I sat at her table, with its mismatched chairs and nicks and scratches—I couldn't quite tell whether they were artfully done or it was just an old table. Either way, I liked the look.

Sylvia had given me some clothes to wear, so I was no longer in bell bottoms and my bloody thrift store shirt. I didn't know if wearing Vince's old clothes was much better, but I'd make do, for now. I wasn't up for driving home tonight, not when one of my eyes was on its way to swelling shut and the rest of me felt like I'd been run over by a truck.

"Here you go, one lukewarm cocoa for you," she said, setting a steaming mug on the table.

She sat across from me, taking a careful sip of her coffee. "Do you have questions?" she asked.

A thousand.

"You don't have to tell me anything you don't want to," I said.

Tell me everything.

"I haven't seen Vince in over a year," she said.

"If I hadn't been in the picture, would he have been the one fucking you tonight?"

She glanced away, chewing her bottom lip. "I'd like to say no, but he was a habit. One that's been completely kicked now."

She turned back, her blue eyes on mine. "What happened between you and me was crazy hot, and even though it seemed inevitable, for me, tonight was a conscious decision. I have had to let go of a lot of hurt to let myself be close to you. It hasn't been easy, and I don't fully trust you yet. Not with me, and not with Emma. I want to, though. I really do."

God, Sylvia was really amazing. I'd been floating through life, bumping into people as I went, while never looking back. And she had been here, this complete, deliberate person, making decisions with her brain instead of her gut—or, in my case, my dick.

"I want you to trust me too. I'm not out to hurt you."

"Well..." She turned her mug in a full circle on the table. "What do you remember from my engagement party?"

"Sadly, all of it."

I walked into the restaurant that night, already drunk. That was the only way I could face that shit. I wouldn't have shown up, but Emma had really tugged at my heartstrings, begging me to be there. She never asked for anything, so I couldn't say no.

I sat there through speeches and toasts, trying to pay attention to my kid, all while watching her mother fake her way through the night. She'd looked so pretty in her red dress and red lips. I don't know if it was the booze haze I'd been in making me see things, but I thought she looked sad too. That motherfucker Vince looked like he'd won the lottery, though, staring at Sylvia like she was his prize.

I'd gone outside to smoke on a private, darkened patio, and Sylvia had appeared like the ghost she was. She'd taken my cigarette from my fingers and crushed it on the ground. I drank my beer and watched her in the moonlight.

"Married, huh?"

Her eyelashes brushed her cheeks as she looked down. "I think so."

I barked a laugh. "You don't sound so sure."

"That's because I'm not. How can I know if I love him enough to love him forever?"

"I think that's one of those things you should answer before slipping his ring on your finger and throwing a big party."

She looked up. Really stared at me. "Why are you here?"

"Em asked me to be."

"I don't believe you. Why are you here, David?"

I tossed back the rest of my beer, my brain just the right amount of hazy to make all this bearable. Setting my bottle down on a table nearby, I stepped into her space. I hadn't been this close to Sylvia Price in years, but fuck if I hadn't thought about it. Every time I saw her, she consumed my brain for weeks afterward.

"We should be a family," I blurted.

She stumbled away from me. "What?"

I grabbed her elbow, steadying her, then pulled her against me. "The three of us should be together. It's what's right. Fuck that guy in there."

She laughed softly. "Just how drunk are you?"

"Not so drunk. Just the right amount to tell you what I've been thinkin' for a long time."

"That's crazy, David. Why are you doing this?"

I pushed her silky hair off her shoulder and bent down to kiss the side of her neck. She hissed, but didn't stop me. "I could love you, Syl. I really think I could."

She put her hands on my shoulders—either to push me away or hold me there. I wasn't sure, and it seemed like maybe she wasn't either.

"You don't know me, David."

"I want to. Won't you let us be a family?" I pleaded.

"You're a few years too late for this kind of talk." This time, she did push me away.

"Just...come over to my place later. Let me talk to you." I got out my phone and texted her the elevator code to get up to my condo. *"Come over tonight."*

She sighed. *"I can't."*

"You can. Please, Sylvia."

With tears in her eerily beautiful eyes, her gaze locked on mine. *"No."*

She'd gone back in, and a minute later, I'd gone in too. I'd seen her in Vince's arms, fake smile plastered on. I'd kissed Emma goodbye, then went home and got shitfaced.

"Why'd you do it, David? Was it because of your drinking?" Sylvia asked.

I plowed a hand through my hair. "No, I...remember Paris?"

"Of course."

"I planned that day for the three of us. Had three tickets to everything. I thought it'd be this family thing. I was really fucking excited."

I could picture, clear as day, walking into their hotel, holding two berets, to pick up my girls. Only...when I got there, it was obvious Sylvia had other plans. That big oaf Vince had his arms around them both, looking like this happy nuclear family. I tossed those stupid berets in the trash, put my game face on, and spent the day trying, but probably failing miserably, to be cheerful and fun for Emma.

"I had no idea. Vince didn't think we should travel internationally by ourselves and I wasn't crazy about it, so we made it a family vacation." Her eyes widened with realization at her own words.

"Doesn't matter now. I was trying to give context for what I did at your engagement party. I was scared shitless, and my head was up my own ass. In my imagination, *we* were a family. Us three. I never liked thinking about you having your own lives that I wasn't the center of...or even a part of." I moved my mug around, the cocoa sloshing dangerously close to the top. "Could be I got so used to the adoration I received while on the road, I expected it when I got home too. But you had your own man adoring you, and I wasn't needed."

"Emma always needed you."

"I get that now. But I was an angry, bitter drunk with a big head. All I saw was my family slipping through my fingers and a replacement stepping into my spot. I'm sorry I messed up your night."

She was quiet for a bit, taking a sip of her coffee. I couldn't seem to keep my eyes off her. Her normally smooth, straight hair was tousled wildly around her shoulders, spilling down her back like waves in a storm. She only had a T-shirt on, and even in the middle of the serious conversation I was relieved to be having, I was itching to get my hands on her again.

"I followed you out there, you know," she said.

"Yeah?"

"Yeah. I needed a break from smiling."

I chuckled. "So you came to me?"

She smiled sheepishly. "I was spoiling for a fight. But then you said all those things and touched me like that...well, I'd been unsure what to do before that, but I was resolved when I went back inside."

"You told Vince I was in love with you?" I asked.

She huffed a laugh. "That's what he heard, but it isn't what I said. It was another few days before I broke up with him. I told him about our conversation, and how I hadn't resisted when you held me. I was trying to illustrate why we shouldn't be together, to show him my heart wasn't committed to marrying him. I did him wrong, David."

I tapped the table in front of her. "Any goodwill he had left evaporated tonight. I'd say you're square, huh?"

"I think so, yeah."

"I stayed drunk for an entire year after that. Messing up hotel rooms, getting into fights, just fucking it all up. Poor Nick had to follow me around, cleaning up my shit. I scared the hell out of us both."

"What made you stop?"

I held her eyes. "You don't know?"

She shook her head.

"Emma called. Wasn't her usual time, and I shouldn't have answered. I was already wasted, but I wanted to talk to her. She was telling me about a part she'd gotten in a play—Mary Poppins, I think—and I set down the phone and wandered away. Nick had to take over. 'Course, I don't actually remember any of this. The next morning, Nick told me about it, all matter of fact. But I saw it. He was starting to hate me. And it dawned on me right then, Em would hate me pretty soon too."

Sylvia climbed into my lap, hugging me fiercely. I stroked her back and arms and cheeks—everywhere I could get to. I knew how lucky I was to have her right now. I'd fucked up her life at every turn, yet here we were, starting this really big thing.

"Tali helped me find a therapist who treated me by video chat when I was on the road. In those early days, we talked all the time. I probably should've been in rehab, but I couldn't do it. My therapist—Mark—really pulled me through it. He got me looking at myself, my childhood, my fears, what I was numbing with alcohol, why I was acting out. I mean, we all know part of it is I'm just an ass." She hugged me tighter, laughing softly against my neck. My heart and dick throbbed equally.

"What were you numbing?"

Leave it to Sylvia to want to know all my shit. "I have this thing about being alone. And nights. I fuckin' hate long, quiet nights where all I have are my thoughts."

"Why?"

I sighed, sliding my hands under her shirt to rub her back.

"My dad left when I was eight. Mom had nothing. No money, no family. Just this crazy, heartbroken kid. She had to work nights, and yeah, I was left alone. I know she really didn't have a choice, but I was a little kid, hiding in my bed night after night, scared shitless of every sound. I never really grew out of it. If I'm home, I have to sleep with a noise machine, even now."

"You haven't used one when we've slept together."

"Don't need it with you. Just need to have my hands on you," I said.

"Do you still hate being alone?" she asked.

"I haven't had to do a lot of it, to be honest. On the road, it's easy. There are always people around. And I...I don't stay home long enough to really feel it. I'm working on it, though. I still see Mark. I tried meds, but I do better with weed for my anxiety. Got my very own medical card."

"I know this is going to sound like a mom thing to say, but I'm really proud of you. I know facing all that can't have been easy."

"Sylvia...you shouldn't be proud. I've been the bull in your life's china shop. Even sober, I'm still crashing around, being an idiot."

She kissed my throat and jaw, her lips warm from her coffee. "My eyes are wide open. You don't have to tell me your short-comings; I'm well aware. I can still be proud of you."

I slid my fingers through the sides of her hair, letting it spill over my hands.

"I like how you don't mess around. You just say shit. It's really refreshing," I said.

Her lips curved into a pleased smile. "I think you were cursed with a similar affliction."

"Yeah, but the shit you say is all wise and mature. Mine's like *I wanna fuck your tits.* Not quite the same."

She burst out laughing. "I feel sorry for you if you had plans of fucking my tiny tits. Now, if you said my ass..."

My eyebrows shot up, and my hips jerked involuntarily. "Sylvia Price, that was mighty filthy."

She shifted to straddle me, rolling her hips. "And it was mighty true. I might not quite trust you with my heart yet, but I trust you with my body."

"And that is an incredible honor I absolutely don't take lightly. I don't take anything with you lightly."

"Me either," she murmured, right before she crushed her lips to mine.

We kissed until kissing wasn't enough, then we fucked and fucked until we were both sore and exhausted. And still, in the middle of the night, we both woke up and had frenzied, dream-like sex.

And then I held her. She might slip back into the ether tomorrow, but for right now, she was real and solid and *mine*.

TWENTY-TWO

DAVID

IN MY BORROWED CLOTHES, which were way too big for me—major blow to the ego—I stepped outside Sylvia's house, shutting the door behind me. Even at ten in the morning, her street was bustling. People raking, couples out for a jog, kids jumping in piles of leaves, dogs racing through yards. It was the picture of domesticity, and there was this deep, yearning part of me that really loved it. Another part, a lot closer to the surface, was mildly terrified.

This was the 'burbs, but with charm and personality. Still the 'burbs, though.

Walking down the old, cracked sidewalk, I made my way to Suz and Mika's. A man walked by with his dog, smiling like we were old friends.

"Good morning! Nice day, huh?" he asked.

I scowled, hoping to fend off any autograph requests. "Sure. See ya."

"Have a great day!" he said as he kept walking.

So strange. The 'burbs, man.

I knocked on Mika and Suz's door, not sure of my game

plan. I just knew I felt pretty damn contrite this morning for messing up their party.

The door swung open to a grinning Mika. "David! To what do I owe this pleasure?"

"Hey, man. I came by to see if I could help clean up."

He looked behind me. "No Sylvie?"

"Nah. Emma called this morning asking to stay with Avery another night, so Syl's taking her some stuff. She made me stay home, with my busted face."

I'd felt like a shit parent when Emma called, because all I could think was I'd get another full day of Sylvia all to myself. Thank Christ Sylvia had been equally excited about the idea. 'Course, I was ready to drag her back to bed immediately, whereas she sprang into action, talking with Avery's mom, then packing Emma a bag for the night.

"Well, come on in. Suz is out with Evan grabbing some bagels and coffee." He held up a black garbage bag. "I'm just getting around to clean up duty. It was a late night."

I pointed to the bag. "Got another one of those?"

Mika grabbed another garbage bag, and we went outside to the deck where there were cups strewn everywhere.

"Your face looks like hell. How's it feel?" Mika asked.

"Feels better than it looks." I tossed a stack of cups in my bag. "Sorry that happened here. Wasn't my intention."

He chuckled. "In my younger days, I wouldn't have blinked. Hell, I probably would've jumped into the fray. But you know, now I've got Suz and Evan to think about, and with her being pregnant, I gotta be careful."

I paused. "You're having a kid?"

Mika rubbed the top of his bald head. "Oh shit. She hasn't even told Sylvie yet. She's waiting to get through the first trimester. She just took the test a couple days ago and...I'm kinda excited, if you can't tell."

I shook his hand. "Congrats. That's awesome news. I guess next year's Halloween party is gonna be a little more low key."

He laughed. "Right? Probably gonna have to press pause on the parties for a couple years." He moved around the deck, bagging trash while I did the same. "I didn't think I'd be a family guy until I met Suz. Then it was like some biological imperative kicked in. I guess it's how the human race has survived, the urge to go forth and multiply."

We went down by the firepit to bag up the trash down there. "You guys been married long?" I asked.

"Newlyweds. We've been married six months. Together two years," he answered.

"Oh, I thought you'd known Syl a lot longer than that."

"Yeah, Sylvie and I go way back. Met her through Vince, that fucker. Both are my friends, but I never thought they were a great match."

I nodded. "He ever get like he was last night with her?"

Mika paused what he was doing to look right in my eyes. "I'd have killed him if he ever tried it."

"Good. Glad she had someone looking out for her."

"Sylvie's got a lot of people in her corner these days. She's a good one," Mika said.

We moved inside, tossing cup after cup. People were fucking slobs, especially drunk people.

"The bagels have arrived!" Suz walked in the living room, holding a paper bag up high. Her smile dropped at the sight of me. "David."

I tipped my head. "Suz. Hey, Evan."

Evan lurked behind his mom. "Hello, Mr. Wiesel."

I snorted with laughter. "Come off that Mr. Wiesel shit. It's just David."

"Ah, okay. I'm sorry," he said.

"Don't be. It's fine," I said.

"Are you joining us for bagels?" Suz asked. "And where's Sylvie?"

I rubbed my stomach. "I could eat. And Syl should be home soon. She's dropping some stuff off with Emma."

Her eyes narrowed. "Fine. You can stay since you helped clean up." She started toward the kitchen, tossing over her shoulder, "You look like shit, by the way."

"Should'a seen the other guy," I muttered.

BY THE TIME Sylvia tapped on the door, I'd tossed back an everything bagel and cup of coffee, and Mika had shown me his collection of guitars. Turned out, he'd been in a band all through his twenties and the guy could really play.

Mika, Evan, and I were out on the deck, talking about music when Sylvia came out, followed by Suz. Evan took one look at all the adults and went back inside.

I stood, but I had no idea how to greet her. All I knew was, with the fall sun shining down on her smiling face, she both took my breath away and gave me life.

She came to me, giving me a hug. "Hey, you."

"I suppose making out isn't an option right now?"

She laughed. "Nope."

"Is Emma good?"

"She is. Avery lives in a rancher, so Emma's hobbling all over with her crutches. I'm going to pick them up for school tomorrow."

"*We*," I corrected. I'd missed a million first days of school, but I could be there tomorrow.

I sat back down in my chair. I wanted to pull Sylvia into my lap, but luckily, she was a lot smarter than me and pulled a chair up next to me instead. I was crazy for her. The need to feel her skin filled me. She knew it too and offered me her hand, which I gladly took, weaving our fingers together.

"David helped Mika clean up this morning," Suz said.

Sylvia patted my thigh. "That was sweet."

I winked at her. "I'm the sweetest."

"Well, he *did* contribute to some of the mess last night," Suz said dryly.

"Yeah, well, you'd have probably thrown down too if you'd heard what that douche was saying. I *am* sorry it happened, though," I said.

Mika grabbed his wife's hand. "We're straight, man. I had some words of my own with Vince. He knows nothing like that will ever happen again."

I picked up the guitar I'd brought out with me. "You interested in jamming?" I asked Mika.

"Hell yeah. I've been trying to teach Evan so we can play together, but he's more interested in his phone," Mika said.

We played some Nirvana and Green Day, then went classic with a little *Stairway to Heaven*. I paused for a second, tuning my guitar, when Mika broke into some Blue is the Color music.

"Holy shit, don't let my band hear you playing or they'll replace me on the spot." Dude's fingers were fast and strummed each note with precision. It was actually really cool to watch.

Sylvia sighed. "I love this song."

"If I weren't already pregnant, I'd be begging you to knock me up," Suz said, her eyes all dreamy.

Mika set down his guitar. "Babe. You're a bean spiller."

She rolled her eyes. "Oh yeah, no, I told Sylvia days ago. I told *you* it was a secret so you didn't blast it to everyone we meet."

Sylvia laughed. "Congratulations, you two."

"Guess I shouldn't have had so much wine last weekend, huh?" Suz joked.

Sylvia shrugged. "Mika's from hardy stock. The baby will be fine. Maybe let's not make it a habit though, okay?"

Suz arched a brow in my direction. "He told you, right?"

"Yep," I confirmed.

"See, babe? You've never kept a secret in your life," Suz said to Mika.

"I told *one* person!" Mika said.

"*One?*" Suz asked.

He exhaled and slumped back in his chair, defeated. "Okay, more like three or four. But I had to ask the deli guy about listeria. That shit is dangerous."

Suz climbed into his lap, circling her arms around his neck. "You are going to be the best dad to this bean, you know that?"

"Yep," he said proudly.

And fuck, my chest actually ached for something I'd never get to have. I wished Sylvia and I could've had Emma fifteen years later so we could've been thrilled rather than horrified.

I had no idea where those thoughts came from. I mean, I knew, but it wasn't anything I'd ever thought or felt before. I kinda chugged through life. My motto had always been "It is what it is." No changing it, so why worry about it?

These days, there were more things I wanted to change than keep the same.

DAVID and I were stretched out on my couch, watching TV while he absently toyed with my hair. After the mess of last night, today had been a good day. I never imagined we'd click like we did. He was easy to be with, and he'd even worn Suz down. There was just something about him. It would be patronizing to call it an innocence, because he was far from innocent. But it was like he was seeing the world for the first time and I got to see it along with him.

I slid my hand under his shirt, resting over his heart. I liked him—I couldn't bring myself to say I loved him anymore, because that was too big and scary at the moment—but I was under no illusions he was an entirely different person just because we were sleeping together. He might decide tomorrow he was bored and head out on the road.

The truly sad part was, I wouldn't have been surprised. Destroyed, but not surprised.

In my head, I could hear Suz asking how I could be with him if I was expecting him to leave me, and the answer was David and I were inevitable. This was going to happen now or ten years from now. We had been heading toward each other for years, just missing each other by millimeters each time our paths crossed. This time, at least for a while, our paths were running parallel. Next time, our course just might be set for collision.

"Do you know how much I love having my hair played with?" I asked.

"That works, because I have somewhat of an obsession with it. How's it so shiny?"

"I think it's a trick of the light."

"When I start touring again, I'm gonna have to take a lock of it with me, like a soldier." He held a long strand of my hair up, then let it fall slowly.

I scratched my nails on his chest and snuggled closer to his side. "I don't really want to think about that."

"Yeah, me either. It's gonna happen eventually, though. But I'll always come back to you," he said.

I didn't respond. How could I? I knew he believed what he said, but he'd probably believed what he said the night of my engagement party too. And that hadn't been true. As soon as I was out of sight, I'd been out of his mind.

"I chose my song for the showcase," I said.

At the abrupt change in subject, his hand on my jaw flexed for a beat before he let go. "Oh yeah? You can tell me, but I'm not gonna know it."

"Then it'll be a surprise." I paused, propping myself up so I could see his face. "You're coming to the showcase, right? I kind of assumed."

"I want to. When is it?"

"Three weeks."

He tapped his temple. "Got it filed away. I'll be there."

"What are you going to do this week with no Emma to cart around?"

He gave me a slow, happy smile. "Don't know. Probably

pine for my girls all day. Play some guitar and try not to get into trouble. Maybe a little harmless stalking."

I dragged my finger down his nose and tapped the end. "There's a lot to unpack in those plans. Who are you stalking?"

"You, obviously. I know which bench you eat your lunch on, so I'll just hang out on it all day."

"How do you know that wasn't a one-time thing?" I asked.

"I'm feeling optimistic."

"We didn't have the best luck on that bench last time we shared it."

He pulled me onto him so we were lying chest to chest. "I don't know. We said a lot of things that needed to be said. Turned out pretty okay." His hands slid down my back, stopping at my ass.

"Tell me more about how you're not going to get in trouble. Is that difficult for you?"

He cocked his head. "Did you not know trouble is my middle name?"

"Is it? Gwen was feeling creative on the day of your birth, huh?"

He chuckled. "It's actually Edgar. Named after my fuck up of a dad."

I scratched his whiskers, and he leaned into my hand, closing his eyes as I moved my fingernails back and forth on his cheeks. I'd learned over the last week that David couldn't get enough of my touch. He was starved for it. Even if I was brushing by him, he'd lean in to feel more of me.

"You know your initials spell 'dew,' right?"

He opened his eyes to roll them. "I'm aware. Nick tried to call me Dewie in middle school when he found out. I had to kick his ass to get him to stop."

"What if I called you that?"

"I wouldn't kick your ass, but I sure as hell would spank you."

I pulled my knees up to straddle him. "What if I said I liked that...Dewie?"

His hand came down swiftly, making a loud smack. I bit my lip, my eyelids fluttering.

"Fuck...you're really into that, aren't you?" His voice came out deeper than normal.

"Sometimes, yeah. I think I'm into anything with you," I said honestly.

I leaned forward on his chest. "Dewie," I whispered.

David sat up so fast, my breath caught in my throat, but then I was laying over his legs, ass in the air. He pushed my T-shirt up, skimmed his knuckles over the backs of my thighs, and palmed my ass. Just when I started to breathe normally again, his spanked me three times in quick succession.

I moaned, rubbing my thighs together.

"Do you have any idea how hot you are, Sylvia?"

I arched my back in response, pushing my ass higher.

He spanked the other cheek—one, two, three—then rubbed the burn away.

"Do you like this?" I asked.

He laughed once, then thrust his hips, his erection brushing against me. "What do you think?"

"I think you should take my panties off so you can see if my ass is pink enough."

He slid my boy-shorts down my legs, and I wiggled them the rest of the way off.

"Hmmm..." His hands slid over my backside, spreading me, checking me out thoroughly. "I'm not sure I'm satisfied with the pinkness of your skin, Ms. Price."

I wiggled my hips again. "I want you to be happy, Mr. Wiesel."

His hand came down again and again. I knew I'd feel it tomorrow, but what I felt right now made it worth it. I could barely stay still in his lap, writhing around with the heady combination of pleasure and pain coursing through my veins.

"Oh, I'm utterly delighted right now," he said.

David was as savage as he was gentle, slapping my butt and thighs, then caressing my fiery skin and leaving sweet kisses on my shoulders and back.

Just when I was about to tap out of the spanking, David plunged a finger inside me. My head shot up, and my grunt filled the room. I pushed back against his hand, making him chuckle all low and growly.

"My girl likes that, huh? You're so wet, I just slid right in."

He worked another finger in, curling and pumping, hitting something magical inside me. I'd already been losing my mind from the spanking, but now I was on a different planet.

I almost cried when his hand left me, and he shifted me on the couch. "Why?" I whined.

From behind me, David slid a hand under my belly, lifting my hips up, and then he plunged inside me. I grabbed onto the arm of the couch, bracing myself so I could push back against him.

"I love being inside you. I love how wild you are. I think you were made for me." With each statement, he thrust into me, stretching me around his thick cock.

I looked over my shoulder at him and almost came on the spot. His brow was pinched, his bottom lip caught between his teeth as he concentrated on the spot where he ended and I began. Each of his muscles were taut and at attention, the ridges in his stomach rippling with every thrust. He had one foot planted on the floor and held my hips in his big, strong hands, digging his thumbs into the rosy flesh of my ass.

My head lolled on my shoulders, and I let out a long, low

moan. I completely gave myself over to David, letting him move me where he wanted, letting him dictate the pace and depth of our fucking.

It was a relief to let go for this brief span. I could be mindless, my only focus receiving the pleasure he gave me so willingly. I trusted David in this. My instincts said he knew how far he could take me, skating the edge, but never going over it.

David was strong, but so was I. With each pump of his hips, I ground my tender backside against his pelvis.

"Give me your hands, Sylvia," he gritted.

I offered one hand, then the other. David cuffed my wrists together with his thick fingers, the other hand cupping my throat, taking complete control. He used my arms to pull my body back each time he slammed forward, pushing the air and thoughts out of me.

My mewls sounded foreign to my ears. My clit throbbed between my legs, but I had no hope of touching it. Right now, my pleasure belonged to David, and he would do with it what he wanted.

"Please," I panted. "I need to come."

"Ooh, I like how polite you are. You feel how hard that makes me?"

I moaned at the sound of his flesh slapping against mine.

"Sylvia...I asked you a question." His hand on my throat tightened slightly. "You feel how hard you make me, sweetheart?"

I squeezed my eyes shut, a tear dripping onto the couch. "Yes...oh god, yes, I feel you."

His hand left my throat, dragging down to my breasts, toying with my nipples, before finding his way between my legs. His fingers skipped my clit, moving to explore my lips stretched around his cock.

I didn't ask again. I waited. I knew it was coming.

"If I touch your clit, are you gonna squeeze the hell out of my cock?" David's voice sounded slurred, like he was drunk on me.

"Mmm...yes." I flexed my inner walls, giving him a preview.

He tsked and plunged into me even deeper. "Fuck, Syl, I'm gonna come before I'm ready if you keep that up."

"I'm ready," I said.

Thankfully, David had mercy on me, circling his fingers around my clit until a groan ripped through me and my legs threatened to collapse. I came hard, my face contorting as my orgasm took over every muscle in my body. I was one big contraction, tight everywhere.

"Oh, Jesus, fuck, Sylvia!" David bellowed, jerking out of me. He pressed me down on the couch, his cock wedged between my ass cheeks, the unmistakable warmth of his cum spilling on my back.

His breath was hot on my neck, whiskers scratching. Neither of us spoke. Words weren't needed. I wasn't sure I even remembered any words.

But then, the cum on my back registered.

And how good David had felt inside me.

No condom.

He'd pulled out, though, so it was probably okay.

"David...you forgot a condom," I said, my face against the couch cushion.

He pushed my hair out of my face and kissed my cheek. "I know, I'm sorry. I got caught up...I swear to god, Syl, I never go without one. Ever. I get tested all the time, I'm clean."

I let out a slightly delirious laugh. "I didn't even think about it. Why didn't I think about it?"

He stroked my cheek with a gentle touch. "You were as caught up as me. I'm gonna get something to clean you up. Don't move."

I laid there, boneless, not letting myself worry. What was the point now? David had worn a condom when I got pregnant with Emma, so it's not like they were one-hundred percent anyway.

I laughed to myself again. Yeah, definitely delirious.

David came back, standing over me. "I have to look at you for a minute. I don't think I've ever seen anything sexier than your rosy ass and my cum all over you. I'm gonna need to lock this image up for eternity." I rocked my hips back and forth, to give him something to think about.

Finally, he knelt next to me, carefully wiping my back with a warm washcloth.

I closed my eyes, smiling. "Mmm...thank you. This is first class treatment."

He palmed my backside. "Anything for you, my beautiful girl."

"I think you might have to carry me to bed."

He chuckled. "I think I can do that."

UPSTAIRS, I woke up a little as I washed my face and brushed my teeth. David stood behind me, watching me in the bathroom mirror.

"You okay with everything that just happened?" His eyebrows were knitted with concern.

I turned, meeting his gaze. "Yes. So okay." I rubbed the spot between my eyes. "I guess I should get back on the pill. I mean, if this is going to be exclusive, I'm okay with ditching the condoms in a couple weeks—"

He gripped my jaw. "Sylvia, I know you're unsure, but, sweetheart, I'm sure as hell. Nothing has ever touched the way I want you. There won't be anyone else."

I brought my hands up to his wrist, and the grip on my jaw

eased. "I'm not unsure about wanting you, David. That's never been an issue."

His eyes traced over my face. "Oh yeah? Never?"

"Never. And now that I know how good it is..."

His thumb stroked my cheek. "Kinda crazy how good it is, isn't it? I meant it when I said you were made for me. I believe that's true."

"Do you think *you* were made for *me*?"

He released a long breath. "I really fuckin' hope so."

I laid my hand on his chest. "I hope so too...Dewie."

He growled, and I made a break for it, screaming with laughter and running toward my bedroom.

I let him catch me...again and again.

THE FOUR OF us watched Tali expectantly.

"I have contracts." She pointed at my healing face. "Do I need to know about this?"

"Nah, problem has been handled."

Explaining to Emma what happened to my face hadn't been the most fun, but it also hadn't seemed right to hide it from her. Although I'd wanted to. If I'd been on my own, I'd probably have made up a mugging incident or tragic weightlifting accident. Luckily, I wasn't on my own and Sylvia insisted we tell Emma what really happened.

She'd mostly been concerned about me, but also sad at how Vince had behaved. Though he'd been out of her life for a while now, he'd been a pretty big part of it for several years—bigger than I'd been. We'd been vague about *why* Vince had been so angry, and Emma had accepted our answers.

Tali laid a thick stack of papers on Nick's table, then split them up into four piles, passing them to each of us.

She continued. "These are just a basic business agreement to get the ball rolling. Your lawyers will draw up more detailed contracts once we know precisely how we're doing this."

"Rein Records" was emblazoned at the top of each contract. The back of my eyes burned, seeing it there. Every single one of us would rather have Reinece back than a cool name for our record label, but I was well aware her passing had been the kick in the ass all of us needed to face a lot of shit in our lives. She brought us together, even though she wasn't here. I could almost hear her telling us how silly it was to name the label after her, while looking pleased as punch about the whole thing.

If Heaven was real, Reinece was smiling down on us. She was also telling Ian to sit up straight, Nick to get married already, Jasper to stop looking so sad and get some sleep, and me to treat my girls right.

We all signed our papers. I didn't do a lot of reading—I trusted Tali and Nick.

"So, now what?" I asked.

"We're going to see Flashing Numbers play next weekend," Nick said. "I have another idea for someone we should check out."

"Who?" Jasper asked.

Nick leaned back in his chair, hands clasped on his stomach. "Malka. She left her band, and she's chilling in Baltimore. I think she could be big solo." His attention landed on Ian. "You cool with that?"

Ian shrugged. "Whatever."

"Man, I don't know. Last thing Ian needs is to get tangled up with Malka again," I said.

Malka and Ian had been playing the relationship merry-go-round for a couple years, breaking up and making up repeatedly. He'd finally broken free—or she'd set him free, who knew—and I loathed to see him get sucked back in.

On the other hand, Malka was Janis Joplin reincarnated. She had the kind of voice that rattled your soul. She'd had some success in the past, but had never had quite the right sound.

"If Ian's cool, I think we should talk to her. Her vocals are so dope," Jasper said. "When we were on tour over the summer, she and I talked about recording a duet."

Tali stacked our contracts and slid them into her briefcase. "I think that's an excellent idea...if Ian's okay with it."

Ian shrugged again. "I won't be around a lot anyway. Go for it."

I smacked him on the shoulder. "You sure? You're not putting on a brave little face now only to go sobbing in your pillow when you get back home?"

An eyeroll was his only answer. That fucker.

Jasper kicked me under the table. "Dude. Leave Ian alone."

I held my hands up, giving him my innocent eyes. "I'm just looking out for him."

"Since when are you all sensitive?" Nick asked.

"I've always been sensitive as fuck, Nicky."

He shook his head, smirking. "Nah, I know a bastard in love when I see one."

I snorted. "*Okay,* dude. Are we gonna paint each other's fingernails and discuss our feelings next?"

I didn't know what I was. Definitely obsessed. I couldn't get enough of Sylvia. In love? What did that even look like? We weren't anything like Nick and Dalia.

There were days over the last week I thought I was trapped in hell, living with Sylvia but not being able to touch her. She'd been adamant about keeping us a secret for now. Nothing in front of Emma. Not even holding hands. She didn't seem to understand the visceral need I had to touch her. Our contact was limited to nights in her bed. It wasn't nearly enough for me.

Was that love? Or physical attraction on steroids?

Ian tapped his fingers on the table. "Nothing wrong with a little nail polish, boys."

I glanced down at his hands, smiling at the black polish.

"You make it look good," I said.

"Nice dodge of the question," Nick said.

"I heard no question. Just a ridiculous accusation," I said.

"Doesn't seem that ridiculous," Jasper countered.

I stared into Jasper's eyes. "Fine, I admit I'm in deep, deep love with you."

He looped his arm around my neck, and laid a big, wet kiss on my mouth. I pushed him away, laughing.

"You think I'm easy?" I asked. "You gotta wine and dine me before you get this sugar."

The four of us busted out laughing while Tali gathered her things. "I'm really glad to be getting a break from you fools. It's like I work with high schoolers."

I raised my hand. "As the father of a high schooler, I can attest they're much more mature than us."

"How was Emma's first week back at school, by the way?" Tali asked.

"No problems. Her doctor is kinda amazed at her progress. She's still got a lot of physical therapy to do, but she'll be able to go to her homecoming dance next week and actually dance with her crutches."

I felt Ian looking at me, so I turned, raising a questioning eyebrow. "Yes?"

"Do you realize your face and voice completely changes when you're talking about Emma?" he asked.

"Uh, no, I didn't."

His mouth curved up. "It's fascinating."

"Cool."

"Well, I for one am glad she's on the mend. But tell me more about this dance. Does our daughter have a date?" Nick asked.

I snorted. "Holy shit, she's got a full-on boyfriend!"

I filled them in on the last couple weeks, keeping a smile plastered on. Syl had mentioned moving back to her place last night, and she might as well have punched me in the gut. Made me wonder if this thing between us was temporary to her while I was ready to call the movers and bring all her shit to my place. Hell, I'd even move into her rickety house if she asked me to.

She wasn't gonna ask me to, this much I knew.

As Tali left, Dalia came in the door, pulling along a little white dog with a smiling face and bat ears.

"No one told me there was going to be a party," she said, unclipping her dog's leash.

The dog ran straight for Nick, who picked him up and cradled him like a baby. I'd been aware of the existence of this dog, but this was my first time seeing them together. Nick had been wanting a dog since we were kids, so it warmed the cold, dead cockles of my heart to see his wish finally fulfilled. Because as much shit as I gave him, he was my brother, and I'd always root for him.

"What is that monster?" Ian asked.

Nick held the dog up for everyone to see. "This fine gentleman is Flamingo."

Dalia stood behind Nick and bent down to kiss his cheek, but he tilted his head back and got her on the lips.

"He's our son, *Ian*. Sadly, we now share custody with my sister Melly and Malka, so we only have him half the time. But I think he likes us better, right, babe?" Dalia smiled down at Nick.

"How could he not like us better?" Nick asked.

"We were just talking about Malka," I said.

Dalia sat down at the table. "Oh yeah?"

"How's she doing?"

"Pretty good, actually. She's living with Mel, writing music. She's happier than she was on tour," Dalia said.

"Aren't we all?" I asked.

She lifted a brow. "Are you?"

I scrubbed my jaw. "Oh god, when did we get all touchy feely? Yes, I'm happy. No, I don't know if I'll remain that way when Sylvia and Emma leave. Yes, they'll leave. No, I don't want them to. Did that answer your questions?"

A laugh bubbled out of her. "Well, damn. I wasn't expecting all that. Nick, I think David needs the Mingo treatment."

Nick plopped his dog on my lap, and the thing stared up at me with wide, black eyes. I swore he was smiling at me, maybe even laughing. I ran my hand down his back, and his warm, compact body *did* soothe some of my troubles.

"Is this dog magic?" I asked, only half joking.

Dalia reached over and rubbed his head. "He's just Mingo."

JASPER and I walked into the back of the theater, rehearsal already in full swing. A young black man who rivaled Ian in the height department stood in the center of the stage, singing a song I recognized from *Rent* in a deep, powerful voice.

"Whoa," said Jas.

He'd been at loose ends after we left Nick's place, so I invited him to come watch Sylvia's theater group. I spotted Emma in the front row, bouncing a baby in her lap.

"Yeah, whoa," I agreed.

The kid—Omar—had a voice to be reckoned with. He had the kind of rare talent, that if nurtured, would take him places. The trick was keeping it nurtured so it'd blossom instead of wither. I'd been lucky to have good teachers, a mom who forced me out of bed every morning for school and Nick cracking the whip at practice. I could've gone the other way easily.

"You cool if I talk to him after this? See if he'd be interested in coming into the studio?" Jasper asked.

I thought about it for a second, and I was really intrigued by the idea. "Yeah, go for it. See what he says."

We made our way up front as Omar ended his song and Sylvia talked to him about his performance, making grand gestures with her arms. I didn't fail to notice her also wiping her eyes.

I slid into the seat next to Emma, and her shoulders jumped in surprise. "Dad!"

Jas sat on her other side, and she jumped again. "Uncle Jasper!"

I laughed, nodding at the chubby baby in her lap. "Who's this?"

She held up his little fists. "This is my buddy, Xavier. His dad couldn't watch him today, so I get to hold him while his mom sings. Cool, huh?"

I had to wonder why the hell his dad couldn't give his mom a couple hours to rehearse, but I stopped myself in my tracks. How many things like this had Sylvia missed while my life barely changed?

Xavier smiled at me, drool bubbling on his lips. "Hey, buddy. You gonna watch Mommy sing?" He squealed and reached for me.

Jas leaned over, knocking my knee. "I think he likes you."

"Shhh!"

I looked up to see Sylvia watching us from the stage, her finger at her lips. "Quiet in the audience," she said.

I smiled and mimed zipping my lips.

"Hey, Jas," she said,

He saluted her. "Hey, Syl. Sorry we're interrupting."

"You're right on time to watch Xavier's mom, Monique, perform. You're in for a treat. She's singing 'I Dreamed a Dream' from *Les Mis*. My favorite," Sylvia said, winking at me.

A young, light-skinned black girl with a ponytail full of braids strode forward, finding her spot on the stage. She was tiny, barely five feet tall, with a delicate bone structure. I knew she was older than she looked, but seeing her and knowing this chubby baby was her son stirred a sadness in my chest. And when she began singing in a voice more powerful than her slight body should have been able to contain, I fucking choked up, especially when I heard the lyrics.

Life killing dreams.

Dreams unused and wasted.

She owned the stage, belting out these words that should have meant nothing to a girl her age, but she probably understood more than most. Her life wasn't over, of course it wasn't. Look at where Sylvia had gotten herself.

Before I got too far in my own wallowing, Xavier reached for me.

"I think he wants you, Dad," Emma whispered.

Holding him under his arms, I lifted him onto my lap. We watched his mother sing together, his little head resting on my chest. I dipped my head, inhaling his curly hair. He smelled like Emma had as a baby, clean and powdery. Delicious.

"This brings back memories," I whispered.

"You should have another baby. I've always wanted a brother or sister. I'd babysit," Emma whispered back.

I kissed her hair. "Don't think that's in the cards."

When Monique's song ended, we stood, Xavier bundled in my arms, and clapped for her. Jasper whistled and stomped, making Monique blush and giggle.

AT THE END OF REHEARSAL, I handed Xavier back to Monique. "His dad doesn't know what he's missing. He's a gorgeous kid," I said.

She grinned, rubbing her nose on his cheek. "Thank you. Hopefully he'll get it right soon. We don't need him if he doesn't. Do we, Xavi?" The baby cooed, laying his head on her chest.

After everyone left, including Jasper—who'd offered Sylvia whatever help she needed in the future for her program— Emma, Sylvia, and I headed out. I got Emma settled in the back-seat of my car, then walked Sylvia to hers.

She touched my cheek briefly, then twined her fingers with mine. "Don't be sad for Monique."

I bowed my head. "She's just so young."

"Seventeen. Older than I was. And she has a mom who helps when she can."

"You're doing such a good thing here."

She smiled. "You know I love it, right? It's my absolute plea-sure to work with those kids. They blow my mind."

I squeezed her hand in mine. "I really wanna kiss you right now."

She went up on her toes, peering over my shoulder at Emma in my car. "She's not looking. Go for it."

Not wasting a second, I pulled her against me, kissing her deeply. She wouldn't give me long, so I slid my tongue in her mouth, needing as much of her as I could get. She sighed, clutching at the front of my shirt as she leaned in to the kiss.

I had to rip my mouth off hers, because there was no part of me that wanted to end it. She felt too good in my arms. Tasted too good on my tongue.

"See you at home?"

She bit her bottom lip. "Yeah, see you at your place, David."

With her very deliberate words, any high I'd gotten from that kiss faded. *My place.* Right.

TWENTY-FIVE

SYLVIA

GOOD THING there was caution tape around my heart, or the sight of David Wiesel, tattooed rock star and my one weakness, snuggling with a baby, would have flattened me.

I was well and truly armored.

As real as this tender side of David felt and looked, it wouldn't last. This was a smooth spot in fifteen years of tumult. A month was nothing.

I couldn't let myself believe otherwise.

Even though this last month had felt like everything.

After dinner, I left David and Emma playing video games and hid in my room. I needed Suz. She'd talk me out of my flights of fancy.

It took two rings for her to pick up my call.

"What's up, stranger?" she answered.

"Hey. I'm just here in this fancy condo, missing my old house and my best friend. How's the bean?" I asked.

"The bean is homicidal. Or is it matricidal?"

I laughed. "Does it matter? You're telling me the bean is attempting to murder you?"

"That's right. Don't give me that tone. This first trimester shit is for the birds. I'm exhausted and my tits are killing me. Of course, Mika wants to touch them all the time because they're already two times their normal size."

I sat in the chair in the corner of my room, smiling. "I never got pregnancy boobs. I did have the barfs, but I chalked it up to my mom's terrible cooking."

"The denial is strong with this one," she said.

"Cheers!"

"Anyway, I'm just going to warn you, being pregnant at thirty-seven is far different than it was at twenty-one. When I made my first appointment with my doctor, the nurse informed me this is a geriatric pregnancy, so I'm higher risk. Geriatric, Sylvie! Can I borrow Emma's walker? I'm going to need it, since I'm geriatric!"

"You're still almost a decade younger than my mom was when she had me," I said.

"Wonder what they called her pregnancy? Tales from the Crypt?"

I snorted. "Is Mika taking good care of you?"

"Are you kidding? He's so in love with me and this baby. I swear, he walks around with a permanent smile on his face." Her voice lowered. "It's so damn different than when I was pregnant with Ev. Chris tried to be happy, but his next fix was always going to come before being a dad. It's cool not being scared this time."

A lump formed in the back of my throat. I didn't know what that was like, and I couldn't say I wasn't just a tiny bit jealous, but mostly, I was happy for my friend.

"If you're crying, I'm sending my homicidal bean after you. You're not allowed to make me cry, Sylvie!"

I choked out a laugh, wiping away the one tear that had escaped. "I'm not crying, you're crying!" I said.

"Bish, you better not make me cry."

"Okay, mama. There was a reason for this call, besides getting threatened."

"David, right?"

I sighed. "Of course."

"Don't hate me, but I kind of like him."

"Suuuuuz..." I groaned. "You're supposed to be talking sense into me!"

"Tell me what you want me to say and I'll do my best."

I got up, pacing the length of my room. "First of all, you're not supposed to like him."

"I know. I really tried. He's a bastard, but a likeable bastard. I mean, he came over to help Mika clean up. And then he talked music with Evan for a solid hour. Ev's ready to plaster his room with Blue is the Color posters."

Needing more room for pacing, I went into the hallway. The sound of video games carried from the living room, so I had privacy, even out of my room.

I rested my forehead on the wall, gathering my thoughts. "What I'm feeling can't be real. And it's definitely not smart."

"What are you feeling, honey?"

"Big, life changing things. But I don't want to change my life. I love my house and my neighborhood and the quiet of it all. It's the kind of life I dreamed of when Emma was a baby."

"Except the dream wasn't for it to be just the two of you," Suz said.

"Maybe. But that was a dream. This is real life. And he's always going to be the man who broke my heart."

I wandered into David's room, not turning on the light. We were so high up, the street lights didn't reach. The glow of the full moon was the only light in the room.

"Does he know what happened after the engagement party?" Suz asked.

I walked over to the window, staring up at the moon. It

looked so pretty from here, all smooth and radiant. I was drawn to it, even though I knew up close, it was cratered and bumpy, and the gleam wasn't its own. But those craters didn't make it ugly, not when you knew they were from being battered by passing meteors for its entire existence. The craters were its story, its battle wounds.

"No. There's no point in telling him," I said.

"There is if that's what's holding you back."

"*Everything's* holding me back. I want stability. I want someone who's going to be there, without question."

"You had all that with Vince."

I sat down on the edge of David's bed. "Yeah, I did. But..." Absently, I played with the drawer of the bedside table, sliding it open and closed until something inside caught the reflection of the moon.

"But David."

"Right. David." When I pulled the frames from the drawer, I nearly dropped my phone. In the first, there was a picture of Emma and me at the beach last summer, each of us holding a giant ice cream cone. We'd asked someone to take our picture on the boardwalk. The second picture was from the same trip. Emma and I had taken a walk on the beach at sunset. She'd just gotten a new phone, courtesy of David, with a fancy camera attached. We took turns taking pictures of each other, and she'd caught one of me laughing, the sky behind me appearing to be on fire.

David had it framed, in a drawer next to his bed.

"I...can I call you tomorrow, Suz? I need to do something."

I hung up after saying goodbye and sat there with the picture in my shaking hands.

"I put them away because I was embarrassed for you to see them."

His low voice jolted me. I twisted on my spot on the bed, watching David approach.

He sat next to me, glancing from my face to the picture. "Emma probably sent me fifty pictures from your trip. When I got to this one...I don't know how to explain it. It was like my heart got stuck. It didn't skip a beat, it just couldn't move on."

"I didn't know you ever thought about me."

"Yeah, well...is it weird I thought about you all the time? I always have. A lot of it was curiosity. I wanted to *know* you. I'd see you over the years and wonder what you did the day before and where you were going the next day. I'd be on tour, drunk, high, homesick for a home I never had, and all I could do was fantasize about being cozy with you and Emma." He laughed to himself. "I remember being in London...probably seven or eight years ago. It was dreary as hell and I was sitting in the hotel lobby so I wouldn't be alone, and I pictured you making soup. I could almost smell it, it was so vivid. No one's ever made me soup before, unless it came from a can. But I was positive you'd make homemade soup. I would've cut off a limb or summoned forth a hell demon if I could've been beamed into your kitchen."

My breath caught. "That's..."

"Weird, right? I was most likely on a cocktail of drugs at the time, but—"

I covered his mouth with my hand. "David. Stop. I don't care if you were high. And maybe it's weird, I don't know. It's definitely the least sexy thing someone's ever said to me. And yet...I really need you to kiss me right now."

He leaned in, smiling against my mouth, then his lips took mine. He didn't pussyfoot around when it came to kissing me. There were no teasing nips and nibbles. His tongue went deep, and he claimed my entire mouth as his.

"Em?" I murmured between kisses.

"Her room. My door's locked."

I pulled my T-shirt over my head and climbed on David's lap. I held his face in my hands, kissing and kissing him. Overcome from his admission and story, the only way I could deal with the surge of emotions powering through my system was to replace it with passion.

David shifted, laying me on the bed and kneeling between my legs. With his eyes locked on mine, he hooked his fingers in my panties and inched them down my legs. I knew I was wet. I knew I could take him easily. But from the hungry look in his eyes, he was going to take me first.

He kissed every inch of my torso, tugging my nipples between his teeth until I had to muffle my screams with my fist, licking each letter of the lyrics tattooed on my ribs, circling his tongue inside my belly button.

I spread my legs wide in invitation. He settled between my thighs, drawing in a deep inhale of my scent. "I love the way you smell." He dragged his tongue up my center. "And taste. You taste like my favorite memories."

I rolled my hips involuntarily, and he caught me, hands sliding under my ass to hold me up to his mouth. I ran my fingers through his hair as he lapped at me. He didn't tease; my clit was the main attraction. His tongue was genius, working me so quickly, he had me coming in minutes, my thighs clamping around his head.

He let me ride his face, eking out every ounce of pleasure from my climax on his tongue.

When my hips collapsed, David laid his head on my belly, his breath hot on my skin. I ran my hands through his hair, and in those seconds in between, I'd never felt so close to another human being, besides my child.

"Come here," I whispered.

He crawled up my body, and I pushed at his shirt. He reached behind his head and yanked it off, then pressed his chest to mine. My arms circled his neck, and his hips settled between my legs. The weight of him was glorious. I loved being pressed into the bed, no hope of getting away.

David's hands bracketed my face, and our eyes were locked. Everything stopped. No more ticking clocks, no more spinning Earth, no more tides in the ocean. Only his breath and mine, his heartbeat and mine. I nudged my chin against his, and his mouth curved into a smile.

"It'd be a crime if I looked away from you right now," he said, voice thick, like it was full of the words he wasn't saying.

"So don't." Mine was just as thick.

Reaching between us, I freed his cock from his sweatpants and positioned him at my opening. He pushed into me, more gentle and caring than he'd ever been, never looking away from me.

This was something we'd never done. We'd fucked every which way from Sunday, but we'd never gone slow, never made love.

The tenderness in his gaze was almost too much. I closed my eyes, but David's fingers fluttered over my eyelids.

"Look at me, Syl."

I opened my eyes, meeting his.

"Yeah," he sighed. "There you are."

His movement was languid, rotating his hips in a way that had my back bowing and fingernails digging into his shoulders. "Keep doing that," I urged.

Again and again, he brushed against my clit. Just a brush. A feather light touch. But I was throbbing and swollen, and *just a brush* meant touching a thousand live wires directly under my flesh. Little tremors shot through me each time he pumped into me.

"I'm staying here all night," he said.

I nodded. "Okay."

I wouldn't argue. I never wanted this to end. Not the way he looked at me, not the way he touched me, and never the way he made me feel.

David touched my face and hair, his fingers tracing the outline of my ears and lips. I pulled him down and sucked his bottom lip between mine. He moaned, his fingers curling in my hair, his brow pinching. Finally, he gave in and closed his eyes, pouring himself into our kiss.

I closed my eyes too, surrendering to him completely. I felt cherished and desired....and maybe a little bit loved. Lifting my legs, I wrapped them around David's waist, writhing when he plunged even deeper inside me.

He dragged his callused fingertips between my breasts, resting over my heart for several beats before moving to cup my breast. The feel of his rough fingertips on the delicate skin had me whimpering.

I came again when he reached between us, rubbing slow circles around my clit. And then again when he used his talented tongue on my nipples, teasing and lapping until I thought I'd die.

We were both sweaty, but still, he stayed. Twin lines formed between his brows as he concentrated on staving off his orgasm.

David rolled us to our sides, his big body practically covering my back. He kissed the back of my neck and along my shoulders, goosebumps spreading across my skin.

"David," I sighed.

He rested his face next to mine. "I know, sweetheart. I know."

His hand pressed on my belly as his hips finally picked up the pace, plunging in deep and hard. My pussy was so sensitive, it was almost painful. But the good kind of pain. The *best* kind of pain.

He pumped into me once more, then swiftly pulled out, his cock jerking between my folds, cum spilling down my thighs.

Careless.

We were being so careless.

It scared me. I wasn't a careless person. I was deliberate in my actions, but I'd gotten so caught up, the consequences didn't seem to matter. When David was touching me, he became my world.

I pressed my face into his pillow, the scent of him filling my nose. My hands trembled as I clutched the pillowcase. I couldn't keep doing this.

If he was my world, what happened when he went away? What happened when he left me drifting in space, no air for my lungs, no ground for my feet?

David kissed my shoulder and pulled me against him.

"Turn over, Syl. Let me look at you," he said.

I closed my eyes and pulled in as much air as my lungs could take, then I wiped away whatever worries were lining my face and turned, wrapping my arms around him. I'd let myself have tonight. Tomorrow I'd be deliberate.

TWENTY-SIX

DAVID

THEY WERE LEAVING.

I had them for one more week, and then they were moving back home.

Something changed after Sylvia saw the picture and we had sex. I saw it the second it was over. Her expressive face went blank.

She waited until the next day to tell me Emma's doctor said she'd be fine climbing steps now. I knew that was true; I'd been to almost every physical therapy session and saw the progress she'd made. What I didn't believe to be true was her reason for leaving.

There was a disconnect between us—something I wasn't getting, and she wasn't sharing. I'd fucked up a lot over the years, but when Sylvia had told me I wasn't too late to set things right, I'd been hoping she hadn't just meant with Emma.

I had another week with her, but she was already fading at the edges, slowly disappearing.

Sylvia still welcomed me into her bed and body, but I couldn't stop her from looking away.

It made me panic. A chilling, consuming panic. The

thought of Sylvia going back to being a stranger, of my relationship with Emma becoming stilted, of sitting in this giant condo
day after day, all alone.

And I was angry. So fucking pissed.

I had no say in this shit. What Sylvia said went. She didn't
ask what I thought. She just informed me of what was
happening.

I couldn't even bring myself to try to convince her to stay
because as her edges faded, mine darkened and closed in. On
the road, when I got like this, I'd smoke a blunt, fuck a random
chick, or take it all out on stage. I didn't know what the hell to do
at home, so the darkness kept right on seeping in.

I WAS PULLING on my boots when Sylvia walked in. She
took a half-step back when she saw me in the foyer.

"Oh, hey. Am I late?" she asked, glancing down at my shoes.

"Nah. Wasn't sure if you were coming," I said.

Her mouth curved down. "I told you I'd be back after I
dropped Emma off..."

I stuffed my hands in my pockets, watching her blankly.
"And now you're here."

She stepped into me, laying her hand on my chest. "Are you
okay?"

"Yep. I'm cool. Was Emma excited?"

She peered up at me, concern stamping her face. I could
barely look at her.

"Yeah. Evan gave her a corsage and his tie matched her
dress. Suz and I both cried. I wish you came," she said.

"I'll see the pictures. Glad she's happy."

Sylvia had driven Emma to Suz's house to take pictures
before she and Evan and a bunch of their friends left for the
Homecoming dance. I'd wanted to go, but my mood was so piss

poor, I'd passed. Seeing the way Sylvia and Emma weren't surprised that I declined the invitation made me loathe myself more than ever.

I probably should've locked myself in my room. I wasn't fit to be around people. Yet here I was, taking Sylvia out on the fuckin' town.

Sylvia seemed flustered, and I didn't blame her. I was being an ass.

"Um, I'm going to go change into different jeans. Give me five minutes." She gripped my shirt as she searched my face. "Five minutes," she repeated.

When she left, I leaned against the wall, deflated. We were going to see Flashing Numbers play with my boys from Blue. I'd been looking forward to tonight for weeks—to taking Sylvia out, listening to some good music, hanging out with friends.

Now, it felt all wrong.

All the shit I thought I felt, thought I could have, was unraveling, and the only thing I could do was watch.

"Okay, I'm ready."

Sylvia came hurrying into the foyer, hopping as she pulled on an ankle boot. She hadn't changed into jeans, but a little red dress, not unlike the one she'd worn at her engagement party.

"You're so pretty, it hurts sometimes," I said.

She straightened, her icy eyes unreadable. "I don't want you to hurt."

I scoffed softly. Too late for that. "Ready?"

Slipping on my leather jacket, I held the door for her, and she walked by me, her hands trailing over my stomach.

A car waited to take us to the venue downstairs, and when we got in, Sylvia snuggled up to me, weaving her fingers with mine. I stared down at our hands, studying the delicate veins running under her smooth skin. My hands were rough, thickly callused from my years on the guitar. They didn't have any business holding a hand like Sylvia's.

"David," she said softly.

I brought my eyes up to hers, raising a brow.

"Are you...am I misreading things? Are you tired of me?"

My heart clenched, and I cupped her cheek. "Never. Not possible."

"Will you talk to me?"

"Later. I'm just a grumpy asshole right now. I'll be better later, after the show."

She sighed, leaning back in her seat, slightly away from me.

THE VENUE WAS CROWDED, thick with shiny, happy people getting drunk and listening to music. We found the boys at a private table, elevated to give a decent view of the stage. An opening act was already playing, but they didn't grab my attention.

Nick stood first, clapping me on the back. "My man. Our cover's been blown."

"No shit?"

"Yep, their manager knows we're here. We've been invited on stage with them."

I nodded. "I could use some stage time. I'm down."

"I'm gonna sit this one out. Ian too," Nick said. He looked over my shoulder. "Hey, Sylvia."

She stepped in front of me, giving Nick a brief hug. Then each of my bandmates took their turns hugging her, completely ignoring my presence. I got it. I really did. Sylvia had a quality that drew people to her, me included. She cared, and she wasn't afraid to show it. She asked questions, remembered details, and was unfailingly kind. Even to motherfucking Ian.

Syl and I took our seats between Ian and Dalia. She leaned

in to ask if I minded if she had a drink, and I told her to go ahead. I almost told her to funnel that shit down my throat while she was at it, but I refrained.

I'd be calling Mark tomorrow, because this feeling wasn't good. I needed to talk it out, ease my way through it. I just had to get through tonight.

I sat there, listening to the opening act, not really attempting to be part of the conversations around me. I felt Nick watching, and I was glad for it. My ass needed to be watched. I needed those pecks at my feet to keep me on my toes, because falling back into old habits was always gonna be the easiest route.

Sylvia leaned in, speaking against my ear. "Want to come dance with me?"

I turned, my nose brushing hers. "Nah, baby. I'm good."

Her frown was immediate, and her rebuke was sharp. "Don't call me that, David."

"Sorry, Syl. Won't happen again."

"Don't be sorry. Just dance with me."

I twisted her hair around my fingers, playing with it lazily. "You go, I'll watch."

"Fine. I'm going."

I know. You were always gonna go.

She and Dalia ventured into the crowd together. The band, whoever the fuck they were, played a decent beat, and Sylvia knew how to move. She whipped her head back and forth, sending her silky strands flying around her face. Dalia cozied up behind her, grabbing Syl's hips and grinding against her.

They were quite the pair. The contrast of the two was unbelievably sexy, with Dalia's mane of red curls and naughty cherub face, and Sylvia's unusual beauty and black glass hair. Sylvia's dress rode up her thighs as she swayed her hips, and Dalia laughed from behind her, saying something to make Sylvia laugh too.

I felt actual yearning for her. My stomach rolled with it. It was hard to breathe.

A distraction came in the form of James Ishimura, Ian's friend and lead singer of Ginza Daydreams. He sat down in Sylvia's vacated chair, greeting everyone at the table. We'd toured together a couple times over the years, and he always had good stories.

Nick's eyes were glued on Dalia, but I turned away from the dancefloor, talking with Ian and James.

When I said Sylvia was so pretty it hurt, I meant literally. My joints ached, my heart was tied in barbed wire, my gut was on fire, and my head was in a vise. It was like I had the flu times a thousand. My thoughts weren't quite my own. They were muddled and slow.

Ian told James about the project he was working on composing. I was interested in what he said, but his words had to fight against the thick mud filing my skull.

I nodded along, trying my damnedest to pay attention.

Nick slid over a seat, drawing my attention. "You look like shit."

"Why thank you."

"You thinking about taking a drink?" he asked.

I sighed. "Maybe. I won't, but the thought is there."

He gripped my shoulder, his face somber. "What's happening?"

"Syl and Em are going back to their place."

"Why? Did you ask them to stay?"

I shook my head, the barbed wire around my heart pulling. "It's just time. Syl wants to go. Not much I can say."

"David, that's some bullshit. Syl can't read your mind," Nick said.

"Man, fuck off. I don't wanna talk about this anymore. It's really none of your business anyway." I shrugged his hand off.

"You know I'm not gonna fuck off. Have I ever?"

I scowled and slammed my fist on the table in front of me. "Do what you want, Nicky. I'm done being your pet project."

"Jesus, and I thought you were an asshole when you were drunk." He stared me down, but I was the one who broke, turning away.

He and I had been down this road. His disappointment killed me. I'd rather he punched me in the gut than see him look at me like that.

James grabbed my attention, giving me a diversion from Nick's constant worry, just when I didn't think I could take another second of it.

"I heard Blue is the Color is taking a year off," James said.

I leaned in, nodding. "Yep. That's the plan right now."

His head bobbed. "Cool, cool. Ginza Daydreams is taking a break too. We're all pursuing other projects, which is what I wanted to talk to you about."

I quirked a brow. "Yeah?"

"Yeah. You know Rico Almada?"

"Drummer from Blossoms and Bones?"

He pointed at me. "You got it. So, we're doing something like Audioslave...you know, guys from different bands recording an album together. Only, this would be a one off. None of us want to leave our bands, but we're all looking to diversify. Interested?"

The idea intrigued me. My fingers were itching to play, and I could really use that high from getting on stage. "Hell yeah, I'm interested. Would we record in Baltimore?"

"That could be negotiated. Do you need to stay local?"

I shrugged casually. "Nah, I could travel. What would touring look like?"

"We're thinking three to four months. Hitting all the major U.S. cities, then a few in Europe and Asia. Not stadiums. We'd go intimate, play in clubs like this one." He gestured to the walls of the venue.

"I could do that. I'd need to know specifics, but like I said, I'm definitely interested."

Right now, I would've probably taken any job that didn't leave me sitting alone in my empty condo.

Flashing Numbers hit the stage, ending the conversation. But that was okay. At least I now had something else to think about besides how much I sucked at life.

I sat there, leaning back in my chair, flipping my bottle of water back and forth between my hands, listening to the music. Despite their name, they weren't flashy. There were five of them, and they looked impossibly young. But maybe I'd just gotten old.

They were cool as shit. Rough, but there was something there. I made eye contact with Jasper, and he grinned. He thought so too.

I glanced at Nick to check his reaction, and saw Dalia in his lap, both swaying to the beat.

Where the fuck was Sylvia? I scanned the area around the table, and she wasn't there. I stood, ready to tear the place down to search for her, only to find her perched rigidly on a bar stool behind Ian, a beer bottle in her hand, her shiny eyes on the stage.

I stood there, staring at her, this beautiful, amazing woman who was leaving me without looking back. She wouldn't look at me. But that only made sense. I could barely look at myself.

TWENTY-SEVEN

SYLVIA

I SAT BEHIND DAVID, unseen, blending into the background apparently. Or maybe he knew I was there. It'd been years since I'd felt that invisible, listening to David make plans to go on tour. No hesitation, no mention of his promises to his daughter...or me.

So much for sticking.

My heart didn't break. It had been broken and repaired so many times over the years, this time, it crumbled. Each patch, each fissure, completely fell apart.

I needed some distance from him. Emma and I needed to get back into our routine. I thought maybe if I went back home, we'd see if what we had was real and lasting and not just a byproduct of our proximity.

I guessed my question was answered. No need to wonder anymore.

Reality was stark, and it was gutting.

David was leaving.

I sat on my stool, unmoving, unseeing. Awareness of David's eyes on me pricked at my skin, but I didn't dare look. I couldn't face him, not right now. A scream was stuck in the back of my throat, and if I were to open my mouth, I wasn't sure I'd be able to hold it back.

Eventually, David walked away, heading toward the stage. The band announced his name, and he sauntered on stage, looking every bit the rock star he was in his worn jeans, unlaced boots, and snug T-shirt, displaying arms covered in tattoos.

It was surreal to think I'd slept in those arms last night, because now, I only saw him as a stranger. He was the poster on my wall, the rock god fantasy. He wasn't my man, and it was a ridiculous notion to think he could've been.

When he played his borrowed guitar, the crowd went crazy for him. I knew the feeling. I knew it so well. David was achingly beautiful under the spotlight, his fingers flying over the strings.

That stage was where he belonged. His fans were all the love he needed. Emma was an afterthought, and I...I was a diversion. A warm body to keep the quiet at bay. And maybe being with me had assuaged some of his past guilt, just like the time he'd driven me to buy diapers, then made me go into the store by myself.

Sliding off my stool, I bent down to speak to Ian. He was the closet, and he most likely wouldn't ask questions.

"Hey, Ian, I have to go. If David asks, you can tell him I've gone home."

His head jerked as he met my eyes with a surprisingly sharp look. "Why wouldn't he ask?"

"Doesn't matter. I need to leave."

He caught my wrist, holding it for a beat. "I think you should probably wait."

I'd been mistaken about him, but what was new?

"I'm going. Have a good night."

An Uber appeared in minutes, taking me back to David's condo. Inside, I went to Emma's room first, throwing as many of her things as I could fit into her bag. She'd most likely be back, so if I left anything behind, she could get it then.

I hated thinking about telling her our time with David was prematurely over. She was spending the night with Avery after the dance, but tomorrow, I'd have to face her.

At least I had tonight to cry and scream as loudly as I needed to in my own house.

I left her bag by the front door, then went into my room. I was more careful with my packing, needing to fit everything into my bags. I knew without a doubt I would never step foot in this place again.

My breath caught when I heard the front door slam closed and my name bellowed. I packed faster as David's footsteps pounded in the opposite direction, toward Emma's room. Frantically, I zipped my bag and carried it out into the hall. David was coming out of Emma's room at the same time I reached the living room.

His face completely collapsed when he saw me holding my bag.

"Sylvia," he croaked.

"I have to go. Why wait another week?"

"You were leaving without saying goodbye?"

He stepped closer to me, and I held my bag in front of me, as if it would protect me.

"Were you going to say goodbye before you left to go on tour with that new band?" I countered.

He growled, his hands balling into fists as his sides. "Oh, come off it. You were already leaving. I'm not an idiot. Why shouldn't I consider going on tour?"

I threw my bag down on the ground. I needed my hands for this. "Forget me! Forget this thing you and I started. What about Emma? What about sticking? What about the record label you're supposed to be starting? You *promised*. But I knew.

You're not the sticking kind. You gave me every warning. *Your papa's a rolling stone*," I mocked. "I've had fifteen years of being let down by you, why the hell do I keep thinking it'll be different this time?"

"*Fuck*, Sylvia! It was! It *is*. I'm having some trouble with my anxi—"

I pushed at his chest as a fifteen-year-old avalanche came spewing out. "I don't care! Did you ever ask about my troubles? I didn't sleep for an entire year when Emma was born. I'd stand at my window, watching you come home from parties, drunk and happy while our baby wailed in my arms. Every time you came around, I dealt with the aftermath. Every damn time. You said you felt like you stepped away from your life for a minute and a lifetime had passed—well, how dare you step away. Stepping away should've never been an option; it sure as hell never was for me!"

His head bowed, like he'd given up. It only made me angrier.

"Look at me, David. I need you to hear why I'm packing my shit and leaving right now instead of next week."

Slowly, he raised his head, meeting my eyes. He looked as broken as I felt, but I couldn't let myself back down.

"You were right. You have bumbled around in my life, knocking things over and smashing others to bits from the second I saw you across the street, and I have loved you anyway." He winced at my words, but I wasn't even close to being done. "I came here that night."

His brow furrowed. "What? What night?" he rasped.

I searched his eyes, the same eyes I adored on my daughter, and I felt nothing. My smashed heart had hardened. I wore my armor, and it had come from him.

"You ruined my engagement party," I said.

"You didn't love him, Syl."

I pushed at his chest again, and he caught my wrists, immobilizing me. "You didn't have any right to make that choice! How dare you come and pretend you had some sort of feelings for me."

He shook my arms with each word he spoke. "I did. It wasn't anything like I have now, but I did. I wanted you."

"You wanted what I symbolized. A family. Comfort. It was never me. It still isn't."

His nostrils flared as he inhaled sharply. "It's you, Sylvia."

I barreled on. I had things that needed to be said, and I wouldn't be deterred. "I came here, David. After the engagement party was over, I used the code you'd put in my phone to get up here. Do you remember that?"

A deep line formed between his brows. "No...I don't remember. I know I got fucked up that night. Jesus, Sylvia, you told me no. You said no!"

"Did you hear the part about loving you? How could I not come?" I un-balled my fists, laying them flat on his chest. "Do you want to know what I saw when I walked in?"

He squeezed his eyes closed. He might not remember that particular night, but I was sure he remembered plenty of others like it.

"There had to be fifty people here. The entire condo had a haze over it. I couldn't hear anything with the music blasting. But I saw a lot. I should've turned right back around and left, but I guess there was a part of me that needed to know. So, I walked around the entire place until I found you. You looked really heartbroken, with those two girls in your bed. I mean, clearly you were devastated."

He pulled me into a hug, cradling the back of my head. His arms wrapped around me desperately, clinging to me. And for a minute, I let myself cling back.

"Sylvia, Sylvia, I'm so sorry, sweetheart. I'm so fucking

sorry," he murmured against my hair.

"I know you are, David. I know. But you see, I can't trust you."

"That's not me anymore, Syl. You know that."

I shook my head and pushed away from him. "I *don't* know that. You might not be drinking, but you're still careless."

"That's why you're leaving me?"

"I was moving back into my house, like we'd always planned! How can you call that leaving you?"

"You were pulling away and you fucking know it!"

I huffed, incredulous. "So you just decide, because you didn't like the way I was acting toward you, instead of calling me on it, or asking me to stay, or saying *anything*, you'd shut down and go on tour for months? You told that guy you had nothing keeping you in Baltimore! Do you have any idea what that felt like to hear? I'm *wrecked*, David. This is the very last time I'll let you do this to me."

"Shit, I didn't mean it like that. Even if I went out on the road, I'd come back between shows..."

I bent down and picked up my bags. "You can email me your plans once you know them, and we can make a schedule for Emma to stay here."

"Sylvia, don't. Don't do this."

I met his eyes one more time. "I might've let you talk me into staying had you not come inside me multiple times over the last week, like you were in this with me for the long haul. Like if you got me pregnant, you'd be here."

He reached out, but I jerked away.

"I got my period this morning, so you're off the hook. Still only one kid. I recommend wearing a condom in the future, though. Less messy in every way."

With those final, ridiculously bitter and ugly words, I left...and he let me go.

TWENTY-EIGHT

DAVID

MY MOM SHOWED up at ten the next morning.

I was sitting on my couch, staring blankly at a wall. At some point, I'd fallen asleep last night, but not for long. Maybe a couple hours. I woke up with a pounding heart, searching my blankets frantically.

But the thing I was searching for was gone. Or maybe I'd never had it.

After that, I couldn't stand to be in my bed. I could barely stand to be in my own skin. The panic from last night had abated, leaving nothing but a raging emptiness.

When my mom walked in with two yoga mats under her arm and a takeout tray holding two coffee cups, I barely acknowledged her.

She set everything down, then sat next to me on the couch, wrapping her arms around my neck. I leaned into her, laying my head on her chest.

I was a thirty-three-year-old man being held by my mom and I didn't give one shit, because I needed it. Little by little, as she stroked my hair, I came back to myself.

"How did you know?" My voice was unrecognizable to me. I sounded weak and pitiful.

"Oh, honey, Sylvia called me and told me everything. Through it all, she was worried about you."

I sat up, nodding. Of course she'd called my mom. Of course she'd been worried. That was Sylvia. I'd broken her heart, and she couldn't stop herself from caring.

"She okay?"

Mom sighed. "Yes, she's okay. Sad, but she's really strong. I'm in awe of her strength sometimes."

"Yeah, well, I'm falling apart here."

"That's bullshit."

My eyes shot to her at the harshness in her voice.

"You think Sylvia doesn't want to fall apart?" she asked. "When you're a mother, falling apart isn't an option. You think I didn't want to lay down and die when my husband, my love, slowly slipped away and became a monster? I wanted to. Every day, I wanted to give into the pain. But I had you, and you needed me. I had to get my shit together. Falling apart shouldn't be an option for you either."

I leaned my elbows on my knees, scrubbing at my bleary eyes. I heard her, knew she was right, but I wasn't quite ready to acknowledge just how right she was.

"I can't really talk about her right now."

She rubbed my back. "Then let's do some yoga."

I scoffed. "Nah, I'm not doing yoga."

"Why not?"

"Not into it."

"David," she said, voice stern. I turned, meeting her stare. "We're doing yoga. If it doesn't help, then we don't have to do it again."

"Help what?" I asked.

"Help you deal with the quiet and the noise."

I blinked at her, disbelieving. How'd she know?

As if hearing my question, she explained. "Before your dad started shooting heroin, he'd get these migraines that started after he got a concussion at work, and any lick of noise would send him into a blind rage. And I do mean blind, because he'd be in so much pain, he couldn't see. He became an entirely different person than the one I married."

She breathed in and out for a moment, and I held her hand. Because I was a self-centered asshole, it'd never occurred to me to think of my mother's pain. How it must've felt to see her husband consumed by addiction. And then later, to see her son consumed by his own addiction and anxiety. I'd hidden it, but there was no question she knew.

"From a very young age, you learned to stay as quiet as possible. We both did. And then, when he finally left, it was like you had to make as much noise as possible to make up for it."

"I can't stand the silence," I said.

"I know, honey. I was the same way until I started yoga. And now...the quiet is peaceful. And those noisy, anxious, angry thoughts that used to fill my head...they're still there sometimes, but I have techniques to ease them."

Jesus Christ, easing those thoughts sounded like a fairytale.

"I'll try it. At this point, I'll do anything."

She smiled, rubbing her hands together. "Yay, I'm so excited! I love practicing with a newbie."

I was dubious, but I was also pretty fucking desperate just to be able to function.

My mom set up our yoga mats facing each other, and I stood on mine. She took me through poses, her voice low and soothing. I wasn't convinced, but if nothing else, it felt good to stretch my tight muscles.

Finally, she had me on my knees, body folded forward, arms stretched in front of me—child's pose. The only sound was the faint traffic outside and our breaths. It made me uncomfortable, but I fought through it, letting my entire body release.

"Now, lay on your back. We're going to practice mindful breathing," she said.

I rolled over, stretching out flat on my back, hands pressed to the floor.

"When you're panicking, when everything feels too big, I want you to try this. Be mindful of one breath, and then the next. Not what is happening ten minutes from now, not what happened in the past. Only your breath. I promise you, there is peace to be found if you're able to stay in the now."

We were quiet for a moment, then she spoke again. "Feel the air entering your nostrils and traveling down to your lungs, filling your body. Feel it coming back out of your nose. When you breathe in, say, 'I am calming the feelings I am experiencing now,' and say it again when you breathe out. Don't control your breath, only be aware of it. Be comforted by it. Find peace in it. And surrender your pain to the peace. Let it go. Let it fade. There is only the next breath and the next."

I laid there for a long time, taking note of every fucking molecule of oxygen in the air. And the hell of it was, it *did* help. Even if it was temporary, some of the ache in me floated away. Some of the rattling in my brain was soothed. Being able to focus on something else other than my inner turmoil and heartbreak was a relief. The task of getting from one breath to the next wasn't insurmountable.

When we finished, I went to take a shower and get dressed, then my mom and I went out for lunch. It felt good to get outside, away from my condo and those walls. I figured I'd sell the place. Too many bad memories. And I didn't know that it was my style anymore.

Sitting across from each other, my mom covered my hands with hers.

"I made a lot of mistakes with you," she started. "I didn't shield you enough when you were little, and then I didn't push you hard enough when you grew up."

I chuckled under my breath. "You pushed me."

"But not in the right way! I was mentally fried from always working, I barely had the capacity to care for myself. Back then, in my mind, if you gave Sylvia money and watched the baby a few hours a week, you were doing your part. I take the blame for letting you get away with that. Yes, you were a father, but you were also still a kid."

"Mom...it doesn't matter whose fault any of it was. The fact is, I wasn't there when I should've been, and I keep messing up. I'm fucked."

She crunched on a piece of ice from her water as she looked me over.

"Do you love her?"

"Yes."

No hesitation. I did. I loved her. It was just that it didn't matter. When I thought of her seeing me with other women that night...how the hell could I expect her to get past that? I'm not sure I could if it were the other way around.

"Does she love you?"

"Why would she?"

She frowned. "David—"

I shook my head. "No, I'm serious. I've given her no reason to love me. I'm this fucked up guy who keeps coming in and out of her life, in and out of my kid's life, expecting them to be there at my whim."

"Okay, well, let me ask you this: do you want Sylvia to love you?"

I exhaled, squeezing my eyes shut. "Yeah. How could I not want that? I think I've always wanted that, I'm too much of a fucked-up asshole to figure out how to go about it."

"So, figure it out," she said.

"Real simple," I said dryly.

"It can be. You have all these reasons why Sylvia shouldn't love you, so make them not true anymore. Be steady. Find peace in your quiet. Talk to Emma, set up a schedule with her. Let her know you're committed to being here, whether you're with her mom or not. Find yourself. Make music, be happy. I think...if you do those things, and it still doesn't work out, then at least you'll be in a better place than you are now."

Our food came, and we ate, talking about other things. My mom was kind of incredible. She really practiced what she preached. She'd started over a decade ago, devoting herself to yoga and fitness. She taught classes at a gym, but she also went into schools to teach kids. Growing up, she'd always had a hard edge about her, a simmering anger I had to watch out for. I knew why, and I didn't blame her, not really. But it was impossible not to be inspired by the way she'd changed herself so completely.

It might take me a decade to be worthy of Sylvia...hell, it might take me a century, but I'd try. I had no choice in the matter. She was it for me. The beginning and the end.

Back home, I went out on the balcony and called my girl.

"Hey, Dad."

"What's shakin'?" I asked.

She giggled softly. "It's weird to be back home. I was surprised when Mom picked me up this morning. I thought we'd be coming back there."

"Yeah, well she thought it would be better for you guys to get back to normal. How're the stairs?"

"Surprisingly okay. I mean, it takes me ten minutes to get to my room, so I'll probably only go up there when it's bedtime, but it's no big deal."

"Good. I'm glad you're adapting." I rubbed at my chest. As

good as it was to talk to her, I missed her so much, it physically hurt. "Did you have fun at Homecoming?"

She sighed. "Oh my god, Dad. It was amazing."

I listened to her tell me every last detail about dresses and decor and how she'd managed to slow dance with Evan, even with her injury. I was smiling, despite myself. This kid was everything. *Everything*. How I thought for one second I should hit the road again when this time with her was so fleeting...

"I miss you, kid."

"Miss you too, Dad."

"You think you could come spend the night here after the showcase on Saturday? Maybe stay the weekend and I'll drive you to school on Monday?"

"Yes! Let me just ask Mom."

I heard her yelling to Sylvia, asking her if it'd be okay, and hearing her murmured response had me dizzy and seeing stars.

"She gave me the craziest look, but she said it would be fine," Emma said.

"She doing okay?" I couldn't help it. I knew I shouldn't be asking, but I had to know.

"Dad..." Emma's voice lowered, "did you two have a fight last night?"

"Aw, Em, don't worry about it."

"I'm definitely going to worry about it. I know you two are... or were, like, together, or whatever. Did you break up?"

I froze. This was one of those pivotal parenting moments, and I had no idea what the hell to say.

"Why do you think we were together?"

"First of all, you didn't deny it just now, and secondly, I mean, come on. I'm not dumb. It was obvious, with the way you were drooling over her and buying her flowers and kissing her when you thought I wasn't looking. And don't tell her I told you, but she looks like utter crap today. Do you look like utter crap?"

I had to laugh. "Yeah, Em, I think I do. But I really don't want you to worry about me. Nothing's changing. I love you like madness. In fact, I'm hoping we can set up a more regular schedule, so I can make sure we see each other as often as possible."

"That would be amazeballs. Will you help me with my homework?"

"You want me to help you with your homework?"

She snorted. "Not a chance! That was a trick. Want to take me out to dinner on Wednesday?"

"Abso-fuckin-lutely."

I DIDN'T SEE or talk to Sylvia for a week. Instead, every morning my mom showed up, we did yoga and I breathed. To tell the truth, I'd been doing a whole hell of a lot of breathing lately. Letting go, letting go, letting that shit go. Saying goodbye to the fear. Letting my anger drift away. With each breath, I pushed more of it out.

When I wasn't breathing, I was writing music or playing with Jasper. I had these words pouring out of me. A lot didn't make sense, a lot was shit, but there was some gold there too. And behind every lyric was Sylvia.

Emma nudged my knee. "The show's about to start."

I checked my phone. "Yep, it's time."

She bounced in her seat a little. "I'm really excited."

So was I. After a week of no Sylvia, I was gonna get to see her under the spotlight, singing her mystery song.

The kids from the theater group were amazing as always. Monique had the entire audience in tears and Omar blew the roof off. Emma grabbed my hand when it was time for Sylvia to take the stage.

My breath caught when the lights came up and she was

revealed. Monique and another girl were on either side of her, and the three of them swayed to the beat.

"Boy, you got me helpless..." she sang. Only, it wasn't quite singing, it was more of a slow rap.

From my weeks of living with Sylvia, I knew this song was from *Hamilton*, and she was singing the part of Eliza Schuyler falling helplessly for Alexander Hamilton. It struck me that Sylvia chose this song when we were getting started. If things had gone differently, I'd be taking her to my bed tonight, showing her just how helpless *she'd* made *me*.

Instead, all I could do was watch. She looked happy up there, and when Omar came out to rap Hamilton's part, the audience went crazy, and my heart went *boom* at the sight of her smile.

My world was a better place when she smiled.

Emma convinced me to come backstage with her after the show. I clutched a bouquet of wildflowers in my sweaty palms. I wasn't the guy who got nervous. Not on stage, and never with women.

But this was Sylvia Price, love of my fuckin' life. I was nervous as hell.

We found her surrounded by her performers and their families. Emma dove into the fray, hugging the kids and congratulating all of them, but I hung back.

I probably would've left if I hadn't been taking Emma home with me for the weekend. I'd have slunk out like a thief in the night, so I didn't have to see the flash of pain crossing Sylvia's face when she noticed me.

I saw it, though. And I felt it.

Eventually, Emma brought Sylvia over, and I handed her the flowers. Every muscle on her face was tight as she accepted them.

"Thank you. They're lovely," she said.

"Of course." I had to shove my hands deep in the pockets of my jeans so I didn't reach out for her. "I was...I was blown away by the show. Really, it was incredible."

She glanced back at the kids, finally allowing the smallest of smiles to break through.

"I'm very proud of them. They worked really hard." She wrapped her arm around Emma, giving her temple a kiss. "Have fun with your dad this weekend. I'll see you Monday."

That was that. She wasn't giving me anything else. And truly, I deserved less than I got.

Luckily, this was only the beginning.

If it took a hundred years, I'd wait a hundred years.

TWENTY-NINE

SYLVIA

My broken path was always leading to you.

I'D GIVE DAVID CREDIT. The man had a way with words. He'd slipped a card inside the flowers he gave me, and that one sentence had tears welling in my eyes. I'd promised myself I was all cried out, but that was apparently not the case.

This past week had been a jumble of emotions. Heartache and anger took the top spot, but confusion and I guess surprise he hadn't tried to reach out to me were also there. He'd talked to Emma almost every day, made plans with her and stuck to them. I think I'd expected him to fade back out of our lives, but he'd only faded out of mine.

I should've been grateful for it. This wasn't what I wanted, but it was what had to happen. My lingering questions about David had been answered. He wasn't ever going to be the man I needed him to be. I wasn't sure if he even wanted that role.

Monique came to hug me again, this time holding baby Xavier. I took him from her, needing a baby snuggle to set me right again.

"I'm going to miss you, Miss Sylvia," she said.

"Honey, this isn't the end. I'll still be at your school every other week, and I'm hoping you'll apply to the Hippodrome's intern program. And I'm always a phone call or text away. You need help with Xavier, or just to talk, don't hesitate. Got it?"

She laughed. "Got it."

I wasn't worried about her. She reminded me of myself in many ways; she was stronger than she even realized. Omar, though...I'd always worry about him.

He stood between two older people, so I went over to them, introducing myself.

"Thanks, Miss Sylvia. For everything."

His grandma nudged him. "Go on. Tell her."

He stared down at his sneakers. "Mr. David and Mr. Jasper asked me to record some vocals for them. Said they have some ideas for my voice."

I gasped. "Did they? When did they ask you that?"

"Mr. Jasper asked for my number when he came to rehearsal, and Mr. David called my grandma a couple days ago. You think he's serious?" Omar asked.

I reached out and squeezed his arm. "I do. David is pretty serious about music."

Omar nodded. "He's kinda famous, isn't he? I'm not into that music, but I've heard of his band."

I grinned. "Yeah, he's kinda famous."

His grandparents thanked me, and I made sure they had my contact info, even though I was completely thrown. I mean, Omar was amazing, and out of all my theater kids, he had a voice that could translate to rock or pop—he could be the next Khalid—but in a million years, I never would have expected David to contact him.

I went home, alone, elated, and more confused than ever.

. . .

MONDAY, I woke up to hammering outside. Mika had finally convinced me to let him and a couple guys replace the boards on my deck before it got too cold to work outside. I'd been expecting him today...just maybe not at seven in the morning.

Rolling out of bed, I got dressed for work since there was no hope of sleeping now. Luckily, I didn't have any meetings, so I went casual in jeans and a cozy sweater, my hair pulled to the side in a braid.

Downstairs, I made myself some coffee before I went to check on my deck. I couldn't be expected to be a polite human being without it—especially not when I'd been woken up forty-five minutes early.

With my mug in hand, I peeked through my sliding glass door. Mika and two heavily tattooed guys were working on ripping off the boards from the deck. Probably guys from the shop who didn't have to be at work until later in the day.

I slid the door open and leaned my head out, smiling. "Good morning! I have coffee if anyone's interested."

The three men turned at the sound of my voice, and my eyes skated over each of them. Mika, Trace from the shop, and...*David*? I almost dropped my mug.

"Wha—?"

Grimacing, Mika came to the door, blocking my view of the other guys. Of David.

"Did we wake you up?" he asked.

"No...yes, it doesn't matter. Why is he here?"

Mika glanced over his shoulder. "You have a problem with Trace?"

I glared at him. He was trying to be cute. He knew full well what had gone down between David and me. Had witnessed me sobbing in Suz's arms when I came home last weekend.

"I'll kick you," I warned.

Exhaling, he glanced over his shoulder again. "Look, he called, asked to help re-build your deck."

"This was his idea?" I hissed.

"Yeah. I know he's not your favorite person, but he's going to be out here. You don't have to see him at all. I'll tell him to leave if you want, but frankly, I need the extra set of hands."

"Fine. He can stay, but I'm not giving him coffee."

Mika gave me a crooked grin. "Then I suppose I shouldn't tell you he brought all of us coffee this morning. And donuts."

I put my hand on my hip. "Where's my donut?"

From behind Mika, David said, "Here, Syl."

Mika stepped aside, revealing David holding an open Dunkin' Donuts box. I didn't meet his eyes. I hadn't been prepared to see him, and my armor was still put away. I focused on his hands instead, but that wasn't better. My heart clenched behind my ribs. I could almost feel his callused fingers on my skin.

I quickly grabbed a bear claw from the box and started to slide the door closed, but David put a hand out to stop me at the last second.

"I dropped Em at school early. She said she had some study group."

I stared at his hand on the door, willing him to move it. "Thank you," I whispered.

He took a step closer, until the glass was the only thing separating us.

"I know you don't want to see me right now, so I'll do my best to respect that, but I'm not going anywhere. I'm in this for the long haul."

My breath caught in my throat at his use of the words *long haul*. It was what I had said to him that last night in his condo. I didn't know whether to be angry or completely demolished that he was saying it back to me.

"You're right," I rasped. "I don't want to see you. Please move your hand so I can close the door."

David took his hand back immediately, but he watched me as I slid the door the rest of the way closed. As I walked away, I felt his eyes on my back. *Damn, I'm going to need curtains for that door.*

EVERY MORNING for the next week, I woke to hammering. I didn't even mind it, since I'd taken to going to bed early and waking up with the sunrise. The nights were too long and lonely to stay awake. Even with Emma at home with me, I still ached.

I knew it would get better. I wouldn't always feel so gutted. It was just a matter of giving myself time. I'd been through upheavals before—too many to count.

But this one...oh, this one would take some time to move on from.

It was next to impossible not to spend my days thinking of David. He was right outside my door when I woke up. He called Emma after school, took her out to dinner. He was everywhere —even on the radio in my car.

Sometimes I'd think maybe I could soften, maybe I could speak to him, then I'd remember how into the idea of going on tour he'd been and got pissed off all over again.

I gathered my things for work, clacking around in high heels. This morning, I had to attend a board meeting to discuss our fundraising goals for the next year. My head was muddled— I hadn't even gone over the latest financial reports—but I looked good in my red pencil dress and black leather blazer. I didn't know the exact amount of money we had to raise, but I was aware it was a hefty, intimidating sum.

There was a tap at my front door, and I hurried to open it as I pushed an earring in my ear.

The smile fell from my face when I saw David on my porch.

His mouth opened in an O as he scanned me from head to toe, settling on my eyes.

I didn't give him an inch. My gaze was hard as I stared him down. I was glad to be wearing leather right now—it wasn't armor, but it made me feel badass.

"Yes?"

"You take my breath away, Sylvia."

I hated that I smoothed a hand over my hair, feeling an ounce of thrill at the way he looked at me.

"David," I sighed sadly.

He rubbed his eye with the heel of his hand. "Sorry, I didn't mean to say that. I mean, I meant it, but I hadn't planned on it. You're wearing red and I...sorry." He held up a sweater. "Em left this in my car last night. Thought she might want it."

I took it, and the very tips of his fingers grazed the very tips of mine, sending tingles down my spine.

"Thank you," I said, backing up from the door.

He leaned his head against the frame, watching me, but it was as if he had no choice in the matter. Like he was fighting, trying to look away, but his body wasn't cooperating.

I found I couldn't close the door. I wanted to. The urge to run and hide was strong, but my limbs weren't cooperating.

David was the first to break the spell. "I'll see you, Syl. Have a good day."

"Bye, David."

MY MEETING WAS...SURPRISING. Shocking, really. For the second time, I was glad to be wearing my leather, because when I went over the fundraising numbers for the community outreach department of the theater, I was completely flabbergasted. My face surely looked stupid as my jaw hung open, scanning the numbers again and again, but at least the rest of me looked badass.

I had to sit through the meeting, listening as the board fawned over the anonymous *celebrity* who'd donated five million dollars to the community outreach program. They fawned, I fumed. By the time I left the meeting, I was infuriated.

I locked myself in my office. This was not going to be a phone call fit for public consumption.

He picked up right away. "Sylvia? Is everything okay?"

I breathed in quickly through my nose. "Yes, David, everything's fine. However, I just left a fundraising meeting at work..."

He cleared his throat. "Yeah?"

"How could you?" I seethed.

"Uh, how could I what? You're gonna have to be more specific, 'cause there's a lot of shit you could be talking about right now."

"Did you think you could buy your way back into my life by making that donation?"

"What the hell? You're actually angry I made a donation?"

"Yes! You don't get to sweep in and act like the hero. First, you call Omar behind my back, and now this. You're not a savior. Neither I nor the kids need to be saved."

"Whoa, whoa, whoa. Cut that shit out right now. I already told you I made a donation weeks ago." David's tone had taken an edge.

"You didn't tell me it was five million dollars. I'm not...that ludicrous sum of money won't make me not hate you."

I heard his heavy sigh through the phone. "You know what, Sylvia? Not everything has to do with you. Yeah, I made a donation weeks ago, and then saw those kids, watched them perform, and I donated more. I never want that program not to exist. If someone else was teaching them, I'd feel the same way. And you wanna know about Omar? You actually think I'd get his hopes up because of my feelings for you? Listen to how that sounds. I *know* you hate me, and have every reason to, but this right here is not one of them. Omar blew me away from day one, and when Jasper saw him perform, and we both agreed to work with him in the studio, to see how it goes. It's kinda like we're starting a record label and looking for talent or something."

I slid down in my chair, my anger dissolving into embarrassment. This was one of those instances I should have counted to ten and thought things through before acting. But David made me lose my mind sometimes.

"Say something," he said.

"I don't know what to say. I'm feeling like an ass."

"A gorgeous ass."

I rolled my eyes. "Don't be flirty just because you have the upper hand at the moment."

"Don't worry, I am keenly aware of where I stand with you."

"Yes, well, you did a good thing, and I shouldn't have yelled at you. I'm sorry for that."

He chuckled softly. "Are you gonna think I'm a masochist if I say it was worth it to hear your voice?"

Ignoring his question, because it warmed my chest in a way I didn't want, I asked, "Are you taking Em this weekend?"

There was a long pause, probably from me giving him whiplash at my swift change in topic. "Uh, yeah. On Sunday. She has plans Saturday, apparently."

When he stopped speaking, I realized I'd been scribbling so hard on a notepad, I'd broken the tip off my pen and ink was spilling everywhere. "Crap, I made a huge mess..."

"Didn't think it was that bad," David said.

"What? No...well, yes, I made a mess with this phone call, but I also just broke a pen and I—" I waved a hand around, swiping at the air. "Doesn't matter. I have to go."

I hung up as quickly as possible and covered my face with my hands. My desk was a mess, that phone call was a mess, and *I* was a mess. I missed David more than I was prepared for, and I couldn't see myself stopping anytime soon. I'd have to buy stronger pens.

"DID you have a good weekend with your dad?"

Emma smiled at me from across the table. "Amazeballs. He's really taking to this dad thing."

I almost choked on my pasta. "Was he not taking to it before?"

She tilted her head, seeming to contemplate my question. "Before, it felt like music was his full-time life, and being my dad was a side gig. I know that sounds harsh, but it's true. We had a really good talk about it this weekend. And guess what else we did?"

Trying to keep any shakiness out of my voice, I said, "What did you do?" Turning my head, I wiped the damn tears from my eyes.

"Yoga."

"Yoga? With your dad?"

"Yep," she said proudly. "Grandma's been teaching him. He's even practicing mindful breathing and taught it to me."

"Wow. I'm...I don't know what to say. That's cool."

"Isn't it? We had probably the best time we've ever had together. It was almost as good as when I'm with you."

My heart swelled at how open with her feelings she was. I'd never been like that. From the time I was little, I'd learned that *big feelings* were the devil infecting me, and I should rid myself of them.

To this day, I sometimes still had to remind myself to share, with Em, with Suz, even with Gwen.

I smiled at her fondly. "That's all down to you, Em. I don't think it's possible to have a bad time with you."

She set her fork down and wiped her mouth with her napkin. "So..."

I scrunched my nose at her. "Oh no, were you just buttering me up?"

She peered sheepishly from under her eyelashes. "Maybe. But it's for a good cause."

"Yes?"

"Thanksgiving."

I was hosting Suz's family plus Gwen. Suz and I hadn't missed a Thanksgiving together since we became roommates all those years ago, but we'd graduated from turkey sandwiches to a full spread.

"Yes?" I repeated, brows raised.

"Dad doesn't have anywhere to go, and since Grandma's going to be here..." she trailed off, blinking her beautiful brown eyes at me.

I sighed. I didn't want to say yes. It would absolutely kill me to have him here, but how could I say no?

"Fine."

She sprung up, hobbling around the table to hug my neck. "Thank you, thank you! Can you text him to tell him he's invited? I don't think he'll believe me."

I closed my eyes, releasing a slow breath. "Yes, I'll text him."

She kissed my cheek with a loud smack. "Love you, Mom."

"Love you the most," I replied.

When Emma was busy with her homework and I'd procrastinated for as long as possible, I sent David a succinct text.

You're welcome to celebrate Thanksgiving with us.

Less than a minute later, he texted back.

David: *I almost said that's amazeballs, but I stopped myself.*
Me: *Emma kind of wears off on you. We'll have dinner at five, but everyone will be hanging out all day, so feel free to come whenever.*
David: *What can I bring?*
Me: *Are you going to cook?*
David: *If that earns me a seat at the table, I will.*
Me: *I'm intrigued. What can you cook?*
David: *I make a mean lasagna.*
Me: *Will it be conveniently portioned into single servings?*
David: *Damn, my plan to thaw all my pre-made meals out and pass them off as my own has been ruined. Now how am I gonna earn my seat?*
Me: *Fruit? Can you bring fruit?*
David: *I can, but are we talking like a bag of apples (I know about your fondness for Honeycrisp), or like chopping shit up? I've got my sleeves rolled up, and I'm ready to dive in, just tell me what I should be doing.*

I laughed, then covered my mouth to stop myself. How could I be laughing at David? Then again, how could I be inviting him to spend the day at my house? That brief glimpse I got of him each morning when he was helping Mika with my deck was enough to make me ache for the rest of the day.

Me: *I think I'll leave that up to you and see what you come up with.*
David: *Can I Google this shit?*

Me: LOL...it's possible.
David: Seriously, thank you. I know you don't want me there, but I appreciate you letting me be there anyway. It means a lot.
Me: It's not that I don't want you here. I'm just...not really over anything yet. But truly, I'm happy we'll all be together, and I expect it to be a lovely day.
David: I'm never gonna be over you, Syl. It hurts to see you, but I'll take the hurt. You're my reason. You and Em. I'm not asking for you to say anything back right now, but I want you to know I'm not giving up.

I read and re-read and re-read his message. I'd thought, maybe, since he hadn't been pursuing me, and with a few exceptions was mostly leaving me alone, he was moving on. And now...as steady as I was in my conviction I was finished with him, he had me feeling shaky.

Me: I don't know what to say.
David: You really don't have to say anything. I have no expectations, just hope. I'll see you Thursday.
Me: See you Thursday.

DAVID WAS the first to arrive on Thursday. In fact, he came to the house so early, I hadn't showered or gotten dressed. I opened the door in my flannel pajamas, hair piled in a messy bun on top of my head and a stalk of celery in my hand.

"Hi," I said, blinking rapidly.

"Hey..." He scanned me from messy head to bare toe. "I've messed it all up already, huh?"

I pulled the door open, waving him inside. "No, you haven't. There's nothing wrong with being early."

He nodded at the celery I held. "You've graduated from shivs to celery?"

A smile tugged at my lips. "Maybe. I've taken a grown man down with less." It was the wrong thing to say, considering, and I regretted it immediately, especially when David's shoulders fell. "I promise not to hit you with my celery if you come in."

He stepped over the threshold, and I pointed to the platter in his hands. "Can I take that?"

He stared down at it like he had no idea how it had gotten in his hands, then he held it out to me. "I hope I did it right."

After he kicked off his boots, I led David into the kitchen and lifted the plastic wrap off the tray.

"Is it okay? It's hella cheesy, right?" He stood next to me, the sleeve of his button-down brushing mine. I lifted my eyes to his, my lips parted in a gasp.

"You did this?" My words were barely audible. My nose tingled, and I had to press my lips together in a tight line to stop them from quivering.

His eyes widened with concern. "Are you about to cry?" He glanced down at the most outlandishly beautiful turkey—the body was a pear with chocolate chip eyes and beak, and then surrounding it were grapes, kiwis, strawberries, and melon making up the feathered tail—and then back up to me.

"Shit, sweetheart. Tell me what I can do. Want me to throw this out?"

I shook my head and gripped his arm, stopping him from tossing the platter in the trash.

Sucking in a deep breath, I attempted to speak normally. "No, please don't. I didn't expect you to go all out like this."

He tugged at the sleeve of my pajamas, then lowered his hand, his pinky brushing mine. "Told you I was gonna Google this shit."

I tried to laugh, but a tear slipped out at the same time. "You did. You certainly did." I wiped my cheek with my sleeve. "I should probably go shower now. Would you mind grabbing the door in case we have any other early birds? Emma's still sleeping."

His eyes moved to the stairs and he grinned crookedly. "Damn, I really *am* early."

WHEN I'D SHOWERED and gotten control of my urge to cry over turkey-shaped fruit and the man who made it, I came back downstairs to find David at the dining room table sipping a cup of coffee.

David glanced up as I approached, and the searing look he gave me forced me to retreat into the kitchen.

He followed me, and I tried to make myself busy, blindly chopping my poor, mistreated celery. He stood behind me while I hacked away, sending bits of celery flying, until finally, he laid his hands on my arms, and I froze.

"Red," he whispered next to my ear.

Dropping the knife, I held onto the counter. "I've heard it's my color."

He ran his hands up my arms to my shoulders before letting me go and leaning a hip against the counter next to me.

He fingered the hem of my sweater. "You know how I feel about you in red. I'm trying to be a good guy and stay away, but damn, Syl. You're killing me here."

I turned to face him, not even close to casual enough to lean. "I'm so confused. How can the man who makes adorable, thoughtful turkey fruit be the same guy who ripped my heart to shreds less than three weeks ago? I can't seem to reconcile the two."

David breathed in, then out, in, then out, his eyes darting over my face. "There's no two. They're both me. The dad and the heart shredder. This is just who I am, Sylvia. It's not all a wrapped up in lovely package, that's for damn sure, but I'm hoping there are some parts that are redeemable."

"Well..." My chest rose and fell faster than normal. Our proximity in my small, warm kitchen wasn't doing me any favors. "I wish I knew that breathing technique. I could use it right now."

His palm skated over my hair and I closed my eyes at the barely-there contact.

"I'll teach you," he murmured. "I'm becoming something of an expert. Lots'a fuckin' breathing lately. Works for me, though. Helps get my head outta my ass and pushes away some of the panic."

The sound of the front door opening and Suz's boisterous voice had me smiling up at David before I could catch myself, and the look he gave me was so filled with hope, he might as well have said the words out loud.

I glanced over my shoulder. "I need to play hostess."

He tipped his chin. "Have at it."

THE DAY WENT...WELL. Actually, it was wonderful. Despite the somewhat awkward beginning, David was on his best behavior, and I could tell both Gwen and Emma were absolutely over the moon to have him there.

Suz was a little less convinced. She gave David a lot of dirty looks on my behalf. Or maybe her own behalf, since he'd hijacked Mika to rebuild my deck, causing him to have to leave her bed at the crack of dawn each day—Suz was cold-blooded, and Mika was her heater.

We were all around the table, forks scraping the remains of Thanksgiving dinner off our plates, when she brought up the subject.

"How goes the longest deck project in the world?" She directed her question toward David.

He wiped his mouth with his napkin, nodding. "Almost done. Probably would've been done sooner if Mika didn't have to teach me everything. And if we could've worked on it more than two hours a day."

Mika shrugged a brawny shoulder. "Some of us have day jobs, my man. Two hours is all I have to spare."

"How many more days are we talking?" Suz pressed.

"Two or three, tops," said Mika.

"Then I'll do the stain," David added.

"And then you'll stop hanging around my girl's house?" Suz asked pointedly.

David's eyes shot to mine. "Yeah, I'll stop hanging around so much."

I hated myself for hoping there was suddenly a shortage of stain, causing this to be the project that never ended. I was so hooked on this man, I needed my daily fix, even if it was only a glimpse, even if it hurt like hell at the same time.

"Mr...erm, I mean, David, have you recorded any new music yet?" asked Evan.

Slowly, David turned away from me to answer him. "Not anything for Blue. My friend Jasper and I are working with a new artist, making a demo. He's completely fresh and untrained. Reminds me of how we were in the beginning."

"Is that Omar?" I asked.

"Yeah, Omar. Jas and I have been working with him after school for the last week. The kid actually cracked a smile the other day. We were pretty damn proud of ourselves."

"I'd love to hear some of it," I said.

David cocked his head. "Yeah? I could manage that."

"Me too," Evan said.

David laughed. "Not sure I wanna go spreading around his demo just yet, but I'll see what I can do."

Sliding down in my chair, I listened to the conversation around me, but I had trouble looking anywhere but at David. If we stayed in this one moment, it would be easy to forget how invisible and uncared for he made me feel in the end. But it was better to remember those moments, because they never went away. Not really. Just like the image of David in bed with other women was forever burned in my brain, so too was the way he'd treated me at the Flashing Numbers show.

I could pretend he'd changed, that he'd had some magical transformation—and maybe he had—but our past still existed. He'd still hurt me in very real ways.

Still, it was a relief not to be angry, even if it was just for a day. In my head, I listed *that* as something I was thankful for when we went around the table. Out loud, I'd said the theater and my family.

The fact that David had also said family while looking directly at me did not go unnoticed.

Gwen pulled out every single stop for dessert, gifting us with pecan, pumpkin, and cookie pies, plus homemade whipped cream. I helped her bring it all to the table once we'd stacked the washer full of dinner dishes, then she followed me back to the kitchen to grab plates.

Pulling David's fruit tray from the fridge, I showed it to her. "Guess who made this."

Gwen smiled down at the platter. "How cute! I'd guess Emma."

I raised my brows. "Nope. It was your very own son."

Her mouth fell open. "No way! Do I have another son I don't know about?"

I laughed. "It was the one and only David Wiesel."

"Well, isn't he surprising."

"Yeah, he is."

WITH BELLIES full and smiles on their faces, my guests retreated to their homes. David lingered, hanging out with Emma on the couch. They'd gotten engrossed in watching *Die Hard*, and I had zero interest in breaking up their time together.

I made myself busy, wiping counters that didn't really need to be wiped again, and scrubbing pans that had already been scrubbed. When I exhausted my kitchen options, I decided to cart the folding chairs back down to the basement for storage. I carried two down, stowing them back in their spot, and when I went back to the stairs to grab two more, I found David waiting for me, the other three chairs tucked under his arms.

"Where do these go?"

My hand shot up to cover my pounding heart. "Oh, I'll show you."

He slotted the chairs into their spot, closing the door to the storage area when he was done.

"Thank you, David." My basement was unfinished, dim and kind of spooky, but that wasn't the reason my hands were trembling. It was the longing look in David's eyes, his nearness, and the feeling of being slightly removed from the rest of the world.

I reached out, snagging the front of his shirt, my breath coming in little pants. David's jaw ticked as he watched me. I didn't know what I was doing, only that I wanted to touch him.

Moving into his space, my breasts skimmed his shirt, and I concentrated on the V of skin peeking out of his unbuttoned collar. There were goosebumps blossoming along his flesh, and even though it was chilly down here, I didn't think that was the cause.

"Syl," he rasped right before his mouth covered mine in the tenderest kiss he'd ever given me. His lips were soft, his tongue tentative as it swept over mine. His hands were in my hair, not pulling, but careful.

If he'd ravaged me, pressed me against a wall and fucked me with his tongue, I would have been swept up, letting my good sense be overtaken by desperate need. It was his gentleness that had me pulling away.

"I can't. I'm sorry," I said.

"Don't be sorry. You didn't do anything wrong," he said.

"I don't want us to become like me and Vince, clinging to something that needed to be over. I know what lies at the end of that road, and it's nothing good."

David ran his knuckles down my cheek, his eyes intent on my face. "Here's the thing, Syl, you and I are nothing like you and Vince. I fucked up big time, but I'm not gonna go round and round in circles with you. When I get you back, it's gonna be forever. No wishy-washy bullshit. I'm in this for marriage and babies and picket fences. You're the only possible woman in the world I'd want that with, and damn do I want that. If you wanna talk, we'll talk. If you need time, I'll give it to you. But I'm here, and I'm not going away. This is me laying all my cards on the table right now. I've got nothing else."

"That's a lot," I whispered.

"I know. I'm feelin' a little intense these days."

There was no mention of love. Even with all the wonderful, enticing things he said, that he loved me wasn't one of them. It was better that he hadn't, because if he had...I might've folded, and then...I didn't know what would happen. How I'd possibly survive him if he loved me and then left me anyway.

He must've read my hesitation, because he backed away and tucked his hands in his pockets. "Mind if I finish the movie with Em before I head out?"

"Sure. Yes, definitely. I'm going to go up to my room and read for a bit."

We went back upstairs, and just before David went to rejoin Emma in the living room, I grabbed his hand. "Happy Thanksgiving, David. I'm glad you were here today."

He squeezed my hand before he dropped it. "Happy Thanksgiving, Syl."

THIRTY-ONE

DAVID

TO BE HONEST, I'd been dragging my feet working on Sylvia's deck. It was my last excuse to be anywhere near her. After this, I'd go back to seeing her through cracks in the curtains—although I wondered if she'd even give me that.

Today was my last day. I couldn't really think of a way to extend the project anymore. I wasn't ready to accept we were really done. Not when I'd only just found this life I hadn't known I always wanted, with the women I would've designed for myself if I could've.

Feeling like a fool, I stared up at her house from the curb. The last thing I had to do was stain the steps, and that'd take me no time. My gut churned at the reality of losing Sylvia for good. Not because I couldn't function without her—I could. I'd gotten into a pretty good groove over the last few weeks on my own. I mean, I'd still rather be with other people than by myself, but at night, when all I had for company was my own breath, I didn't loathe it. I didn't go crazy and call up the usual suspects to party. I didn't get the urge to crawl out of my own skin.

I managed. I lived. Jas and I had some good shit going at the recording studio we were using, with Omar and on our own. We were writing, both for Blue and other artists. He needed it just as much as I did, and it felt good to be there for my friend, my brother who'd lost so much.

Thinking I was seeing things when the curtain on the front window moved, I rubbed my eyes. But then the front door opened, and there stood Sylvia, looking as pretty as ever, with her glassy hair tumbling over her shoulders and a smile on her face.

"Are you going to stand on my sidewalk all day?" she called.

I chuckled. "Hadn't quite made up my mind. Seems like I'm delaying the inevitable."

To my absolute surprise, she waved me closer, so I wasted no time climbing the steps to her front porch.

"Hey," I said.

"Want a cup of coffee before you get to work?" she asked.

"Are you kidding me? Hell yes I do." I was taken aback by the offer, but no way would I be turning it down.

Following her inside, I asked why she was still home since it was after nine.

"Working from home." She gestured to her clothes. "Hence the casual attire. I took Em to a follow-up ortho appointment this morning and decided to treat myself to a day on the couch with my laptop."

As she poured two cups of coffee, she told me about the appointment. I listened, because yeah, I did care how my kid was healing, but now that she'd drawn my attention to what she was wearing, it was hard to pull my eyes away. I thought Sylvia in red was my favorite, with her in workout clothes coming a very close second, but Sylvia in ripped and faded jeans and a plain white T-shirt a touch too short, revealing a sliver of stomach when she moved...well, it was something else entirely. My cock stirred, but so did my heart. I wanted her, with her pretty, painted toes, and old, worn out jeans, padding around my house every damn day for the rest of my life.

I just didn't know if I'd ever make that happen.

We sat in her living room, a cushion between us on the couch, and she turned toward the sliding glass door.

"The deck looks amazing. I don't know why I resisted for so long," she said.

"I know why." Her head swiveled back, one eyebrow raised in question. "What you had before worked. It was fine, functional. You didn't know how good it could be with a little effort."

She sipped her coffee. "I think you're right. Familiarity is comforting and asking for more is scary."

What came next was a mystery. There were a million things I had to say, but she wasn't ready to hear them, and I wasn't quite ready to say them. Because if I said them, and she didn't say them back, then that was it. It was truly over.

"I have a song for you to listen to." This was a safe topic. Neutral. Also fucking terrifying.

She grinned, straightening. "Oh my god, yes! I've been dying to hear this." She set her mug down on the side table, leaned her head back on the cushion, and closed her eyes.

"Take pity on me because this is the first song Jas and I ever produced—with a lot of help from an actual producer because we don't know shit. Omar and I wrote this together, so it's kind of a mix of both of us and—"

Sylvia cracked an eye open. "Just press play, David."

Taking a deep breath, I hit play on my phone. Omar's voice was ridiculous. He had his own style, a mix of rock and rap, and the kid could write. We sat down together and whipped out the first draft of a song in twenty minutes. Turned out, he had a lot to say.

Sylvia smiled when she heard him begin to sing.

Walking on crooked paths, stumbling
broken feet and I'm headed somewhere
Home is the other way, crumbling
around the edges, and I'm lost

These streets ain't made of gold
Not even twenty, but I'm feelin' old
There are no more picket fences
With you, I throw out all my defenses

Living in your memory, shaking
off the hurt, and I'm harder now
Heart not ever the same, aching
Just to see your face, my own ghost

Love like magic
Broken heart tragic
stretched thin like elastic
And I broke

Watching the stars at night, feeling
insignificant and I've been humbled
Pressing on my shoulders, reeling
from the weight of my world.

These streets ain't made of gold
Not even twenty, but I'm feelin' old
There are no more picket fences
With you, I throw out all my defenses

Hope like winning
Head goes spinning
one extra inning

And I'm gonna play

SYLVIA WAS CRYING—I seemed to be making her do a lot of
that lately. When the song ended, she opened her wet eyes and
held her arms out. I scooted closer, accepting her embrace, and
wrapped her in one of my own.

"That was beautiful, David. I'm really proud of you and
Omar. Tell him that for me, okay?"

She laid her head on my shoulder, and I stroked the silk of
her hair. "Yeah, sweetheart, I will. And Jas too."

She let out a sob mixed with a laugh. "Definitely Jasper too."

"You liked it then?"

She pulled back, her blue eyes stormy. "Yeah. How could
you think I wouldn't?"

I wiped a tear from her cheek with my thumb, and her
eyelids fluttered momentarily. "I'm feeling a little vulnerable
here. I haven't tried something new in years, and I don't have my
band to stand behind, you know? But I'm also so fucking
inspired right now."

Sylvia's arms slowly loosened until she let go, and it
would've been creepy as hell if I didn't follow her lead. Reluctantly, I let go, but I didn't move away. Her leg was pressed
against mine, and I did take note of the fact that she didn't move
away either.

"Being vulnerable is good. I'm just a little...I guess I'm trying
to catch up. You're not touring with that other band?" she asked.

"No, Sylvia. I'm not. That night was a panic attack on
steroids. I want you to understand I wasn't in my right mind.
I've lived with low-grade anxiety pretty much my whole life,
but sometimes, when I'm really stressed or worried or spiraling,
I go into panic mode where the only thing I can think about is

trying to escape. It's hard to explain if you've never experienced it, but it's this physical and visceral feeling that is so real, it can't be logiced away. I'm gonna be straight, it scares the shit out of me when it happens. And I never talk about it because it's embarrassing for me to have so little control of my own brain."

She inhaled sharply, her eyes searching my face. "I wish you would have told me before. I wish we could have talked like this. I know you're embarrassed, but I'd never judge you for something you can't control."

I laid my hands on my knees, bowing my head. "I know, Sylvia. But I didn't want to be that guy with you. I couldn't lay my shit at your feet and ask you to accept it. Not after I'd already laid so much at your feet. I wanted to finally be the one to take care of you."

Her hands covered mine, her thumbs hooking my thumbs. "I was done with you, David. Really done. Your name on my heart was crossed out with permanent ink."

I raised my head to look at her. "Are you not done now?"

"I don't know," she whispered.

I bobbed my head, seeing that sliver of a chance and hanging onto it with all my might. "We can go slow. I don't know, date or something?"

The corners of her mouth pulled up slightly. "Date or something?"

"Yeah." I laughed at how I always managed to fuck this up. "Will you go on a date with me? On Saturday night?"

"Can I think about it?" she asked.

"Yeah, of course." My eyes flicked to the deck outside. "Guess I should get to work."

Sylvia kept her hands on mine. "Can you stay here for a little longer? Tell me about music or yoga or whatever?"

I turned my hands over to weave our fingers together and

grinned. "Yep. You know how much I like doing *whatever* with you."

She bit her plump bottom lip, holding back a smile. "There will be none of that, sir."

I brought our joined hands up to my forehead, utterly grateful and kinda overwhelmed by this moment of lightness and levity. We'd needed it.

I stayed a little while, telling her more about the music Jasper and I had been making and what our plans were. God, it felt so good to sit with her and *talk*. Not about all the shit I'd messed up, but about life and the things I was actually proud of.

When I headed outside to work on the deck, I promised to text our plans for Saturday. And as I rolled the stain on the steps, I knew the flutter of the curtain wasn't my imagination. Sylvia was watching.

SHE WANTED to think about it, but I wasn't gonna miss my shot. I waited exactly forty-eight hours to text her.

Me: *How do you feel about* Phantom of the Opera?
Sylvia: *Love it. What theater nerd doesn't?*
Me: *Want to pop my theater cherry and accompany me to a show at the Kennedy Center?*
Sylvia: *OMG, I love first timers! I promise to be gentle.*
Me: *Was that flirtation?*
Sylvia: *You're taking me to see Phantom...I think that deserves a little flirting.*
Me: *So musicals were the way to win you over this whole time? Damn.*
Sylvia: *If you didn't know that, you weren't paying attention.*
Me: *I promise you I was.*
Sylvia: *Are you really taking me to the Kennedy Center?*

Me: I really am...if you're still into the dating thing.

Sylvia: I am. I kind of missed having you lurk around my house this week.

Me: I'm willing to lurk. Name the time and place. I could probably tackle some more projects on your house if you want.

Sylvia: Without Mika's supervision?

Me: Definitely not. That dude is handy as hell. Glad you have him in your life.

Sylvia: Me too. I know my way around a drill, but I wouldn't have survived without Mika these last few years.

Me: I'm gonna learn from the master so you can call on me from now on.

Sylvia: I'd like to be able to call on you.

Me: In my dreams, you wouldn't have to call. I'd be there with you.

Sylvia: Sounds like a lovely dream.

Me: I know we're going slow, but I meant everything I said on Thanksgiving. You're everything I want.

Sylvia: David...

Me: I know. Too soon, too much. That's me.

Sylvia: I like that you're too much. It's you.

Me: And you like me?

Sylvia: Sometimes. Sometimes an unhealthy amount. Lately, a lot.

Me: Jesus, Syl, I need to see you.

Sylvia: Slow, remember?

Me: Believe me, sweetheart, I remember. I just wanna touch your face.

Sylvia: That's all?

Me: Oh, not even close. Don't think you want me naming all the other things I want to do to you.

Sylvia: Better not. But I'm sure I can imagine.

Sylvia: Thank you, David.

Me: *What for?*

Sylvia: *I don't know...for not moving on. For trying. For taking me to see Phantom.*

Me: *For the fruit turkey?*

Sylvia: *Haha...you laugh, but that damn fruit turkey really moved you up in my esteem.*

Me: *I'll make you a veggie Christmas tree next, try to get you to love me.*

Sylvia: *I don't need a veggie tree for that, but I'll take one anyway.*

Me: *Did you just...?*

Sylvia: *I wouldn't have said something like that over a text message. But maybe.*

Me: *I'm gonna have to touch more than your face, Sylvia. FUCK!*

Sylvia: *I should go before I let my fingers get away from me again.*

Me: *Yep. I'm two seconds away from sexting you.*

Sylvia: *LOL...boner killer, I'm sitting next to Emma right now.*

Me: *Yep, that did it. Never getting hard again in my life.*

Sylvia: *See you Saturday, David.*

Me: *Sweet dreams, Syl. Give Em a kiss for me.*

I DROVE to Sylvia's house at midnight. Texted to see if she was awake, and she replied, "Just barely." Taking a deep breath, and then another, I asked her to come to the front porch. A minute later, she opened the door, looking so sleepy-pretty wrapped in a huge fleece robe with knit booties on her feet.

"Hey...you okay?" she asked.

"Yeah, but I forgot to tell you something," I said.

She leaned her shoulder against the doorframe, frowning in confusion. "And it couldn't wait?"

"No, not sure it could." I shoveled my fingers through my hair, then said what needed to be said. "See, the thing is, Syl, I'm completely in love with you. When I said I wanted all those things with you, the future, I forgot to tell you how much I love you. I'm going to love you for the rest of my life, no matter what happens next. It's written in stone."

Her lips parted, not to speak, but in what looked like shock. I held a hand up, then let it brush her cheek.

"Maybe it's not fair for me to tell you that right now, when you're still undecided about me, but I thought it was information you should have. My heart is yours, Sylvia, and that's a fact." I glanced over my shoulder. "I'm gonna go. We're still on for Saturday?"

She nodded, her lips pressed tightly together.

I touched her face one more time, because I had no choice. "All right. I'll see you in two days."

FEELING slick and confident in my suit, I picked up my phone, checking it one last time before I went to pick up Sylvia. I had a text from her, and dread coursed through me. *She's cancelling. Doesn't want me. Fuck!*

When I checked it, the words weren't what I expected.

Emma got her heart broken today. She's asking for you. Can you come now? She's really upset.

With a hammering heart, I went to my girls.

I SHOULD'VE KNOWN how to handle a broken-hearted teenage girl, but all I wanted to do was curl up and cry with her. At least I knew that was the wrong thing to do. She needed me to be strong, to be her calm in the storm.

But when she asked for her dad, I almost broke. Her voice was so small, it took me straight back to all the times she'd asked for him when she was little and I had to tell her she couldn't have him.

This time was different, though. This time when I asked, he was pounding on our door in less than half an hour. I left Emma wrapped tightly in a blanket on the couch to answer the door. When I pulled it open, I almost broke again at the sight of David in a suit, eyes frantic, chest heaving.

One look at me and he took me in his arms. "What happened?"

I shook my head against his shoulder. "Evan broke up with her."

I felt the entirety of his body clench, and I tightened my arms around him. "That little shit. I'll fucking kill him," he growled.

"No, honey. No. He didn't do anything wrong. He was really sweet about it, but he's sixteen and he didn't love her like she loves him." Saying the words aloud soothed me as much as they soothed him. Teenage relationships weren't meant to last forever. They were about learning your heart, maybe learning to love....and a whole lot of lust.

"How can I help her? I don't know what to say."

I tipped my head back to look up at him. "Just be here."

His gaze was fierce. There was possession behind his eyes, but also the utmost tenderness.

"I'm here."

When Emma saw her dad coming to the living room, her tears started all over again. He sat with her for a long time, holding her and stroking her hair. First, she cried, then she melted against him.

I sat down on Emma's other side and laid my head on her shoulder. When she was little and inconsolable, I used to sing her showtunes. Most of the time, she'd get distracted from whatever was ailing her and sing along. But this time, David did the singing. So quietly, I had to lean in to hear, he sang her the song he'd written for her.

I loved this man. Like Evan and Emma, what we had as teenagers was never supposed to last...and it hadn't. The love I had for him was new and based entirely on who he was today. It wasn't the kind of love I'd get over. But I really didn't want to either. David was the end and the beginning.

The three of us spent the rest of the evening eating pizza and ice cream and talking.

"The worst part is, I feel like I'm losing my best friend at the same time," Emma said before glumly chewing on her crust.

"Maybe. But I doubt it. The two of you have too much history to never speak again," I said.

"But it hurts. Like, my heart actually hurts." She rubbed her chest. "I never knew that was a thing."

David rubbed her back. "Hell yes, it's a thing. But here's what I know: those cracks you're feeling in your heart? You need those to let the ache out, and then, to paraphrase my boy, Leonard Cohen, the cracks let the light in."

Emma nodded. "That actually makes sense."

It actually did. My broken places had only made me stronger. And I thought, even though it took him longer to realize it, David's broken places had strengthened him too.

I hated that Emma was going through this at fifteen, but I had no doubt she'd come out the other side knowing herself better and realizing her own fortitude.

Suz called to make sure I didn't hate her, and I assured her we'd still be friends forever. She said she'd told Evan he'd never do better, but I could tell she was just as sad as I was their fledgling relationship had come to an end.

When Emma was all cried and talked out, David helped her upstairs while I cleaned up the kitchen. He was gone so long, I started to think about checking on them, but then he came trudging down the stairs, his eyes red and bleary.

When he saw me waiting for him, his mouth lifted in the corners. "I stayed with her until she fell asleep. I took her through some mindful breathing, and I think it helped," he explained.

He picked up his suit jacket and tie, which he'd slung over a dining room chair at some point in the evening. "I guess I'll head out."

My heart thumped. "Please stay."

He raised both brows. "Yeah?"

"Please."

He tossed his jacket down and tucked his hand in his suit pants. "Of course, Syl."

"Are you tired?" I asked.

"Nah. I mean, I'm worn out, but I'm not going to be sleeping any time soon." He pointed at the ceiling, toward Emma. "That was...I'm glad I was here for it."

I sighed. "Me too. I'm really glad you're here."

"I'm not going anywhere, Sylvia. Even if you and I don't work ou—"

"I don't want to date," I blurted.

His eyes went just as wide and frantic as when he'd first arrived. He scratched at his chest, eyes darting. "Okay, that's...okay. I'll probably go then."

I rushed to him, grasping his arms. "No, you misunderstand. I don't want to date because I just want to be with you."

One second passed. Then another. In the third second, I was in David's arms, his lips at my ear, telling me how much he loved me, telling me it was forever.

And I believed him. I just did. I'd been through enough, seen enough, that I should be cynical, and in a way I was. But this moment rang true. David's promises felt irrevocable.

"I love you too," I whispered into his mouth, right before he kissed me breathless. This wasn't the tender kiss of Thanksgiving—and thank god for that. He kissed me like he was absolutely starving for me.

We broke apart, foreheads pressed together, his hot breath on my lips. "Love you, sweetheart."

I smiled into another kiss, then one slower, more languid, but still as passionate.

"Ah, god, can I take you to bed?" he asked.

I chewed on my bottom lip for a second. "I don't think we should...if Em wakes up—"

"I know. I'm not asking to fuck you." His hands moved down my waist, thumbs brushing the skin under my T-shirt. "I wanna lay with you and hold you. Can we do that?"

"We can definitely do that."

THIRTY-THREE
DAVID

I SAT on the corner of Sylvia's bed, watching her undress. I'd already rid myself of my suit, stripping down to my boxer briefs. It was a relief—I was never gonna be a suit guy.

Sylvia's T-shirt fluttered to the floor, then she inched her jeans down her hips until they were on the floor too. She wasn't putting on a show, only getting into her pajamas, but my cock was stupid. It saw this pretty, warm, sexy woman and wanted inside.

My hands, though, that was where my desperation mostly laid. I gripped the bedspread to stop myself from touching her. These last few weeks without her had felt longer than the fifteen years before. Because I knew her, knew what it was like to have her, to touch her.

"Sylvia."

She arched an eyebrow, smiling. "Yes?" Her bra dropped, revealing her perfect little tits capped with tight, brown nipples. She quickly pulled on a tank top, which barely covered anything.

There was no disguising the tent in my boxers, so I didn't

try. I wanted her to know how fucking beautiful I found her. I laid down on top of the covers, patting the spot beside me.

"Gonna need you right here, sweetheart."

She came to me, in just her tank top and underwear. It was torture not to be able to sink inside her, but it was the sweetest kind of torture, because I had her. She was mine.

Sylvia settled beside me, slinging her leg over mine. I gripped the side of her thigh, holding her there.

Her hand settled over my heart. She had to hear it pounding. My heart was getting used to the surge of emotions I'd been feeling lately. It probably wouldn't want to go back to its normal, steady life. It got used so much more these days.

I slid my hand under her tank top, settling on her breast. She let out a short laugh, but didn't protest.

"I need to feel you, Syl."

"Me too, David."

We laid there quietly touching each other for a while. My heart slowed, matching the rhythm of hers.

"I got so used to my life. All the craziness, the traveling, the people—that was my normal. It didn't fill me up, but it was safe. I never panicked, because nothing was at risk, you know?"

Sylvia propped herself up on my chest, watching me as I spoke.

"But when you and Em came to stay with me, I loved it from day one. But the entire time, I was so focused on it ending, I didn't even realize how terrified I was. There's risk in loving you."

She started to protest, but I held a finger to her lips.

"There is, Syl. Nothing is assured. Look at Em's accident. We could've lost her, but nothing would ever stop me from loving that girl like madness."

She kissed my chest, and I cupped her cheeks, holding her

clear blue eyes with mine, making sure she understood every-thing I was saying.

"I just know I'm always gonna love you. I might be struck down by lightning tomorrow, or live to a hundred and two, and my last thought will be of you. That's the assurance I can give you. I am committing to loving you the best I know how for every single breath I take for the rest of my life."

Sylvia blinked and blinked again. "That's a lot to unpack."

I chuckled, a lot of tension flowing out of me. "Yeah, that's kind of my thing."

"I used to think we were inevitable, like two trains careening toward each other on the same track."

I pushed her hair away from her face and down her back. "And now?"

"Now, I don't accept that. My love for you is deliberate. It's a choice I'm making and will continue to make until the end of time."

With both hands, I squeezed her plump ass, holding her against me. "God, I love you, Sylvia. I think we should probably just get married."

"Get married and make babies and have picket fences?" she clarified.

Moving my hand behind her neck, I pulled her down on top of me, kissing along her jaw.

"Picket fences optional. The rest, hell yes."

"Yes. Let's do that," she said.

I growled into her neck, then flipped her over so I was on top. "I really need to be inside you."

She hitched her legs up, rocking her core against me. "I need you too."

Our clothes were removed in a frenzy, and when I sank inside her, her wet heat enveloping my cock to the root, going without a condom was another deliberate choice. I kept my eyes on hers as I moved inside her, knowing this was the one woman I'd ever do this with again.

And fuck if that awareness didn't make me even harder.

Sylvia was everything, *everything* I'd always wanted. Here, in bed, and out there, in life.

I held her hips in my hands, and we both watched where I slid into her. It was perfect, the way I stretched her and filled her, and the way she took me.

She sighed, tightening around me, and I fell on her, kissing her while she shuddered. I slowed my thrusts, letting her catch her breath and catching my own. I wanted to look at her—remember this moment, with her hair fanning around her face, her lips swollen and red, her eyes glazed and satisfied. And then she smiled at me, and my heart tripped, and my cock surged.

I said things, things about loving her forever, telling her she was an angel, that her pussy was made for me, then telling her I'd love her even past forever. She murmured in agreement as her nails dug into my shoulders and her ankles hooked behind my back.

I made it last as long as I could, but I finally gave in, spilling deep inside her until I saw spots behind my eyelids.

I pulled her with me when I collapsed on the bed, my cock softening inside her.

"Love you forever, sweetheart," I said softly.

"I love you forever plus one," she said back.

This was it. The beginning and the end. We weren't stuck together. We'd chosen this—chosen each other—and I wasn't scared. No panic in sight. Because Sylvia was my quiet, but she was also my crazy endorphin rush, and if this all slipped away tomorrow...well, I'd still be better for having had her.

I was cracked as hell, broken all over, but with Sylvia, I'd always let the light come in.

Forever.

EPILOGUE

SYLVIA

Two years later

I CLOSED MY EYES, listening to the music I knew so well, but never, ever got tired of. But closing my eyes was no good, because I couldn't see my beautiful husband working his magic on the guitar when I did.

David was having the time of his life, playing back to back with Jasper, thousands of fans erupting with joy. They'd been waiting for this, waiting for Blue is the Color to get back on the road and give them new music. I had no doubt they were thinking it was worth the wait now.

Tali came to stand next to me, bumping my shoulder with hers. "You know he'd kill me if I didn't tell you to sit down."

I rubbed my round belly, smiling. "Soon. My ankles are feeling pretty large and in charge right now. I just have a better view when I stand."

"You look beautiful, ankles notwithstanding. I've never seen leather maternity pants," she said.

I laughed. "Gotta play the part of a rock star wife, knocked up or not."

Another song, and I gave in and had a seat. Watching David play from the side of the stage had never stopped being thrilling. Tonight, we were in Baltimore, the last show of their North American tour. I'd managed to come to a lot of shows, racking up frequent flyer miles. We didn't like to spend more than a week apart—and even that was pushing it. I was due any day now, though, so this would be my last show for a while.

This baby had been about as planned as it could get. We'd tried the old-fashioned way for a year, with no luck. Turned out, after going through test after test, we had unexplained infertility. The bitter irony was not lost on us. It was our second IUI that did the trick, and baby boy Wiesel was conceived in my doctor's office.

The last two years hadn't been perfect; our infertility had been stressful and sometimes sad. David blamed himself, I blamed myself, but what we didn't do was blame each other. We only grew closer, and through the stress, we let ourselves savor the unexpected time we had as a threesome.

And Emma...oh, Emma. She was amazing as always, dying for her baby brother to be born. Absolutely chomping at the bit to get her hands on him. She'd bounced back from her heartbreak quickly, more emotionally astute than a lot of adults. She and Evan had become friends again when Suz had her baby girl, Matilda. Emma hadn't been able to stay away from Matty, and Evan was part of the package.

The show ended, and my sweaty husband swept me out of my seat—as much as I could be swept at nine months pregnant.

"How was it?" he asked.

"Perfect. The song about Azalea is still my favorite."

"Not your song?"

I pulled his bottom lip between mine. "Mmm...yeah, I like that one too."

His hands slid down my sides to my belly. "Was he dancing?"

I laughed. "I'd be surprised if he doesn't come out with a guitar in his hands."

David's lip curled. "That sounds painful for you, sweetheart."

He nuzzled my neck as he walked us to his private dressing room. We'd developed a ritual after shows. It was a pretty simple one. After the first concert I attended, David discovered how wet watching him perform made me, and since then, he came right off the stage, got me in private, and fucked me hard.

Tonight was no different. Our positions were limited, but he sat me in his lap, my back to his chest, and slid inside me with no resistance. Being married to a rock star was a giant turn on, unsurprisingly.

He cupped my breasts and rocked into me, both of us watching ourselves in the mirror.

"Jesus, I love your tits." He squeezed them, pulling at my sensitive nipples until I squealed. "You're so fucking ripe. So sexy."

I *felt* sexy like this, big belly and all. David never stopped making me feel safe and sexy and wanted.

I caught his eye in the mirror. "Do it. I need it," I panted.

He grinned and bit my shoulder. "You're so pretty, Sylvia." Then, he wrapped my hair around his hand and yanked. My head jerked back, the wind left my lungs, and I came hard, gripping him tightly with my inner muscles. David followed me over, spilling inside me until I was dripping everywhere.

"You're crazy wet tonight, sweetheart," he said.

"I thought that was you."

I looked down at his soaked legs and the small puddle on the floor below us. "Honey, I think my water broke."

He grabbed my breasts in a panic, making me laugh. "Shit. What do we do?"

I wove my fingers with his and collapsed back on him, laughing. "I think we have to go to the hospital, although I'm not sure how I'm going to get my leather pants back on."

LEO WIESEL WAS BORN SCREAMING, with a head full of thick, dark hair and a gorgeous, angry face. Emma had held my hand while David held one of my feet as I pushed, and once the baby was out, David let Emma cut his umbilical cord.

"Hi, Leo," Emma cooed at the baby in my arms. "I'm your sister, Emma, and I've been waiting so long for you."

For the briefest moment, everything stilled. Leo's angry protests quieted, and he stared up at her. Then, I took a breath, and the world began turning again, and Leo rooted madly for something to latch onto, which I gladly obliged.

I'd had thousands of perfect moments in my life, but this one was right on top, with my new baby at my breast, my devoted husband stroking my hair, and my sweet daughter wiping tears of joy from her cheeks.

It felt like we'd come full circle. A circle we hadn't known was incomplete until we completed it. When Emma was born, David had hidden in a corner, pacing, staying away from me. My mom had been there, but I couldn't have felt more alone. But that moment Emma was laid on my chest and David finally came over and our eyes met, the circle was formed. It had taken us a long time to make our way back to the beginning, but here we were.

"You did good, sweetheart," David choked out.

I trailed my fingers down Leo's warm back, soaking in the feel of his baby fresh skin. "I know." I met his watery eyes. "I did so good."

This was it. Another end and beginning. The perfection wouldn't last. It'd get tough again, and it'd get messy. It would also be so beautiful, I'd barely be able to take it. I knew this. I also knew I'd never be alone. Because from the second we'd agreed on marriage and babies and picket fences, and maybe even before then, David had been walking next to me—and our road was endless.

He was David and I was Sylvia—and that was the way our stars aligned.

PLAYLIST

Spotify Playlist

I hate you, i love you Gnash, Olivia O'Brien

You're Somebody Else Flora Cash

Wish I Knew You The Revivalists

Better Now Post Malone

Worst In Me Julia Michaels

Sober Up AJR

I'll Cover You Jesse L. Martin, *RENT*

A Closeness Dermot Kennedy

It's Quiet Uptown Renee Elise Goldsberry, Lin Manuel Miranda, *Hamilton*

Falling Slowly Glen Hansard, Marketa Irglova

Like A Stone Audioslave

Wicked Game James Vincent McMorrow

I Dreamed A Dream Ann Hathaway, *Les Miserables*

The Monster Eminem, Rihanna

Don't Wanna Think Julia Michaels

Helpless Phillipa Soo, *Hamilton*

Take It All Back 2.0 Judah & the Lion

Sorry Nothing But Thieves

Are We Too Late Tom Leeb

Anthem Leonard Cohen

Hello My Old Heart The Oh Hellos

Undone-The Sweater Song Weezer

NEWSLETTER

Sign up for my newsletter:
www.subscribepage.com/t7m4u4

Join my reader group:
www.facebook.com/groups/JuliaWolfReaders/

ACKNOWLEDGMENTS

When I was writing Times Like These, I thought it would be interesting to make this total womanizing, dickface of a man the father to a teenage girl. What I didn't think about was how I was going to write his book when it came time and make him redeemable.

I was scared. I'd never written a parent before, or a kid. It turned out, I didn't need to be afraid. I took my own experiences as a parent, imagined what it would have been like if I'd been much younger and without any support, and the words flowed.

David's anxiety and panic attacks are deeply personal to me. Like many, I suffer from anxiety that can't be logiced away (trademark David). Everyone's experience with anxiety and panic attacks are different, but I wrote David's from my personal feelings. The skull filled with mud, not being able to think of anything else besides the one tiny thing I can't let go of, being irrationally angry or sad. I wouldn't wish it on anyone, but there's comfort in knowing I'm not alone.

All that is to say, I have to thank my husband, Dan. On those sleepless nights where I didn't think I could possibly go on? Dan was right there with me, suffering just as I was. Hey, we have twins. There was no switching off who got to sleep. So we'd stare at each other all bleary-eyed and wonder aloud 'What did we do?'. I wouldn't have survived without a partner I could ask that very honest question to.

I'd better also shout out to my three kids now. They are my biggest fans—in fact, they like to tell pretty much everyone they meet that their mom is an author. However, they have requested far less kissing in the next book...what do you think?

As always, I love my author friends. Marika, Cassie-Ann, Elizabeth, Laura, Brenda, Susannah, Sylvie (and her goat videos), Heather, Rebecca, Jami, Ceri, Molly...and oh my god, I have so many freaking amazing women in my life who love kissing books as much as I do.

To my awesome beta readers, Ellie, Janet, Tonya, and Jennifer, you are my rock stars. I couldn't do this without you.

To my freaking fantastic reader group, I adore you lovelies. Two chuggas forever.

Would it be weird to thank musicals? I'm doing it anyway. Thank you to musical theater for making me happy and for supplying the songs that never leave my head or my heart.

ABOUT THE AUTHOR

Julia Wolf is a lover of all things romance. From steamy, to sweet, to funny, to so dirty you'll be blushing for days, she loves it all.

Formerly a hair stylist, she spent years collecting stories her clients couldn't wait to spill. And now that she's writing full time, she's putting those stories to use, although all identifying characteristics have been changed to protect the not-so-innocent!

Julia lives in Maryland with her three crazy, beautiful kids and her patient husband who she's slowly converting to a romance reader, one book at a time.

Visit my website:
www.JuliaWrites.com

ALSO BY JULIA WOLF

SUCH GREAT HEIGHTS

COMING LATE JUNE 2019

ONE

MALKA

FUNERALS WEREN'T REALLY my scene. I'd been to one in my entire twenty-nine years on the planet, and that had been enough for a lifetime. I made a deal with myself six years ago that I'd never have to go to another one again.

But some deals were meant to be broken. Some exceptions were meant to be made. Jasper Antonio was one of them. We were barely friends, but if I told him right now that I needed him, he wouldn't hesitate to show up. People like him were rare, and not to be taken for granted. So I showed up for him too. Even if we didn't speak, I wanted him to know I was there. That my shirt was his if he needed it.

I took a red-eye to Phoenix from Baltimore, arriving in the wee hours of the morning. My hotel room wouldn't be ready until after four in the afternoon, so I wandered until I found a twenty-four hour diner to hang out in until it was time for the funeral.

After I ordered a cup of coffee and a stack of pancakes, I dozed for a bit, my head flopping forward, hair hanging over my face. My vibrating phone woke me up.

I looked at the screen and cringed. *Merrick.*

"Hey," I answered.

"Your shit's sitting outside my house. You need to pick it up," he said.

"What?" My stomach instantly knotted. "I'm in fucking Arizona for a funeral. I won't be back for two days."

He sighed. "Who died?"

"A friend's mother. Is my stuff really outside?"

"Yeah. On my porch. I didn't know you weren't around." He sounded only slightly remorseful.

"Well, I'm not. I don't have anyone who can pick it up for me." That fact was even sadder than my shit being outside on his porch.

He was quiet for a long beat, but I heard his heavy breaths through the phone. Like the death of Jasper's mother was some great inconvenience to him. "Fine. I'll bring it back in. But you get two days, no more. I don't want it in my house."

"I don't really get why you're acting like this, Merrick."

"Cause I'm done with your hot and cold bullshit, Malka," he gritted.

"I don't know what that means."

He growled loud enough I had to hold the phone away from my ear. "Just get your stuff."

He hung up before I could respond and I sunk back in my seat. *Shit.* I didn't have many possessions, but all my clothes and some of my mother's things had been residing in his empty guest bedroom for the past few months. I really didn't want to have to find a new place to store my stuff, but it seemed like I was going to have to.

I had a new email from my dad, so I opened it, knowing he'd probably sent me another tale of his antics, and I wasn't disappointed. He'd attached an up close and personal picture of his teeth, telling he'd just gotten them whitened. They were so bright, I had to adjust my screen to look at them. In my reply, I told him that, which I knew he'd take as a compliment. He also asked me to come visit, but I steadfastly ignored that part of the email.

"Here you go, hon." My waitress set down a plate piled high with pancakes, a mound of butter melting on top, and a brimming cup of coffee right next to it. "You should eat before you take a snooze."

I smiled at her gratefully. "Thank you. I just flew in, and I haven't slept all night."

She tapped her lip with her pen. "Where ya from? I like that accent."

"Germany originally, but I've been a vagabond for a while now."

She gave me a pinched smile, then glanced over her shoulder. "Go on and eat. As long as my boss stays back in the kitchen, no one will mind if you take a rest. Not like we need the table right now."

I made fast work of my breakfast, scrolling through my phone to keep me company—and to stop me from passing out in my pancakes. I went through my ritual. Every morning I Googled my name and my former producer's. There hadn't been a news story about the two of us in years, but like most rituals, I didn't feel right unless I performed it. Because what if the one day I didn't check, and all hell broke loose again?

Today it was crickets though, just how I liked it.

The coffee and sugar did nothing to ease my bone-deep exhaustion though, so I tucked my phone away and leaned my head against the chrome diner wall and dozed some more.

As a musician, I'd spent my adult life traveling and sleeping in odd places, so I had no trouble closing my eyes in the middle of an all night diner. It wasn't the most restful sleep though. By the time the morning rush started, the bell above the door jingling each time another customer entered, I'd slept off and on for a couple hours and decided that was going to have to be enough.

After I paid my bill, I carried my small duffle bag into the restroom, which was shockingly clean. Sparkling even. Tossing my bag on the sink, I dug through it, pulling out my funeral clothes.

I hated wearing black. Despised it. And Reinece deserved rainbows and sequins. She deserved color and flowers and happiness. The day was sad, but she hadn't been. So I was going to wear Kelly green. I might be the leper of the funeral, but I didn't mind. I'd played the leper before.

After cleaning myself as well as I could in the sink and applying a new coat of deodorant and lotion, I slipped my dress over my head and changed from flip flops to wedges. I smoothed my dress over my hips and attempted to see my reflection in the cloudy mirror. Mostly I just saw green topped with pale pink. I'd gotten dressed in less hospitable environments than this. I could apply my makeup without looking.

Today, I skipped the mascara, opting for just a swipe of lip gloss and a little bit of blush to disguise some of my pallor. I pulled my pale pink hair into a loose braid draping over my shoulder and then I was ready to go to the funeral of the nicest woman I'd ever met.

FOR ALL MY determination to be there, once I arrived at the cemetery, and saw Jasper surrounded by the guys from his band, Blue is the Color, and many, *many* people I didn't recognize, I hung back. Suddenly, I felt out of place and intrusive. Silly, really, for thinking my presence would matter.

Reinece was being laid to rest in a lovely spot, as far as cemeteries go, under a tall tree with views of mountains in the distance. I wondered if she'd picked it. If she thought of people coming to visit her grave and wanting to give them a nice place to spend some time. That sounded like her. Thoughtful to the end.

I stood in the shade of a smaller tree off to the side, the voice of the pastor barely filtering over the warm desert spring air. But I didn't need to hear his words; Reince and Jasper hadn't lived in the state for a long time. Chances were he didn't even know her at all.

I watched Jasper instead. Head bowed, his dreadlocks hanging down his back like thick ropes. From where I was, I could only see his profile, but the tears flowing freely down his cheek were unmistakable, even from a distance.

I trailed my eyes over the other members of the band. Nick Fletcher, lead singer, grumpy as hell on a normal day, was expressionless. David Wiesel, guitarist, looked ready to spring out of his chair and start a fight with anyone who looked at him funny. Unsurprisingly, Ian Grady, drummer and my sometimes ex-boyfriend, stared off into the distance, probably lost in his head. I'd seen that expression countless times over the years.

A small choir sang "Amazing Grace" and I sunk to the ground in my silk dress, quietly crying. That song got to me every time I heard it, but today it broke me just a little.

I wiped my eyes, and when I opened them again, Jasper was looking directly at me. For a second I froze, then I mouthed "Hi". His lips curved up. It wasn't quite a smile, but it was close. He mouthed "Hi" back. I whispered, "I'm sorry." and he closed his eyes and mouthed, "Me too".

His eyes went back to the choir and so did mine. I stayed under my tree until the very end. When Reinece's casket was lowered into the ground, the sobs coming from her mourners filled the air. She was a woman who'd been loved.

At my mother's funeral, it had just been my dad, my brother, and me, plus a few distant relatives. It had been a very staid, German affair. No sobbing, no singing, just a solemn sermon from the pastor of the Lutheran church my mom went to growing up. He hadn't known my mother either. When he spoke of the angels carrying her home, I'd stifled a hysterical laugh. She'd been a devout atheist and I had no doubt if when she died, some ladies in white tried to take her somewhere, she'd have fought them tooth and nail.

I *did* wear black that day, mostly because I'd let someone else dress me. I couldn't find the energy to lift my own arms, let alone choose something from my closet.

I hadn't been able to bring myself to step foot in Germany since then. My dad still lived there, but he flew to the States to visit me, or we met in a neutral place, like England or France when I toured with a band. Germany held nothing for me, and I had no intention of ever returning.

I left the cemetery with the other funeral goers. Jasper knew I'd been there. I didn't need to insert myself any further. And if Ian saw me, if we talked, chances were we'd end up in bed together, and I didn't want that. We'd been broken up for three months, and I wasn't ready to jump back on our endless cycle of breaking up and making up.

This day hadn't been easy, and the sky was still light. What I needed was a shower, and then a place to park my ass and drink my cares away.

———

Add to Goodreads

42877711R00188

Made in the USA
Lexington, KY
21 June 2019